POPULAR PUBLICATIONS   FACSIMILE EDITIONS

Dime Detective Magazine #7 (May 1932)

Dime Detective magazine was the flagship detective pulp in the Popular Publications stable, running for almost 300 issues over twenty years. The May 1932 issue contains stories by T.T. Flynn, Carroll John Daly, Edward Parrish Ware, and J. Allan Dunn, and includes appearances by series characters such as Vee "Crime Machine" Brown.

Authors:

T.T. Flynn, Carroll John Daly,
Edward Parrish Ware, J. Allan Dunn

Illustrators:

William Reusswig, John Fleming Gould

DIME DETECTIVE MAGAZINE
10¢

EVERY STORY COMPLETE   EVERY STORY NEW

Vol. 2   **CONTENTS for MAY, 1932**   **No. 3**

Watch for the June Issue   **On the Newsstands May 20th**

Published every month by Popular Publications, Inc., 2256 Grove Street, Chicago, Illinois. Editorial and executive offices 205 East Forty-second Street, New York City. Harry Steeger, President and Secretary, Harold S. Goldsmith, Vice President and Treasurer. Entered as second class matter Feb. 26, 1932, at the Post Office at Chicago, Ill., under the Act of March 3, 1879. Title registration pending at U. S. Patent Office. Copyrighted 1932 by Popular Publications, Inc. Single copy price 10c. Yearly subscriptions in U. S. A. $1.00. For advertising rates address H. D. Cushing, 67 West 44th Street, New York, N. Y. When submitting manuscripts, kindly enclose sufficient postage for their return if found unavailable. The publishers cannot accept responsibility for return of unsolicited manuscripts, although all care will be exercised in handling them.

"SELDOM SEE AN I. C. S. GRADUATE OUT OF A JOB"

"IN ALL the years I have known of the International Correspondence Schools, I have seldom seen one of your graduates out of a job."

A business executive made this statement in a recent letter commenting on the I. C. S. graduates and students in his employ and expressing regrets that it is necessary to reduce the personnel of his organization.

"However," he added, "all I. C. S. graduates and students will be retained, for I realize their value in the conduct of my business."

The reason I. C. S. men always have jobs is because they are *trained men!* You, too, can be an I. C. S. man. In this age of efficiency and specialization, to be an I. C. S. man means security for the present and assurance for the future.

Mark the subject in which you are most interested. Mail the coupon *today.* There is no cost and no obligation in doing so. Yet it has been the most important act in thousands of men's lives!

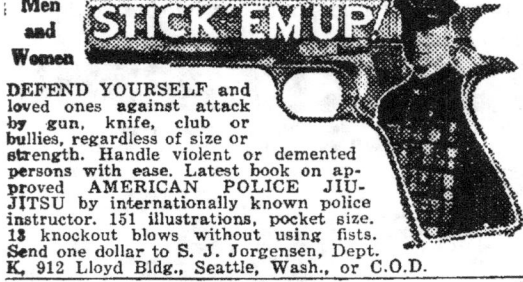

Every Good Boy Deserves Fun

LOOK!
Easy as A·B·C to learn music this way

JUST see how easy it is! The lines are always E-G-B-D-F. Memorize the sentence, "*Every Good Boy Deserves Fun*"—and there you are! Whenever a note appears on the first line, you know it is *e*. Whenever a note appears on the second line, you know it is *g*.

And the spaces—just as easy to remember. The four spaces are always F-A-C-E. That spells "face"—simple enough to remember, isn't it? Thus whenever a note appears in the first space, it is *f*. Whenever a note appears in the second space, it is *a*.

You have learned something already! Isn't it fun? You'll just love learning music this fascinating way! No long hours of tedious practice. No dull and uninteresting scales. No "tricks" or "secrets"—no theories—you learn to play real music from real notes.

You don't need a private teacher this pleasant way. In your own home, alone, without interruption or embarrassment, you study this fascinating, easy method of playing. Practice as much or as little as you like, to suit your own convenience, *and enjoy every minute of it.*

You learn from the start—Previous training unnecessary

So clear and simple are these fascinating "music lessons" that even a child can understand them. You do not lose a minute with unnecessary details —only the most essential principles are taught. Clear, concise, interesting and attractive — that is how each lesson is presented to you. And at an average cost of only a few pennies a day!

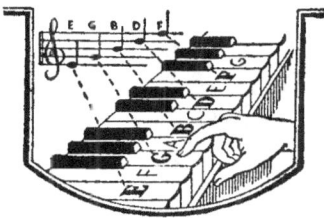

The surest way to popularity

Don't be just "another one of the guests" at the next party you go to. *Be the center of attraction!* The most popular one at a party is always the person who can entertain—and there is no finer and more enjoyable kind of entertainment than music.

Never before have you had such a chance to become a good player—quickly —without a teacher. And this method does not mean that you will be able merely to read notes and play a simple tune or two—but it means you will become a *capable and efficient player.* Many of our pupils now have positions with professional bands and orchestras.

Choose Your Course

Piano	Violin
Organ	Clarinet
Ukulele	Flute
Cornet	Saxophone
Trombone	Harp
Piccolo	Mandolin
Guitar	'Cello

Voice and Speech Culture
Piano Accordion
Hawlian Steel Guitar
Harmony and Composition
Sight Singing
Drums and Traps
Automatic Finger Control
Italian and German Accordion
Banjo (Plectrum, 5-String or Tenor)
Juniors' Piano Course

No alibis now for not learning to play your favorite instrument

Like having a phantom teacher at your side every minute, encouraging you, teaching you, smoothing the way so that it becomes so much easier, so much quicker for you to master your favorite musical instrument.

You simply cannot go wrong. First you are *told* how a thing is done, then by graphic illustrations and diagrams you are *shown* how, and when you play—you *hear* it.

Don't be afraid to begin your lessons at once. Over 600,000 people learned to play this modern way—and found it as easy as A·B·C. Forget that old-fashioned idea that you need special "talent." Just read the list of instruments in the panel, decide which one you want to play, *and the U. S. School will do the rest.*

Send for our free book and demonstration lesson

Our wonderful illustrated Free Book and our Free Demonstration Lesson explain all about this remarkable method. They prove just how anyone can learn to play his favorite instrument *by note* in almost no time and for just a fraction of what old, slow methods cost. The booklet will also tell you all about the amazing new *Automatic Finger Control.*

Act NOW. Clip and mail this coupon today, and the fascinating Free Book and Free Demonstration Lesson will be sent to you at once. No obligation. Instruments supplied when needed, cash or credit. U. S. School of Music, 865 Brunswick Bldg., New York City.

Thirty-fourth Year (Established 1898)

- - - - - - - - - - - - - - - - - - -

U. S. School of Music,
865 Brunswick Bldg., New York City

Please send me your free book, "How You Can Master Music in Your Own Home," with inspiring message by Dr Frank Crane, Free Demonstration Lesson and particulars of your easy payment plan. I am interested in the following course:

.................Have you Instr.?........

Name ....

Address ....

City .... State ....

He half raised up—twitching fingers pointing back at the wagons.

THREE-RING MURDER

by

T. T. Flynn

Author of "Faces in the Fog," etc.

For weeks a pall of mystery had hovered over the big top. Clown and canvas man, ringmaster and roustabout—each sensed the sinister forces which gripped the lot. But no one guessed that human blood would stain the sawdust of the circus ring—that death would crack its whip over the arena.

CHAPTER ONE

Tents of Terror

IT WAS circus day. For a fortnight gaudy posters had informed Midland and the surrounding country of the wonders and pleasures to be displayed before their eyes. And here they were. Lions, tigers, elephants. Beasts of the jungles and fields. Strange and exotic sights. Daring riders. Aerialists. Animal acts. Grotesque clowns. Dashing cowboys and cowgirls from the far west. Sideshows filled with freaks of every kind. Balloons. Popcorn. Crackerjack. Whistles. Hot dogs. Lemonade.

"This wa-y-y, lad-e-e-ez and *gent*-tul-men! See Jumba-a-a, que-e-en of the fat girrrrls. A qua-*tah* of a ton of smiling winsomeness. O-o-nly ten cents, the t-e-enth paht of a dollah, the fifth of a half. Ste-e-ep up . . . "

"Li-t-tle Joe, the Ra-a-attlesnake Boy. See a s-i-ight yo' eyes have ne-evah . . . "

"This w-ay for tickets to the *beeg* show! This wa-ay. Get yo' tickets."

The shrill of whistles. The blare of toy horns. The shuffle of feet. Dust sifting up around the oil flares. Crowds. Noise. Excitement. Everybody happy, gay, expectant. For the circus came only once a year. The big top and adjacent menagerie tent loomed in the night like man-made mountains of pale glowing canvas. A brass band was playing inside. Elephants were waiting. Lions were waiting. Clowns were already grimacing in their before-the-show walk arounds. Circus night.

Early that morning the long trains had rumbled into the Midland freight yards. And at the fairgrounds nearby a white-tented city had sprung up as if by magic. There had been a parade, an afternoon show. And now before the evening show was over the outer tents would be coming down. And by the time the last tired spectator had slipped into bed the circus would be on its way through the night.

But that was still hours away. The big show had yet to near its apex of the day—the night performance. The long rows of wooden seats inside were filling fast. The menagerie was emptying of its staring crowds. The midway was growing more quiet. The red-coated ticket takers in the big marquee were perspiring as they snatched pasteboards and skilfully directed the streaming throngs inside.

Make way for the *beeg* show.

And as the lot grew still quieter and the performance inside began, a stocky young man walked briskly through the midway and stopped before the ticket wagon.

"Yes, suh!" the man inside droned through the small grilled window. "Reserved seat? Still a few left."

"I'm looking for Mr. Brown," said the stocky young man calmly.

"Find 'im in the office, I guess. Back of the wagon here."

"Thanks."

Dan McGrath stopped at the corner of the ticket wagon and looked back along the midway, at the gaudy posters before the sideshow tents, at the lemonade and hot-dog stands. Slowly his eyes swept the big top and past it to the big throbbing light trucks where a gasoline engine whirled the dynamos that supplied light and power to this traveling tent city. That was what it was, a city, a world, a life of its own. People were born in it, lived in it, died in it and without even becoming a part of the world outside. Strange nomads they, who knew every corner of the country.

At one time Dan McGrath had briefly shared it all, and he felt the pull of it again; the old urge to be rolling with the trains to the next stop, and the next and next . . .

Dan's face was round, smooth, cherubic

and innocent. Strangers took in that cherubic innocence, the ready smile, the mild gaze, the soft speech, and thought they knew the man behind it. Soft, wishy-washy, inexperienced. A man who could be handled. And then some day, if there was occasion for it, they received a rude shock.

For beneath the cherubic innocence were muscles that could cord grimly, eyes that could grow cold and shrewd, and lips that could spill concentrated vitriol.

DAN McGRATH walked back of the ticket wagon. A few yards away stood a second gaudy red wagon. It had a door at one end and steps to the ground. And over the door a gilt sign.

OFFICE
Brown's Consolidated Circus

Dan McGrath knocked on the door and a small sliding panel flipped back. A thin, withered, sourish face peered out. Then a dry, rustling voice said through a wispy gray mustache: "Yes? What do you want?"

Dan McGrath smiled vaguely. "Is Mr. Brown in?" he asked uncertainly.

The dry rustling voice asked: "What is your business with Mr. Brown?"

"Is he buying any elephants?" Dan McGrath asked innocently.

A suspicious eye beneath a parchment lid glowed at him. The head beneath it shook.

"No business like that done here, mister. We don't need any animals now anyway. The menagerie is full up. You couldn't sell us an elephant this season."

"Gracious," Dan McGrath said mildly. "Not an elephant this season? *Hmmm.* Well, I left my elephant samples at home tonight anyway."

The parchment eyelids blinked at him. "You, uh, w-what?" the dry rustling voice stuttered.

"Twitty, who is that?" a voice asked from the other end of the portable office.

The face turned away and answered: "A man here says he left his elephant samples to home, Mr. Brown."

A joyful whoop filled the car. "Let him in! There's only one man in this state who would be fool enough to say anything like that!"

A chair kicked back as the door opened. The stooped leathery figure of Twitty stepped aside as a slim well-tailored young man hurried to the door. He met Dan McGrath coming in. He fell on him like a whirlwind, pounding his back, shaking his hand, dragging him to a chair.

"You son-of-a-gun!" Harry Brown cried delightedly. "I knew it was you! Not another egg in the state would have had the nerve to talk elephant samples to Twitty."

Twitty stood beside the door, blinking sourly. He was a man who might be any age. A rusty black suit hung on a frame as thin and spare as the supports of a corn-field scarecrow. His shoulders were stooped. His face was lean and wrinkled, like a piece of very old parchment. Across it his mouth cut like a thin tight gash. And as he stood there peering through half-shut eyelids his whole expression was of outraged sourness.

"Twitty," said Harry Brown, "this is a very old friend of mine."

Twitty raised a clawlike hand and pushed the fingers through six hairs combed neatly across a pallid dome. He nodded slightly. His mouth twitched in a slight grimace that might possibly have passed for a smile.

"Pardon my mistake," Twitty begged in dry, rustling tones. "I did not know the gentleman."

Harry Brown seized a gray hat lying on a desk at the other end of the car.

"I'll be back after while, Twitty," he said. "Get the figures from the ticket wagon as quick as you can and put them in the totals."

"Very well, Mr. Brown," Twitty rustled. "Didn't you tell me you were going to check over these figures before your father came back?"

"They can wait." And Harry Brown went outside with Dan McGrath. He paused a moment at the foot of the steps to shoot a swift glance around the show lot, and then led the way off into the darkness beyond the light wagon. "Lord, it's good to see you," he declared as they went. "I was beginning to think I'd miss you."

"I was out of town when your letter got here yesterday," Dan explained. "Didn't return until an hour or so ago."

"How's the sleuthing business?"

Dan McGrath smiled. "Pretty good."

Harry Brown sobered and looked at him keenly. "Ever hanker to get back in the circus? That year we had together after college seemed to agree with you."

"I was thinking tonight it would be pretty nice to roll out with the show," McGrath confessed.

"Why don't you?"

For a moment Dan McGrath was silent. Then he asked mildly: "Got something on your mind Harry?"

INSIDE the big top the brass band struck up another lively tune. The thud of horses hoofs drifted out through the canvas walls.

"We've been having trouble," Harry Brown said slowly. "The Finke and Streit Circus have been playing this territory on our schedule."

Dan McGrath whistled softly. "Trouble, eh?"

"Yes. You know how it is. It happens now and then in the game. It usually simmers down to war between the billing crews. Each side trying to keep the other's

paper plastered under theirs. We've had that for a month."

"I'd like to spend a day with your billing car," Dan grinned.

"You'd have some fun," Harry Brown assured him. "But we've more than held our own. It's something deeper that's worrying me." Harry Brown sobered. "Dad is pretty old and in bad health, you know. His mind hasn't been what it was since mother died last year. He's—he's a little childish at times. Vague. I don't know—"

Harry Brown shook his head.

"I'm afraid he's losing his grip," he muttered. "Finke and Streit have been trying since last year to buy us out or consolidate with us. Times are hard and shows are doing no more than break even. Some of them are losing heavily. Dad wouldn't listen to their proposition. He told them to their faces they were crooks and he wouldn't deal with them. Chased them out. Made a lot of bad feeling. But then that's always been his way. He won't tolerate a crook."

"I know. He's one of the grand old men of the circus game," Dan nodded. "And so he's in bad with Finke and Streit now?"

"I think they laid their route along with ours on purpose," Harry Brown said harshly. "They're trying to smash us, or force us to sell out or go in with them. And they're using every dirty trick they can think of. I know for a fact that some of our people are taking money from them. But I don't know who. We have been having more trouble in a week than we usually have in a whole season. Everything is wrong. The morale of the whole show is shot."

"Can't your detectives help you any?" Dan asked.

Harry Brown shrugged. "They seem helpless. I've gotten to the point where I don't know who is with us and who is

not. And every time I make a move dad **ties** my hands. He's still the big boss and I'm the youngster who can't be trusted **with** responsibility. I think the way his **mind** is has a lot to do with it. Things **have** been going from bad to worse. It has gotten to the point where something **has** to be done to save the show. Think **of** that, Dan. Brown's Consolidated Circus—forty years out on the road and in danger of going under."

"Perhaps it isn't as bad as that," Dan urged.

Harry Brown struck a fist in the palm of the other hand. "It is! I'm giving you straight dope!"

"I'm sorry, old man," Dan said awkwardly. "I wish I could do something."

"You can!" Harry Brown said vigorously.

"Me?"

"Yes. That's why I wanted to see you."

"What can I do?" Dan countered.

"You know the circus and the routine. You can make yourself at home. And perhaps between us we can spot some of the rotten places and cut them out."

"You'll be gone tonight," Dan pointed out.

"You're coming with us," Harry Brown told Dan calmly.

There was a moment's pause. "Sorry. I can't do that," Dan said.

"Sure you can!"

"Can't make it, old scout. I've got a couple of things in the fire now I can't run away from. The agency can't afford to pass them up."

"If it's money—"

"Not that, so much as sticking here and pleasing the steady customers."

"Hell!" said Harry Brown disgustedly. "I was counting on you."

"Sorry. But you can get a better man **than** me at any of the big agencies."

"He won't know the circus game and fit in like you. Besides, I want you."

"Sorry."

"Rats!" Harry Brown snorted.

Dan fumbled for a cigarette and lighted it. The flaring match before his face showed a slight frown. He felt bad over turning down Harry Brown. They had been good friends. He wanted to help. But he had told the truth. The agency had two cases that needed him. He was in a rut now and couldn't run out on a whim. The circus had plenty of money to hire anyone they pleased. Harry could take care of this all right.

It wasn't that he didn't want to go. The old spell of the circus was getting him again. Sawdust and spangles, hard work and hard play. Here today and somewhere else tomorrow. New sights, people, scenes.

As he flicked the match away and took the cigarette from his mouth Dan's eye was caught by something over in the shadows beyond the office and ticket wagon.

Some of the huge red wagons were over there, lumped around in the night like grotesque creatures. A darker shadow had slipped from behind one of them, appeared for a moment, and disappeared behind another wagon. A stooping, furtive shadow that flitted out of sight and did not reappear.

"Someone is sneaking over among those wagons!" Dan said sharply.

"Where?"

Dan pointed.

"Probably one of the canvas men or roustabouts. They sleep around any place," Harry decided.

"This fellow looked like he didn't want to be seen."

Harry Brown chuckled. "Just how did he look?"

"No wonder you have trouble, if that's

all the attention you pay to suspicious actions," Dan snorted.

"There's no harm anyone can do over there," Harry assured him.

"We'd better go over and have a look, just the same."

"All right, if you insist."

Together they walked toward the wagons. Their course brought them past the back of the office wagon. And as they reached that point Dan suddenly caught his friend by the arm.

"What's that?" he exclaimed sharply.

Out of the night before them a choked, wailing cry had come. A cry that seemed to bubble from a throat in a queer inhuman manner. A cry that ran the gamut of surprise, fright, terror.

"What the devil was that?" Harry Brown rapped out.

"Trouble!" Dan said briefly.

CHAPTER TWO

Murder On the Lot

SURPRISE had stopped both of them in their tracks. And now as they looked a figure came out of the group of wagons. A lurching, staggering figure that seemed about to fall each step, and somehow did not. A figure that clawed at its throat with both hands and made queer gurgling sounds as it reeled toward them.

"Great God in heaven!" Harry Brown cried thickly. "Look at that, Dan. Look at that!"

Dan saw too. He went sick inside. He wanted to turn his eyes away—and could not. His mind seemed to stop as his feet took him mechanically forward at a run. Harry Brown ran at his side, cursing frantically under his breath.

The reeling figure pitched forward at their feet, raining blood.

It was an overalled roustabout, grimy of face, needing a shave. One of the tattered drifters that do the heavy muscle work of a big circus. And his throat had been torn open by a ghastly, terrible slash. Before their helpless eyes his life-blood was draining away, drenching the hands that pawed futilely at the throat, pouring on the ground beneath.

There was nothing they could do. Dan knew it. Harry knew it. They could only stare in horror for a moment. And then as they both dropped to their knees the man struggled over on his side. He half raised up.

A ghastly, gurgling noise came from his throat. He was trying to speak and could not. One wet red arm slowly raised with a mighty effort. Twitching fingers pointed back at the wagons.

And then with a gasp he fell suddenly back to the ground. His feet and body twitched. He gave one convulsive shudder—and then lay still.

Still swearing in frozen, lifeless tones Harry Brown pushed up an eyelid. Slowly he turned and stared at Dan McGrath. His voice sounded flat and thick when he spoke.

"He's dead, Dan."

"Yes, he's dead," Dan nodded. "No man could live through anything like that."

"He didn't have a chance!" Harry broke out, getting to his feet. "It was murder, Dan. Cold murder!"

Dan was already on his feet too, starting toward the cluster of wagons at a run.

"Come on!" he threw back over his shoulder. "Maybe we can get the one who did it!"

They plunged in the thick black shadows among the wagons. They ran here and there, searching for sight of another figure. And they found no one. No one else joined them either. There was still noise in plenty on the midway. Either the cry had not been heard, or had been disregarded by anyone whose ears had caught it.

Panting, the two friends came together and stopped.

"The fellow I saw skulking must have killed him!" Dan rapped out.

"Maybe the man back there on the ground was the one you saw," Harry suggested.

"I don't think so. The one I saw seemed to have a black cloak on. Or something that flapped in the shadows."

"Maybe you didn't see straight."

"Maybe not," Dan admitted. "But I saw enough to make me suspicious. And right after that the fellow was slashed."

"I wonder if he fought with someone," Harry Brown said dully. He was badly shaken by what had happened. It showed in every action and word.

Dan was shaken too, but his mind was working fast, canvassing all the possibilities at hand.

"There wasn't much time for a fight," he pointed out. "Not over thirty seconds. You can't get steamed up to a killing pitch in that length of time. Someone might have been waiting there for him. The man I saw might have been looking for him. Had it all planned out, and when he caught his man he killed him and ran. That would explain what we heard. The poor devil saw what was coming, yelled, and his throat was torn open before he had a chance to finish the yell."

"God, I can't understand it!" Harry Brown muttered. "I've never seen anything so cold blooded and vicious as that, Dan. A bullet wouldn't have seemed so bad. But this—"

"We'd better put in a call for the city police, cover the body up and question those people over on the midway while their minds are fresh," Dan suggested crisply.

"All right. You—you go back to the office, Dan. There's a portable phone there, hooked up with the city system. Call the police. I'll run over to midway and question them. I'll have better luck there than you will."

THEY parted, each running to his task. As Dan came up to the back of the ticket wagon he saw a pile of canvas on the ground beneath it. He dragged it out and spread it over the body.

Queer that no one had noticed the death. Not thirty yards away were people. But they were in the light, and this was in the shadow back here. If they had not heard the cry there was nothing to bring their eyes this way.

The brass band in the tent was playing loudly. It occurred fleetingly to Dan how ironic it was for music, laughter, enjoyment to be so close to sordid death.

He had hardly finished draping the canvas over the body when he saw a big hulking figure striding past the ticket wagon toward him. It was a veritable giant of a man, sleeves rolled up over massive forearms, khaki shirt open at the throat, battered felt hat cocked on the back of his head. And he growled under a close-clipped black mustache.

"Who are you, mister? What are you doin' draggin' canvas around here?"

"Who are you?" Dan returned shortly, for he had little time to waste on this man.

"I'm Gerraty, boss canvas man. You ain't with the show, are you?"

"I am right now," Dan snapped. "What brought you over here to this spot?"

Gerraty scowled at him. His face was a chunky block of weather-beaten meat. It seemed all square beefy angles. His mouth chopped out the words he spoke. "I seen you reach under the wagon and drag out that canvas. What's the idea?"

Dan stepped back and lifted up a corner of the canvas. "This is the idea," he said curtly. "Know who this man is?"

Gerraty gaped, gulped. "Geez!" he breathed. "Who done that?"

"We want to find out. Know him?"

"Wait—sure, that's a guy named 'Spud' Wolfe. He's been with us half the season. Canvas man. Old-timer in the game. Who killed him? Did you do that?" Gerraty swung menacingly on Dan.

Dan dropped the canvas. "I haven't time to argue with you now," he said coldly. "I've got to get in the wagon there and call the police. I didn't kill him. I was with Harry Brown when this fellow staggered up to us. Watch him."

He left the boss canvas man muttering to himself and burst into the traveling office. Twitty jumped off a chair set before a desk and gazed at him sourly.

"Where's the telephone?" Dan demanded.

And then seeing it over in the corner the next moment, he ran to it and snatched it up. In a few moments he was connected with headquarters. He recognized the nasal voice of Sergeant Mason.

"This is Dan McGrath, of the McGrath Agency, speaking," he snapped. "I'm out at the circus grounds. There's been a bad murder out here. Send a homicide detail. The body's back of the ticket wagon." Dan hung up.

"Murder?" Twitty gasped in his dry voice. His eyes seemed to bulge as he stared with head hunched forward.

"Yes. A canvas man by the name of Wolfe. Throat cut. He's out back of the wagon here on the ground."

Twitty's parchmentlike face might have belonged to a mummy as his beady bright eyes gazed at Dan unwinkingly for a moment. And then his breath sucked in audibly. A harsh whisper came through his gash of a mouth.

"*I knew it.*"

"You knew what?" Dan asked sharply.

"Somebody'd get killed before the season was over," Twitty husked.

"How did you know that?"

"It's been plain. The season's cursed. Anybody with half an eye could see it'd end in murder."

"Is that all?"

Twitty nodded.

"Nonsense," Dan said curtly, turning to the door.

But as he opened it and went out Twitty spoke again, in that same dry rustling whisper that might have come from the mouth of the mummy he resembled.

"Mark my words—there'll be more deaths! We're in it now and can't stop it!"

DAN slammed the door. For some reason he did not like Twitty. There was something about the old fellow that grated on his nerves, got under his skin. Twitty didn't seem to belong to this earth. He was like some dry, dusty, taloned apparition out of the shadows. A croaking bird of ill omen.

The boss canvas man was still standing by the lumpish pile of canvas on the ground. Three men were with him now, and as Dan looked he saw several others drifting up out of the darkness back of the light truck, drawn to the spot by sight of the group forming there.

"The police will be here shortly," Dan said to Gerraty. "We don't want a crowd around here. Run those men off as they come up. And keep them from wandering around the wagons over there. If there's any evidence we don't want it stepped on or destroyed."

"I take orders from the guy over me, not a stranger," Gerraty growled.

He was either a surly fellow, or his nerves were raw from what had happened. The men with him seemed little better by the unfriendly glances they gave. And, in a way they were right, Dan concluded. He had no authority around here. So he left them and hurried off toward the midway.

He found Harry Brown just turning away from one of the sideshow booths where he had been questioning the ticket seller in front. Dan saw him, came over to him. He shook his head.

"Not a thing, Dan," he said. "No one admits hearing anything or seeing anyone come out from the wagons."

"Funny," Dan said slowly. "Do you know all those men? Can you trust all of them?"

Harry shrugged. "I know their names, and some of them. But the personnel of this part of the show is always changing. I don't try to keep up with them. Half of them I can't vouch for one way or the other."

"Then someone might have lied to you?"

"Easily," Harry admitted.

They stood in uneasy silence for a few minutes.

"There's no excitement," Dan muttered. "You'd think after what happened the whole lot would be in an uproar."

"I didn't tell anyone why I was questioning them," Harry said under his breath. "They're all busy with other things."

"Your canvas man is over by the body. Some others are with him. He seems like a surly fellow."

"That's Gerraty. He is. I've had several run-ins with him. Threatened to fire him once, but dad kept him on. Says he knows his business and that's enough. Gerraty has quieted down the last month. Are the police coming?"

"Be here any minute."

Harry Brown looked over the black shadows around the looming wagons.

"I can't figure why the poor devil made that effort to point back at the wagons," he confessed. "He seemed to have something on his mind. Something he wanted to tell us badly. It must have been important to take precedence over the fact that he was dying."

Dan frowned thoughtfully as they walked slowly off the midway toward the wagons.

"It might be he was trying to show us where to find the man who cut him," he suggested, but changed that idea almost as soon as it was spoken. "It does look as if there was something else on his mind. If he only had been able to speak . . . "

Dan broke off suddenly. His voice sharpened.

"Say—did it occur to you that whoever cut him might have done so because they didn't want him to speak? A bullet, a stab through the heart, a blow over the head would have dropped him. But he still might have been able to talk. But his throat—no chance then."

"Sounds logical," Harry admitted. "But who didn't want him to speak, and why? What would he have said? Of course . . . What's the matter?"

Dan had left his side suddenly and dashed off at a tangent. The well-dressed son of the circus owner gaped for a moment as he saw his friend dodge behind the nearest wagon. An instant later he appeared at the other end.

HARRY blinked. No man could have made the length of that wagon so quickly, could have disappeared at one end and come out the other almost instantly.

The mystery was solved as a second figure jumped out after the first, catching its arm, halting it. Harry was already on his way toward the spot. He saw now that the second man was Dan McGrath. The first was a stranger who had been behind the wagon, and had run out.

The stranger was protesting in injured tones as Harry joined them.

"Leggo my arm! What's the idea of

grabbing a fellow like this? I was only taking a short cut through here."

"Short cut, eh?" Dan rasped. "Do you always run when you take a short cut?"

"No," said the other sullenly.

"What's the idea of running now?"

"I wasn't running."

"I saw you!" Dan told him curtly, and to Harry he explained: "I caught a glimpse of this fellow hurrying past a wagon. He was trying to get away quick. He must have stopped behind that wagon there when he heard my steps, and then he ran out when he saw I was after him."

As he talked Dan dragged his prisoner out where the light from the midway fell on him. The man was short and shifty looking. He wore a wrinkled suit of old clothes, a dirty shirt and a faded necktie. He was thin, scrawny. His face was lean, almost wizened, and his eyes shifted around with a harried, furtive expression. He gave the impression that he would bolt if that grip on his arm were released.

Harry stared hard at him. "Your face is familiar," he remarked.

"Why shouldn't it be?" the prisoner retorted quickly. "I been workin' with the show all season. Ed Bolen is my name. I work balloons, canes an' whistles for Sam Taylor."

"Oh, yes, that's where I've seen you," Harry recalled. And to Dan he explained: "You remember Sam Taylor. He's the big fat fellow who has the lot concession for slum goods. He's been with the show for years. This man is with him right now."

"Why isn't he over on the midway now?" Dan demanded.

"The towners are all inside," Bolen said hurriedly. "I had a bottle hid over in the weeds, an' I went over there for a drink. I was just comin' back when you grabbed me. Geez! What's the matter anyway?"

The smell of whiskey was strong on his breath, bearing out what he said.

"So eager to get back to work you were running to it, I suppose?" Dan said sarcastically. "I'll just look through your pockets and see what you're carrying."

He did that, despite the prisoner's violent protests. He found no weapons of any kind. But his exploring fingers jerked open the soiled shirt and disclosed a money belt next to the skin. The pocket of the soft leather belt was fat and well filled.

Dan opened it. Inside was a neat wad of bills. When he took them out and riffled through them over a thousand dollars were revealed.

"Pretty well heeled for a slum seller, aren't you?" Dan questioned drily.

The owner of the money tried to grab it. "Never mind about that," he said angrily. "My money ain't any of your business. I earn it an' I save it. By God, I'll make trouble for this!"

The thin wail of a nearing siren drifted through the night. Dan returned the bills to Bolen. "Here come the police," he remarked coldly. "You can tell it to them."

"The police!"

The words were ripped from Bolen's lips involuntarily. There was startled fear in them. His mouth worked as he thrust the bills back in the leather money belt and tucked the shirt in over it. His eyes searched their faces furtively. Abruptly he ducked under Dan's arm and fled.

Harry Brown saw the move. He made a flying tackle that brought the fellow down heavily on the dusty ground. The next moment Dan grabbed the prisoner by the nape of the neck and dragged him up.

"Good tackle, Harry," he grinned approvingly. "You should have gone out for football in college."

Harry got up, brushing the dust from his clothes. His face was hard as he looked at the prisoner. "I guess that settles it," he said shortly. "He's covering something up."

Dan's big hand clamped hard into the scrawny neck of the prisoner. He shook Bolen roughly. "Spit it out!" he ordered gruffly. 'You're on a spot now! What did you kill that man for?"

DAN asked that as a blind shot. He merely wanted to shake the little man's nerve, so he would confess whatever he was trying to hide. There was no thought in Dan's mind that the prisoner had had anything to do with the slashed throat of the dead man. There was not a sign of blood on hands, face, or clothes. He could not be guilty of that without having blood on himself. There had been no time to clean it off.

But the reply to the brusk question staggered him.

Bolen's defiance vanished. He began to twitch and tremble. "Is he d-dead?" he stammered.

Dan shot a swift glance of surprised warning at Harry. He scowled into the face of the prisoner.

"Certainly he's dead! And you killed him! Why did you do it?"

The siren wailed again, much nearer. Bolen collapsed completely.

"I didn't kill him!" he choked. "I didn't, s'help me! I don't know who killed him! I didn't know he was dead! I stumbled over his foot an' saw him lyin' there, an' thought he was a drunk."

"You what?" Dan demanded in amazement.

"I saw him lyin' there, an' thought he was drunk," the prisoner quavered.

"You can't tell a dead man when you see one?"

"I didn't look close, s'help me, mister. I thought he was drunk, an' I rolled him an' beat it. That's where the money come

from. I did that, mister, but I didn't kill him."

"He must be off his head," Harry declared, staring at the twitching wizened face.

Dan was thinking the same thing. This man claimed to have gone through the pockets of the body and taken that large sum of money. But how could he have done that with the boss canvas man and the other men standing around? And whoever heard of a roustabout having that much money on his person anyway? Either the fellow was lying or his mind was wandering.

"Where was the money?" Dan questioned.

"In his coat pocket, mister. He had a billfold."

"Where is it?"

"I threw it away."

"He didn't have on a coat!" Dan said coldly.

"He did," the prisoner wailed. "I can show it to you."

"He must be cuckoo," Harry decided disgustedly. "That fellow didn't have on a coat. And this man couldn't have rolled him without getting blood all over his hands. No roustabout in this show carries that much money, anyway."

The prisoner stared at them, as if they too were out of their heads. He cringed away, in the grip of stark fear.

"He wasn't a roustabout!" he denied wildly. "An' he didn't have any blood on him. He was alive. I heard him breathin' hard. That's why I thought he was drunk. He kinda groaned once, like he was havin' a bad dream! So I rolled him an' beat it. An' you caught me before I got away."

Dan's interest sharpened. "You rolled him just before I caught you?" he snapped.

"Yeah."

"Where is he?"

"Over there," the prisoner gestured back at the rear of the wagons.

"Take us there," Dan ordered.

THE prisoner led the way without hesitation. They went, not toward the office and the spot where that ghastly still figure lay under the canvas, but to the rear of the wagons where the shadows were thickest and darkest.

"I hid my bottle over there in the weeds on the bank," Bolen explained feverishly. "An' I cut right through here comin' back. I stumbled over his foot in the dark. There, he's under that wagon."

Dan had hurriedly passed by this spot, looking for the killer. Failing to find him, he had run on. The shadows were so thick a man lying on the ground under one of the wagons could very easily have been invisible. But now as they halted and he strained his eyes he saw the dark form of a man under the big wagon. There was the foot projecting out by the rear wheel that Bolen claimed to have tripped over. Slow, harsh, labored breathing was audible. The man was alive, all right.

Harry Brown caught the feet and pulled the man out.

"Dan, this must be what that poor devil was trying to tell us," he said excitedly. "He knew this man was here and wanted us to know."

"I was thinking the same thing," Dan confessed. "He sounds hurt. Got a match?"

"Yes."

A moment later a match flared in Harry's hand. It moved over the figure on the ground.

Harry's voice suddenly wrenched out: "Dan! It's my father!"

"Your father?" Dan rapped out.

"Yes! He's hurt! He's unconscious!" Harry feverishly struck another match

and dropped to a knee. Jonathan Brown had been a big man, but age and illness had shrunk his form and put deep lines in his face. His hat had fallen off. His silvery white hair tumbled back in confusion from his forehead. Dust and dirt covered his suit. His face was set and expressionless, in that dull vacant stare of the unconscious. His eyes were closed. His chest rose and fell as uneven labored breathing sucked harshly in and out.

Harry staggered to his feet. "We can't do anything for him here!" he said thickly. "We've got to get him to the hospital. I'll run over and telephone for an ambulance."

The police siren wailed again at the edge of the lot as Harry ran from the spot. Dan hesitated. There was nothing he could do for the injured man either. He hustled his prisoner after Harry.

And as he went his mind sorted through everything he had found out this evening. Trouble. A man killed. The owner of the show unconscious. Old Twitty saying in his rustling tones that more trouble would happen.

Truly a curse had struck this show. No wonder Harry had been worried. Back of all this Dan felt there was much more. Jonathan Brown had not been struck down without purpose. And that purpose had not been robbery. This cringing, sniffling prisoner he was hustling along had found money on Jonathan Brown. A large sum.

Dan believed Bolen's story now. He had gone for a drink, found what he thought was a drunk on his way back, and furtively gone through the pockets. It was just the kind of petty crime Bolen would select. He had been caught trying to get away with his loot, which had doubtless been far more than he suspected. No wonder he had been uneasy, frightened. In the darkness he had not recognized his victim, or he would probably have blurted everything out as soon as he was stopped.

CHAPTER THREE

Sawdust Jinx

THE homicide detail was just hurrying up to the office when Dan got there with his prisoner. Lieutenant Hayes had charge. With him were three men, Langdon, Mitchell and another Dan did not know. All were in plain clothes.

Lieutenant Hayes saw him and veered over. "What's all this?" he queried as he came up. "Where's the body?"

Dan jerked his head at the canvas mound on the ground a few yards away. "Under that canvas," he said. "Take this man and hold him. He's part of the case. We just found Jonathan Brown, the owner of the show, unconscious over there under a wagon. This man had gone through his pockets and was trying to get away when I caught him. He had a sum of money that belongs to Mr. Brown."

Hayes was a grizzled, shrewd veteran of the force, level headed and a good man to work with. A crisp order from him turned Bolen over into custody of a detective. Lieutenant Hayes strode to the canvas.

Gerraty, the boss canvas man, and at least a dozen others were around the spot now.

"Get back," Hayes snapped at them.

They obeyed him. Hayes pulled back the canvas. A low whistle came from his lips as he took in the dead man.

"Nasty, isn't it?" he asked. "What happened?"

Dan quickly and briefly sketched what had occurred. "I think he knew Mr. Brown was over there unconscious and tried to tell us," he finished.

Hayes nodded. Harry Brown had come out of the office, listened a moment as Dan talked, and then hurried back to his father.

Lieutenant Hayes looked at the men clustering around. "Any of these men figure in it anyway?"

"Not that I know of."

"Ummm. Well, the medical examiner will be here in a few minutes. Langdon, put that canvas back and watch the body. Keep these people away. The rest of you come with me."

And as they started toward the wagons, and some of the roustabouts and canvas men drifted after them, Hayes snapped: "Keep back, all of you! The first man who comes tagging along over here will get run in."

That held them for a little. And for some minutes the scene was a busy one. With a flashlight Hayes traced back the trail of blood. It was not hard, for the doomed man had bled copiously. That brought them a few yards from the spot where Harry Brown watched over his father with a flashlight he had gotten in the office.

There, around the end of a wagon, was clearly the spot where the attack had taken place. The ground, cluttered with hoof marks and shoe marks, offered little in the way of evidence, beyond the dark splotches of blood on the dusty sparse grass.

"It looks to me like Mr. Brown was struck down; the other fellow came up, saw who did it, and got his before he could get away," Dan suggested.

Lieutenant Hayes nodded. "That's about what happened," he admitted. "What was Mr. Brown doing over here?"

Harry Brown said soberly: "He had been down town. I was expecting him back any minute. I don't know what he was doing over here. After getting back on the lot he may have decided to look around before he came to the office. He often did that. He tried to keep an eye on everything."

"You have no idea who might have done this?"

"No," Harry denied. "It might have been one of a score of people in the show, or someone from outside, as far as I know. We can't check up on everyone around a crowded lot like this. It may have been a crook belonging in the city here."

But Dan had the feeling that Harry did not mean that. He was reserving judgment, just as Dan was himself. There was no proof of any kind to go on. Mere suspicions could not be uttered recklessly.

The homicide squad looked around. They found the empty wallet that Bolen had thrown away, and that was about all. No knife. Nothing that could have been used in the attack on either man. And it was soon clear they were getting nowhere.

While they were doing that Dan saw two men hasten up. One was a big, beefy mustached, fellow. He was accompanied by an equally tall, thin, gangling man wearing a hat on the back of his head.

They bore flashlights, and they came directly to Harry Brown, still with his father. Dan, standing by, heard Harry say sharply: "Where have you been all this time, Fletcher?"

The big man shrugged. "Lupe and me was over in the menagerie tent, and then inside the big top, keepin' an eye on the towners. I put the finger on a coupla dips, an' run 'em out. I just heard about this, an' I grabbed Lupe an' hurried out here."

Harry said to Dan: "This is Fletcher, our boss detective, and the man who works with him. They're all the force we're carrying this season. Fletcher, this is Mr. McGrath, an old friend of mine. He's with a detective agency here in town."

FLETCHER looked and talked like a gruff man. But his handshake was quick—almost too quick—and his greeting was smooth and cordial.

"Glad to know ya, Mr. McGrath. So you're a detective, eh? Well, you're lucky you don't have to fight trouble in a show like this. Like tonight. Gawd, it's tough! Meet Lupe."

"Howdy," said Lupe briefly.

His handshake was limp. His tall gangling body and ill-fitting clothes made him look like a country rustic in to stare at the show. He had a long, corded neck and when he spoke a huge Adam's apple raced up and down in it. Dan saw all that by flashes of the lights, and not much more.

Fletcher said to Harry: "I see you got the city dicks here. I guess there ain't much we can do now."

"You can circulate around and try to pick up the man who did that killing!" Harry said sharply. "He'll have to get marks of blood off him! Don't come to me and ask me what to do! That's your job, Fletcher. Look alive to it. Don't you get the fact that a man has been killed and—and my father attacked? Get busy!"

"O. K., boss," Fletcher grunted gruffly. He seemed to resent the way Harry had talked to him as he snapped: "Come on, Lupe! Let's do a little Sherlock Holmesing!"

Harry Brown silently watched the two of them walk away. After a moment he said: "That fellow has been in the show game a long time, and it doesn't seem to have taught him much."

The medical examiner came, looked at the body. He was hardly on the lot when an ambulance drove swiftly up. Harry Brown's father was lifted on a stretcher. The white-coated interne who accompanied the ambulance crew made a brief examination and said to Harry: "Concussion. We can tell more when we get to the hospital."

Harry went with them. "I'll be back as quick as I can," he said to Dan. "The show has got to get away."

Lieutenant Hayes said thoughtfully as the ambulance drove away: "The circus goes on tonight, doesn't it?"

"It's scheduled to," Dan said.

"That tangles everything up. I don't see where we can do much. We'll search the show and everyone we can find. But they're all strangers to us. We haven't any leads to go on. And no time to work. We can't hold the show here. There's no evidence of any kind. And as he says, it might have been someone from the town."

And that was what it all simmered down to. The dead body was taken away. Lieutenant Hayes and his men began to round up everyone on the lot and examine them, looking particularly for signs of blood on anyone.

They found nothing. Harry Brown came back from the hospital presently.

"Bad concussion of the brain," he said briefly to Dan. "They think he has a fair chance of pulling through, but it's nothing they can hurry. He may be unconscious until tomorrow. I've arranged for every care to be taken of him, and wires will be sent to me letting me know how he gets along."

"You're going on with the show?" Dan asked.

Harry smiled thinly and swept his hand toward the big top. The show was still going on in there, as if nothing had happened. Outside of the circus people probably no one knew that anything had happened.

"The show always goes on," Harry remarked. "They're striking some of the tents now. We have to keep on schedule. Dad would want me to carry on with it." His face hardened. "Only now I'll be the big boss," he said grimly. "And if

there's any way of getting to the bottom of this I'm going to do it. This wasn't a casual thing, Dan. Much more of the same thing is going to play the devil with the show. Already they're asking themselves who the next one is going to be. When a show like this gets branded with a jinx it sticks. Trouble breeds trouble."

"I think I'll go back and get my bag," Dan decided.

"Your bag?"

"Yes. I'm going on with you, Harry."

Harry's hand met his in a tight grip. "I knew you'd come through," Harry said huskily. "We'll lick this together, Dan."

BEFORE the big show was over, the circus was flowing toward the railroad yards. Canvas billowed down before the staccato orders, and was stowed in the canvas wagons. Men darted here and there, working briskly, efficiently. Torches flared in the night. The led stock filed away through the darkness, following the line of pot flares placed at intervals along the way to the loading runs half a mile distant. Sleek, powerful horses hauled rumbling wagons after them. The show lot began to wear a deserted look.

Dan moved around, looking for suspicious signs, but found nothing. The ticket wagon and office were hauled away. In a few hours the show lot would be dark and silent, holding only the debris of the show and the memory of murder that had been done.

Dan walked down to the yards with his bag. There was nothing more he could do on the lot. If there was a killer in the show he would come along with them. If he did not, they would know who to check on. Every boss had orders to report instantly any member of his crew who deserted this night.

Harry's private car, which he and his father occupied, was coupled on the rear end of the last section. Dan found it with little trouble, gave his bag to the porter in charge of it, informing him he was going on with the show, and went outside to watch the loading further down in the yards.

The flying squadron was just pulling out with the cook tents, horse tent wagons, menagerie tent and sleepers for the men who went with it. In the light of flaring acetylene torches the loading runs were a scene of furious activity. Horses' hoofs trampled heavily. Big wagons rumbled up the loading runs onto flat cars, where they were chocked in place by watchful razorbacks. Pot torches with flaring wicks dotted the night beyond with wavering points of flame.

Steps crunched on the cinders beside Dan. It was Fletcher, the big boss detective. The light here showed Fletcher's face better. Bushy black eyebrows shaded half-closed eyes that broke off into deep wrinkles at the corners, as if the man had a habit of staring suspiciously most of the time. Overfleshed cheeks sagged down into jowls around his collar, and his mouth was thick-lipped and big. A crooked nose betrayed violence in the past.

Fletcher rocked back and forth on big feet, hands in pockets. His squinting eyes dwelt on Dan for a moment, and then shifted away as Dan looked at him.

"Lots of work to load an' unload a show like this," Fletcher commented casually.

"It seems to be," Dan said, forbearing to mention that he had traveled with this show at one time. He had been only a minor part of it then. His friendship with the owner's son had counted for little. Few people still in the show would be apt to remember him at all. And he had changed some, too, with the years.

Fletcher had apparently stopped casually, but as he stood there Dan sensed that he had something on his mind.

"This business tonight was bad," Fletcher observed.

"Nasty," Dan agreed.

"Bad business," said Fletcher again, slowly. And when Dan said nothing, Fletcher observed: "With a show moving around all the time it's hard to get to the bottom of anything like this. Too bad you can't go along with us and work with me an' Lupe."

Dan said casually: "I am going along."

"Say—that's great! I'm sure glad to hear that, Mr. McMath."

"McGrath," Dan corrected.

"McGrath—I'll feel better now, with someone else working with us. If we team up we ought to get somewhere."

Every indication of heartiness was in Fletcher's voice. But Dan merely agreed: "I hope so."

Fletcher squinted at him keenly. "Got any ideas?"

"None."

"Ummm. I was hoping you had." There was reluctant disappointment in Fletcher's tone. "I haven't got any either," he admitted. His eyes strayed off into the night. Casually: "A lot of the show folks are looking for anything to happen. I kind of feel that way myself. Well, guess I'll be getting along."

Dan watched the big detective depart. He frowned slightly. What did Fletcher mean by saying anything might happen? Did a hidden meaning lurk in those words? Had Fletcher stopped to pump him, find out what he was doing here in the yards? Why did Fletcher want to find out what he knew?

TWO figures came walking from the show lot. As they moved into the light, Dan saw it was Harry and a girl. She came about to Harry's shoulder, walked with a smooth, graceful stride as they approached him. Dan saw she wore a sweater and a smart little tam, and carried a light leather bag in her hand.

"Marta, I want you to know an old friend of mine, Dan McGrath," Harry said as they stopped. "Dan, Marta is our star equestrienne, Marta White."

A small muscular hand met Dan's. He recalled her pictures on the twenty-four sheet posters about town. Pictures of a slim, whirling vision in gauzy tights doing breath-taking stunts on the backs of her horses.

He remembered seeing her three years before, with the Finke and Streit Circus, flashing through her daring and difficult act. On the posters and in the sawdust ring she was like some unreal creature from wonderland. Here before him she was a small, slim girl who might be from a select boarding school. Her tam was saucily tilted; big eyes laughed at him from under sweeping lashes; her face was open, frank, pretty. Her voice was a slow, throaty drawl when she laughingly spoke.

"Marta White, professionally, Mr. McGrath. Marta Twitty off the job."

"You met Marta's father tonight," Harry reminded.

Dan remembered, recalled his slight dislike of Twitty. This daughter made him relent a little on that. It took him a moment to get used to the idea that Twitty could be her father. There was no resemblance between them.

"I put my bag in your car," Dan said to Harry.

"Fine. Anything new?"

"No."

Marta White shivered. "This terrible night," she said soberly.

Harry patted her arm. "We'll be away from here in a little while. Go to the privilege car and get some coffee and forget about it."

"I can't," Marta said. "I keep wondering what is going to happen next."

There it was again. The whole circus was permeated with the idea that there was more coming. Dan wondered if she had been talking to her father.

Harry took her arm. "I'll take you over to the car for that cup of coffee. Come along, Dan."

"Thanks. I'll stay out here and look around," Dan said, and as he watched them walk away arm in arm he knew they were not exactly sorry. Harry had said nothing about any affairs of the heart, but this certainly looked as if he had fallen at last.

Dan lighted a cigarette, moved down toward the other end of the train, passing a herd of zebras and a string of camels as he went. On the way he noticed a suspicious figure pass a gap in a string of box cars a couple of tracks over. Something about the way it moved caught his attention. He cut across the tracks, looked cautiously down that drag of cars.

A second line of box cars on the next track formed a long, dark tunnel. The floodlight at the other end of the yards made a background of light silhouetting the figure. It stopped, peered through the gaps between two cars, moved on, to stop again and stare at something. Finally it climbed the steps of a coal gondola and disappeared inside.

Dan's lips tightened. Something queer here. Perhaps a tramp looking for a car to ride out of the yards, but he doubted it. He waited a moment, and then walked quietly forward.

The fine cinders on the ground were close packed; the rubber soles of his shoes made no sound against the background of noise from the loading runs.

He reached the gondola, swung up cautiously. There was his man, peering over the other side at something. Dan vaulted over into the car.

The sound he made caused the stranger to whirl abruptly. A hand went under his coat. It came out with a revolver, ugly, menacing.

CHAPTER FOUR

The Shadow of Death

THE next moment the gun went down. A dry voice said: "I mighty near let you have it then, Mr. McGrath. Better whistle next time. It's risky business slipping up behind a fellow in the dark thataway."

It was Lupe, Fletcher's tall, gangling assistant. Lupe still looked like a farmer and talked like one. But there was nothing rural about the way he had whirled and whipped out that revolver. Dan realized in that moment that Lupe might be a bad man to have trouble with.

Dan stepped over, so Lupe had to turn, getting the light on his features. They were calm. No sign of guilt about him. In fact, he was smiling slightly, with a quizzical look about his eyes.

"Thanks for the warning," Dan said coolly. "Why so nervous? Expecting trouble?"

Lupe smiled. His big Adam's apple ran up and down in his lean neck as he said: "Most folks got a right to expect anything around here—after tonight."

Dan nodded, glanced about the dirty gondola. "I saw you climb up in here and got curious."

Lupe had a quid of tobacco in his cheek. He expectorated expertly over the side, and sighed.

"Funny thing about these here empty coal cars. They seem to work on me. I like to climb around in 'em. Ever get that feeling about an empty car?"

"Now that you speak of it, I seem to feel it myself," Dan agreed mildly.

His eyes went out into the night where Lupe had been staring. A dozen tracks away was the circus train, still the center

of furious activity. A file of elephants padded by, each trunk gripping the wispy tail of the elephant in front. Like great slatey shadows they drifted past, and when they were gone Dan's eyes narrowed.

An odd car was parked on a track just beyond where the elephants had passed. Two people were standing at the end, talking—a man and a woman. The man was gesturing emphatically. The woman was nodding agreement. Dan recognized Fletcher.

A dinky switch engine busily moving about the yards threw a swath of light down the tracks against the two. The woman was wearing a split-leather riding skirt, an embroidered leather jacket, gauntlets and a western sombrero. Her face, visible for an instant, was pretty in a hard determined way. The engine backed away; the light vanished; the two indistinct forms were left there.

"I declare, there's Fletcher over there," Lupe remarked in surprise. "I been wondering where that jasper was."

"And you just saw him?" Dan retorted with a trace of sarcasm.

"Just saw him," Lupe assured him.

The fellow was lying flatly. Dan knew it; and Lupe knew that he knew, for the quizzical smile was on his face as he looked at Dan. Lupe had been stalking Fletcher, spying on his meeting with the girl.

Why?

What significance was there about this meeting of the show detective with that girl dressed in western costume? For that matter, why were the two off in the shadows this way, alone, unheard? It was an unexpected angle that might have any meaning.

"As long as you've found him, why not go over to him?" Dan suggested.

Lupe shrugged. "An' break up that sweet talk? Mister, I pack a tender heart.

I couldn't bear to do that. No sir, I could not. I'll see Fletcher later on."

Lupe was gently kidding him. Dan frowned his irritation. He had a sneaking liking for the fellow. But he tried to remain cold, neutral in this matter.

"Who is the girl?" he questioned.

"Barbara Davis, they say. She's a rider in the western troupe. An' a mighty good one."

"Fletcher's girl?"

"Well, now, I don't rightly know," Lupe denied. "I reckon Fletcher takes 'em as, if, an' when they come."

"Ladies' man, eh?"

"Not being a lady, I couldn't set you right about that," Lupe murmured.

Lupe was playing behind a screen of words, knowing all the time that Dan realized it. He drew out a thick gold watch, held it up to the light, and sighed: "I reckon I'll mosey along. Take good care of this coal car, mister. It seems kind of lonesome, standing all empty and alone thisaway."

Lupe swung over the corner of the car and dropped down into the dark. A thin chuckle floated back, and he was gone.

DAN smiled wryly to himself. Blast the fellow anyway. It wasn't often he met a man who could fence with words so entertainingly. But the smile was replaced by a frown a moment later. Lupe knew he was a detective, yet had said nothing about the case on which he and Fletcher were supposed to be working hard. Dan came to a sudden decision. He left the gondola on the side nearest Fletcher and his companion. As he dropped to the ground and turned to walk toward them, he saw that he had been discovered. They were both looking at him, and as he came up to them they were silent.

"Hello," said Fletcher shortly.

Dan returned the greeting. He stopped.

"Have you a match?" he asked Fletcher. It was an excuse to see the girl closer, and meet her.

Fletcher handed him a match, seemed for a moment unwilling to make the introduction. But he did finally. "Miss Davis, this is Mr. McGrath, a detective who is staying on with the show."

Miss Davis's mouth was rouged; her cheeks were rouged; and beneath the red her face looked drawn, hard. Dan saw nothing to change his first estimation of her, despite the arch smile she gave him.

"And were you detecting over there behind the cars?" Miss Davis questioned innocently. But her eyes were not innocent. Keen, watchful, they studied his face.

Dan smiled easily. "I was looking around," he confessed. "I cut across that car there."

"Oh, I think it's thrilling! Are you working for the police on what happened tonight?"

"Not exactly," Dan smiled at her. "I was strolling around. Thanks for the match, Fletcher. A pleasure to meet you, Miss Davis."

Fletcher nodded. Out of the corner of his eye, as he left, Dan saw the smile wipe off Miss Davis's face. A hard, calculating expression replaced it.

There seemed to be wheels within wheels in this show. The more he saw, the more tangled everything became. And lying over all was a certain sinisterness that was disquieting. Dan had the feeling that others knew more than he did. Knew things they would not speak about. Suspected things they did not put into words. The taint of unseen, hidden menace lay over the show, usually so cheerful and happy. He saw people eyeing one another furtively, as if wondering what their faces were masking.

And something did happen, startling in

its unlooked for suddenness. Terrible in its intent. Ghastly in its planning.

It happened about fifteen minutes later. The show was rapidly being loaded. Dan had continued his strolling about the yards, stopping now and then to watch the workers. He was restless, didn't want to board the train until the last. Out here in the night where he could walk about and exercise, he could think better. And there was so much to think about. So many things had happened in the last few hours; so many things threatened to happen. Harry Brown and his father had been sitting on top of a seething pot of trouble. Despite Harry's delineation of it, Dan doubted that his friend had realized the full danger until death had staggered to their very feet, and violence had been done to Jonathan Brown.

Once or twice Dan caught himself looking quickly behind. He had the sensation that he was being watched, followed. Nothing he saw bore that out. But a moment came when he loitered beside an empty track, at the end of a string of cars.

A switch engine was rolling down the track toward him, its bell tolling warningly, its headlight shining through the night like a staring white eye. Dan idly watched it come.

And when it was hardly ten feet away something struck his back with terrific force. He felt talonlike fingers clutch his neck, hurl him forward. Something crashed against the back of his head. A foot tripped him. He lurched forward in front of the engine.

For one awful instant Dan was dimly aware of hissing steam, rumbling wheels, the swooping advance of the juggernaut.

And then it struck him!

A T SUCH times the mind refuses to work coherently. Single impressions are lost. Everything blends into one kaleidoscopic whirl in which the subconscious takes hold and acts for the brain. The instinct of self-preservation is strong in all of us. It was in Dan McGrath. He knew he had been attacked from behind, knew he was falling forward before the locomotive. The blow on his head seemed to paralyze his body. A flash of stark fear shot through him as he thought of those grinding wheels that would mangle his body the next instant. All that without being able to do a thing about it.

An then in some way Dan struck the cinders and threw himself up. The pilot was on him. His arm flung out, dropped over the coupler. He was knocked over, legs dragging on cinders and ties. The wooden step scooped under his legs. He hung there, rigid, dazed.

The steam cut off. The locomotive shuddered as wheels slid on sanded rails. It stopped many yards down the track. And Dan rolled off the coupler and step to the cinders between the tracks. He was dazedly trying to get to his feet as an overalled figure rushed up from the cab.

A startled oath of relief—strong hands lifting him up—a shaken voice stammering: "You ain't dead! Lord, I thought we'd find you under the wheels! Howja do it?"

A second overalled figure joined them, then two brakemen from the rear. They held him up while his head cleared.

The fireman babbled excitedly: "I caught a slant of you goin' in front of us an' yelled to Jake to throw 'er in emergency! But I didn't think you had a chance."

Dan's head cleared, gave way to a pain in the back. He felt there. No blood. A swelling was raising under the hair. He had not imagined that blow from behind.

"Did you see anything else?" he asked the fireman.

"I just looked out the front window and saw you over the end of the running board," the fireman told him. "I thought I seen a dark kind of shadowlike thing behind you. Somethin' like a man wearin' a black cloak. But after I yelled over to Jake and looked again I didn't see it. Guess I was seeing things. Howja come to stumble in front of us that way, mister?"

Dan stepped over and looked back past the engine. Nothing there. He said slowly to the fireman as he rubbed the back of his head: "I guess I was thinking about something else. Don't see how I came to do it."

The brakeman had seen nothing.

"Better keep your mind about you when you're in the yards this way," the engineer said curtly. It was plain he thought Dan had either been drunk or out of his head. Dan didn't enlighten him.

"I'm all right," he assured them. 'Thanks for stopping your engine as quick as you did. I doubt if I could have held on much longer."

"We got to make a report of this," the engineer stated heavily.

"I'm going out on the circus train. Not much you can report. The name is McGrath. I live here in town. Nothing to say myself."

He left them, hearing as he walked away a muttered remark from the engineer about drunken fools. It was unheeded. His mind was grappling with the matter. He had been right about someone following him. That person had slipped up behind, tried to hurl him under the oncoming engine. Nine times out of ten the attempt would have succeeded, and there would have been only a mangled body left, with every chance of the attacker's getting away unseen. The death would have been put down to carelessness. Yes, a clever idea.

Dan quickly searched the tracks about the track. No one there. No one nearby who could have seen what happened. Death had reached out of the dark night,

and faded back into it. But it was still there, lurking . . .

Dan went to the private car at the rear of the train. They pulled out shortly after that. Harry came in. Dan told him what had happened. Harry's face was grave, disturbed when he finished.

"Murder again," said Harry.

"Yes."

"But why?"

"Plain as day, Harry. More trouble is coming. I'm not wanted around. I'm an unknown quantity. No telling what I'll do, or find out. Better get me out of the way. Another death tonight—an accidental death—would have made every person on the train twice as jumpy as they are."

"A little more of this and we'll have some accidents in the aerial acts," Harry muttered. "They can't do those split second turns if their nerves are shot."

"And that means more trouble—and more worry."

Harry lighted a cigarette, strode back and forth in the small sitting room of the private car. The wheels underneath were clicking with increasing rhythm over the rail joints, and the car was swaying gently.

"We've got to stop this—quick!" Harry exclaimed, halting and glaring. "We haven't got a big city detective department to turn loose on the matter. It's up to us. You—me—Fletcher and Lupe! And we've got to do it quick! We don't know what's going to happen next!"

"No," said Dan slowly. "We don't."

MORNING found the show in Portsmouth. As he ate breakfast at the bosses' table in the cook tent, Dan noticed many curious glances cast at him from the other tables. But he heard nothing more than casual chat as the circus people bolted food and hurried out to their manifold duties. Harry was not present.

Dan walked out to watch the vast cloudlike expanse of the big top rising slowly to the tops of the high tent poles. A voice at his shoulder murmured: "I hear you mighty near got run over last night."

It was the long, gangling Lupe, smiling thinly as his jaws worked slowly on a chew of tobacco.

"Where did you hear that?" Dan asked sharply.

Lupe squinted at a tent stake, neatly nailed it with a stream of tobacco juice. "Fletcher told me," he murmured, and his glance flicked sideways at Dan.

"When?"

"Last night."

Dan's face remained unchanged. Last night he had told only Harry, and Harry had not left the private car after that. How had Fletcher known?

"Whole show is talking about it," Lupe volunteered casually, showing marked interest in the raising of the big top canvas —a thing he had seen scores of times before. "I've heard a few bets made as to where the lightning's goin' to strike next."

That explained the many glances that had dwelt on Dan since he left the private car this morning. "Accidents will happen," Dan shrugged casually.

"Uh-huh. That's what I told Fletcher, in spite of him insisting that you were pushed on the track. Guess I'm the only one in the show that knows it was an accident."

"How do you know?" Dan asked quickly.

"You just told me," Lupe said mildly.

Their eyes met for a moment. Lupe's right eyelid lowered in the barest hint of a wink. "A fellow's got to be careful," he said as he moved away.

Dan grinned wryly at Lupe's back. The man had just given him a gentle warning. And what else? Something about Fletcher? A few minutes later he saw Fletcher entering the portable office parked in its old place behind the ticket

wagon. Dan went there, found Fletcher talking to old Twitty inside. They stopped as he entered. Fletcher's thick lips spread in a grin.

"Morning, Mr. McGrath," he greeted. "Glad to see you're able to walk."

"You know about my accident?"

"Sure," said Fletcher heartily. "I was talking to the crew of that yard engine before we pulled out. They said it wasn't an accident." His habitually narrowed eyes fixed brightly on Dan.

"Bad," Twitty's dry voice rustled ominously. "I warned you there would be more trouble, Mr. McGrath."

The thin, dry, sourish face was more than ever like a mummy's mask this morning. Twitty's eyes were bright points, not too friendly.

"The engine crew were talking through their hats," Dan told the two of them coolly. "How could anyone have pushed me? Why should they? Stop this talk about it."

Dan left them on that, but as he went out the door a rustle of words came through Twitty's wispy mustache: "There'll be more. More."

Confound the fellow anyway, with that sort of talk. If there were many more like him the morale of the show was going to go fast.

That afternoon Marco, the big black-maned lion that was the mainstay of the cat act, fell violently sick shortly after feeding time. In spite of every effort of Doc Ramey, the veterinary, Marco was dead by sundown. The cage had been moved out back of the menagerie tent and surrounded by a picket wall of canvas. Dan and Harry were there at the end.

"Poison!" Doc Ramey said briefly to Harry. He was a little, short, stout man, and he wiped his forehead nervously as he spoke. He had worked hard to save Marco without avail.

Gertrude Ordway, the slender, fearless

young woman who handled the cat act, wiped a tear from her eyes, and then spoke fiercely: "Oh, if I could take my whip to the beast who did that! I'd—I'd lash the skin off his back! Poor Marco—" She turned away, overcome.

Harry's face was tired and drawn as he walked out into the open with Dan. The strain was beginning to tell on him. "Let's try to find out who did that," he said soberly.

All the cats had been fed on horse meat, which had been cut up and thrown into a big tub outside the menagerie tent. The two men who had done that were vehement in their denials of knowing anything about poison.

Fletcher fixed one of them, a short, thin fellow wearing a soiled red-braided coat, with a ferocious scowl. "We're gonna get to the bottom of this!" he rasped. "If you're hiding anything—"

"Don't try to say I did it!" the animal man bristled angrily. "I don't know anything about it."

"Yeah? That's what you say!" Fletcher snarled threateningly.

It looked for a moment as if the smaller animal man was going to start a fight right there. Dan headed it off by asking calmly: "Did either of you chaps leave that meat for as long as thirty seconds after you got it?"

A guilty glance between them showed that the question had gone home. It had been hot work cutting up the meat, they admitted. They had stepped over to a hamburger stand for a cold drink apiece.

"Anyone might have walked past that meat and poisoned a piece of it," Dan shrugged to Harry. "We'd better find out who walked past the tub while these men were gone."

They tried at once. No one questioned recalled looking at the spot where the meat tub was at that particular time. The trail ended there.

CHAPTER FIVE

Sabotage

THAT evening Gertrude Ordway took her cat act on with Tina, a big female lioness, taking Marco's place as leader. And Tina, nervous, bewildered by Marco's absence, fumbled some of her cues and began to lash her tail warningly. And in the space of an eyelash pandemonium broke out in the thickly packed tiers of seats. Tina had leaped as Gertrude Ordway turned her back for an instant. Leaped like a great tawny bolt of snarling death.

The slim, leather-clad figure of the girl trainer went down in a heap, her small whip slashing futilely at the ripping paws and slavering jaws tearing for her life.

Women screamed. Men shouted. Children began crying frantically. The spectators surged to their feet. Wild confusion gripped the whole interior of the tent.

Blank cartridges were fired through the bars of the cage that surrounded the act. Long steel prods jabbed Tina back for an instant. The bloody figure of the mauled girl staggered to a wooden chair, swung it up.

Tina's guttural roars were terrifying as she dodged a steel prod and rushed in at her victim again. Gertrude Ordway jabbed the four sharp legs of the chair into the face of the enraged lioness. Tina fell back in surprise.

And while she hesitated for a moment, eyeing the chair uncertainly, Gertrude Ordway staggered slowly back to the small entrance door, holding the chair ready for another rush. Steel prods, hastily thrust in, covered her retreat. Willing hands dragged her through the door and slammed it against Tina's leap.

And as they bore the terribly lacerated figure away, and clowns trooped out to distract the attention of the audience, there were more screams and confusion at the north end of the tent. A seat had broken under the surging weight of the people on it. Half a dozen spectators had fallen hard to the ground.

One woman had her leg broken. A man had a dislocated collar bone. The others were bruised and frightened.

All were rushed away for medical attention. Dan had hurried there. He pulled away the broken seat, with the help of a pin man standing by. They dragged the two boards under the canvas. Outside Dan threw a light on the broken ends of the boards, and showed them to Harry.

A saw had cut partway through the center of the board, and the cut had been filled with putty and dirt rubbed over it. It had borne weight for some time, until an unusual strain had come on it. There was no telling how long it had been that way.

There was despair in Harry's voice as he said: "Sabotage. This will mean damage suits. Our cat act is gone for a time. No one but Gertrude Ordway can handle them. And for the next week we show in the same towns with Finke and Streit. What's the end going to be, Dan?"

Before Dan could answer, Twitty came picking his way to the spot like a lean dry shadow. "Mr. Finke is at the car asking to see you," Twitty whispered.

Harry swore under his breath, said curtly to Dan: "Come on."

Finke was a tall, smooth, pallid man, close-barbered, immaculately turned out. He seemed perfectly at his ease as he stood up when they entered the office.

"Hello, Brown," he said affably, extending his hand. "I just dropped in for a little confab." He dropped the hand quickly when Harry overlooked it.

Harry eyed him truculently. "What do you want to see me about?"

"Well, I really wanted to see your father," Finke said. "But I hear he has had an accident."

"Call it that if you want to."

Finke cleared his throat. "As a matter of fact I can talk to you, since you seem to be in charge." Finke sat down on the edge of Twitty's desk, drew three cigars from the breast pocket of his coat, returned two of them when they were refused, and lighted the other deliberately. "I'd like to talk to you confidentially," he murmured, eyeing Dan, who had not been introduced to him.

"This gentleman is a friend of mine," Harry said shortly. "Say what you've got to say in front of him."

Finke took no offense at that, beyond a slight narrowing of his eyes. Green-pupilled, they were, flicking and darting here and there.

"I guess there's no harm in that." Finke smiled affably. "It's a straight business proposition. One your father and I have had under consideration for some time. Business in the circus game hasn't been so good the last season or so, and all the signs point to the fact that overhead must be cut down, methods improved. Here we find ourselves routed on the same schedule, with a loss of business, and, er, good will, that does no good. Now if the Finke and Streit show were combined with the Brown show, we would have more than a chance to get back on a profitable basis. I understand your father is rather badly injured. You are a young man. The responsibility of a big show like this is heavy. It makes a man old before his time. Too many things are always going wrong. Briefly, our proposition is this . . . "

Finke paused and lifted an eyebrow as Harry sucked in a sharp breath. Harry had stood there listening, his face getting red and set.

"Never mind your proposition!" Harry exploded. "I can tell you what it is! In fact I can tell you a good many things, Finke! The first is that business is still good enough to get along on. The second is that our routing through this territory was made first. I don't see how your outfit got it so quick, but you did. The third is that you're right about me running this show. I'll be running it a damn sight longer than you can afford to wait for it. The fourth is that I'll stand the responsibility and pull the show through. The fifth is that you and your partner are a pair of dirty crooks. And the sixth is that you are going to get a punch in the schnozzle!"

FINKE sat there in frozen silence, his eyes getting wider as Harry spoke. He let out a grunt of surprise as Harry's fist snapped into his face—and the next moment he was sprawling on the floor.

Twitty had been standing in the doorway, listening sourly. Now he darted forward, gulping: "Oh, my, this is terrible! Your father won't like this!"

Twitty helped Finke to his feet, and got a shove away for his reward. Finke's suit was soiled with the dust off the floor. His immaculate air of jaunty confidence had vanished. A trickle of blood was coming down out of his nose. And he was livid with rage.

"I'd have you arrested for that, you young fool, if I thought it was worth it!" he choked. "I came here with a legitimate business proposition offering peace and quiet! I withdraw that offer! I'll see your show sold at auction before the season is over! I'll break you! I'll see you begging for a job! You and that apple-cheeked detective standing there!"

"Scat!" Dan exploded.

Finke jumped, sidled toward the door and slipped out, dabbing at his injured nose with a handkerchief. Twitty fairly wrung his hands.

"You shouldn't have done that, Mr.

Harry!" he remonstrated. "After all—"

"Shut up!"

Twitty shut.

"Come on, Dan. Let's get out of here." And when the two friends were outside, Harry admitted: "Maybe I shouldn't have lost my temper that way. But he made me see red. He's a rotten crook, looking for my hair. He wouldn't have dared come around here if the old man had been on the job. But he thought he had a young fool to deal with, who'd swallow his line."

"You didn't help the case any," Dan said drily.

"I know," Harry admitted gloomily.

Dan chuckled. "But then you probably didn't hurt it any," he comforted. "It couldn't be much worse."

Joe LeBoyne, the dapper little claim adjuster, bustled up. "I got releases from all but two of those injured parties, Mr. Brown," he said briskly. "Cost fifty apiece, but I figured it was worth it. I'm afraid two of 'em are going to sue."

Harry waved him away.

"Do what you can," he advised.

And as the dapper claim adjuster left, Dan advised: "Tomorrow you'd better have every piece of equipment inspected as it goes up."

"Not only that, I'll have guards posted," Harry said. "Tomorrow we'll be in Homestead, and there we pick up the Finke and Streit outfit for four days. They're showing on the lot right across the street from us. Those two sites are the only ones that can be had in the town. And take it from me there's apt to be excitement. Anything can happen when two outfits who are fighting each other get together like that."

"Finke knew about me," Dan pointed out thoughtfully. "And he's never seen me before. Knew all about me."

"Sa-ay—that's right. I forgot about that."

Dan smiled grimly. "And whoever reported on me doesn't have a very high opinion of my abilities. Seems to think I'm pretty much of a fool."

"He doesn't know what he's talking about, whoever it is."

"I hope he thinks he does," Dan grinned. "What this job needs is a good fool right now—who won't be noticed. Walk back and make yourself small, Harry. I've got a hunch."

"What's that?"

"Back. Out of the way. Scram. Lam. I crave to be alone for a few minutes. There's a nigger in the woodpile over there."

They were standing by the ticket wagon. Harry looked in the direction Dan indicated. He nodded understandingly, and stepped back. Dan walked swiftly around the back and cut down past the midway tents that were about ready to be dismantled.

What he had seen was Finke, walking slowly along and staring about as if looking for someone. Dan cut back of the tents at a fast gait, and by the time he had reached the last one Finke was walking toward the edge of the circus lot and the street beyond. And strolling after him, apparently aimlessly, was the big beefy figure of Fletcher, the show detective.

Finke turned to the right. Fletcher made the same turn a few minutes later. Towners were drifting out of the show lot and Dan fell in behind a small group of them. Across the street were houses; on this side were vacant lots and sign boards. The sidewalk was dimly lighted.

Ahead Fletcher walked swiftly, Finke slowly. Fletcher caught up with the showman. The towners stopped to get into an automobile parked at the curb and Dan stepped behind the machine parked back of it. He saw Finke and Fletcher talking. They looked back along the sidewalk, then stepped over behind the end of a sign

board opposite them and disappeared behind it.

The automobile ahead pulled out. Already large circus wagons were rumbling along the street toward the loading runs. Dan stepped out from behind the machine, starting for the other end of that sign board. And just then a cheerful voice said: "I'll bet you're slippin' up on someone."

It was Lupe, who had come down the outside line of machines parked at the curb and was standing there watching him.

"And who are you watching?" Dan asked slowly moving back.

Lupe laughed soundlessly. "You, right now," he said.

"You know what's over there in back of the sign board?"

"Uh-huh."

"And what were you going to do about it?"

"Wait an' see what you did," Lupe confessed. He stood there in his ill-fitting clothes like a country bumpkin, head cocked forward with interest on his long corded neck.

Dan crouched behind the automobile as he saw the two men coming back to the sidewalk again. They parted, Finke going on and Fletcher turning back toward the circus lot. Dan caught Lupe's arm and urged him to the side of the machine, crouching down. Fletcher passed without suspecting they were out there. He was whistling blithely between his teeth, as if well satisfied with himself and the world.

After he had passed and they had straightened up, Lupe shook his head. "I never would have thought it," he murmured sadly.

"What?"

"That Fletcher could whistle that happy. I've never heard him do that since I've knowed him. Well, good night, Mr. McGrath. You certainly are turning out to be pretty smart."

Was there a trace of mockery in Lupe's voice, Dan wondered, as he watched him depart.

MORNING again—and the small city of Homestead, where Dan woke up with Twitty's dry rasping warning echoing through his sleep-fogged senses.

"Mark my words—there'll be more . . ."

Half the night he had been awake, conning through his mind the few facts he had to go on. And pitifully few they were. Somewhere about the show a murderer was walking openly. Somewhere in the small army of men and women that filled the different sections of the circus, minds and hands were plotting against Harry Brown. Eyes were watching Harry and himself. A vague, inert dread lay like a pall over everything. The fact that so far they had made no arrests or accusations against those guilty ones made it all the worse. They seemed helpless, and they were.

More than one person was connected with this business. There was little doubt in Dan's mind that much of their trouble traced back to the Finke and Streit outfit. The remarks Finke had made about him showed clearly there was a hidden channel of communication between the two big circuses.

And now they were together. All night the sections of the two shows had thundered swiftly toward this converging point. At different ends of the freight yards they were unloading, trekking steadily toward the show lots, across the street from each other. The billing crews had fought it out, plastering paper over each other's signs, to come back and find their own covered up and the job to do all over again. Space had been taken lavishly in the newspapers. Every means of publicity had been used to let the public know that each show was offering them the greatest assortment of wonders and en-

tertainment that had ever been brought under canvas. Homestead was a mere background against which the rivalry of the shows was clashing.

More than one fight occurred as the long strings of cars were being unloaded, for the spirit of the thing had gripped the rank and file of both shows. Nerves were taut. Tempers hair-triggered.

The spreading areas of canvas went up across the street from each other. Harry Brown gave orders that every bit of equipment was to be inspected and tested, and then posted guards to see that it was not tampered with.

Parade time came. Harry got the streets first by starting early. It was a small triumph, but welcome. Dan kept an eye on Fletcher as the day wore on. Fletcher seemed moody, restless. He made no attempt to cross the street onto the grounds of the other show. But he wandered around their own lot, seemingly with aimless purpose. Before the matinée Dan saw him back in the yard talking to Barbara Davis, the hard-faced young woman who rode with the western troupe. He seemed to be giving her instructions. She nodded understandingly as they parted.

Matinée came and passed without incident. Harry again scored, sending his bands out to the front of the show lot and turning loose a score of ticket sellers who ranged as far as two blocks from the lot, selling tickets at cut rates.

"Bad business," Harry confided to Dan. "But every ticket keeps one away from Finke and Streit, and helps fill our seats. If we're crowded and they are empty, the word will get around that we are the biggest and best outfit."

And so it proved. They showed to the bulk of the afternoon's customers. And Harry prolonged his show by every device possible, so that when their customers streamed out in a thick tide, they saw a mere trickle of loiterers across the street, and carried the news away that they had gotten much more for their money.

"I guess we're showing that bunch of crooks a few tricks," Harry grinned to Dan when it was over. "We've got 'em on the run, boy."

"Looks like it," Dan admitted, and added thoughtfully a moment later: "I wonder what tricks they're going to show us."

"Yes, I'm wondering too," Harry confessed bleakly. "Whatever it is, it will be below the belt."

But neither of them was able to foresee the wide gamut of danger and heartbreak, of surprise and terror the evening was to bring.

CHAPTER SIX

Tools of Doom

LOW scudding clouds came racing out of the northwest before dark, blotting out a blood-red sunset. Gusts of wind came with them, kicking up swirls of dust on the show lot, and causing the mountainous big top and menagerie tent to heave and sway uneasily. Guy ropes were hurriedly tightened and strengthened. Harry Brown strode about, watchful, alert. He hailed Dan near the front of the lot.

"Busy, Dan?"

"Just going down to the car to get my pipe."

"Good. I want my flashlight. Marta White has it. She's there, too. Look her up and ask her to bring it back, will you? She's in the third car up from mine."

"Sure," Dan agreed.

He walked the block and a half to the yards, cut across the tracks and was soon in the owner's private car at the rear of the section. It took only a moment to get his pipe and pouch of tobacco, and then he walked forward in search of Marta White, the small equestrienne.

Most of the show people were on the lot, or heading toward it to get ready for the evening performance. The cars were all but empty. These at the back were compartment cars, for the more important performers. A door slammed as he entered the third car, and when he stepped into the long aisle he saw a slim figure walking hurriedly away from him.

"Miss White?"

She turned, cuddling a bundle under her arm. And as Dan came to her he noticed that her face was pale, drawn. Her eyes were red, as if she had been weeping. She seemed uncertain, apprehensive, as she waited silently for him to speak.

"Harry wants his flashlight," Dan said to her.

"Oh—yes, I have it. I'll get it for you."

Dan could have sworn there was relief in her voice. He eyed her curiously as she walked past him to the door of her compartment. It was locked. She fumbled in a stamped-leather purse and brought out a key. Her small muscular hand was trembling violently. Something was very wrong with her. The bundle bothered her.

"Here, I'll hold this," Dan said, slipping it from under her arm.

His action brought an exclamation of protest. She turned quickly, tried to grab the bundle back. Her hasty fingers knocked it out of his hand. It fell to the floor. The thin newspaper around it flew open and the contents fell loosely at their feet. A revolver rolled out on the floor with a little thump.

A gasp of dismay came from Marta White. "I'll—I'll pick it up!" she urged wildly.

But Dan was already bending over quickly. He had seen something else. A large clasp knife and a pair of gloves had also been rolled in a dark raincoat. His gaze riveted on those cheap cotton gloves lying there beside the knife.

Crimson splashes and smears stood out vividly on the cloth. Dan caught his breath sharply. Those stains could be only one thing.

Blood!

Marta White's voice went unsteady with emotion as she begged: "Won't you please let me get them?"

Dan ignored her as he handled the gloves. The spots were dried and stiff. The blood had been there several days. His heart began to race as he realized the significance of this.

Whipping out his handkerchief he picked up the knife.

It was a clasp knife, with a small button set in the side of the handle. He pressed the button and a long blade flashed out, ready for use. Its edge, against the ball of his thumb, was razor keen. And the knife blade and the handle of the knife itself were both covered with dried blood. Spots were on the shiny metal of the revolver.

THERE, in grim and gruesome clarity, was everything he had been looking for. Dan's mind went back to that dark show lot at Midland. It was easy to visualize the revolver crashing against the head of Jonathan Brown, felling him. And a gloved finger pressing the release button of the knife. Then—a slash, and that staggering, stumbling figure that had died at their feet . . .

And the fireman of the switch engine had mentioned a figure that seemed to be wearing a dark cloak. Was it this raincoat?

Little ridges of muscle stood out in Dan's set face as he straightened and looked at Marta White. Her features were like one who had died. Ghastly pale, with wild, mute terror in her wide eyes. She shrank back a step before his look.

"Open that door!" Dan said curtly.

Silently she did so, stepped in and turned on the light. Dan gathered up the articles and entered. The first thing he saw was a small light leather bag on the lower berth. He remembered that bag. Marta White had been carrying it as she came to the train with Harry, that evening when murder had been done.

Dan closed the door, stepped over and looked into the open bag. It was empty. A few dark stains on the lining betrayed what its contents had been.

Dan went a little sick as he thought how like a small, innocent girl she had looked that night. Sweet, pretty, without a care in the world as she walked at Harry's side. And all the time she had been carrying those tools of death in one small muscular hand. Smiling and laughing with Harry while she carried the gun that had felled his own father, the knife that had slashed the throat of one of his men.

Dan had not looked at her hands that night in the darkness. The one that had met his had been cool, firm, strong. A hand trained by strenuous exercise that could easily strike a death blow . . .

"What have you to say?" Dan asked her harshly.

Marta White had backed into the corner of the small compartment. Her face was still waxen pale; stark terror was still in her eyes. She looked at him mutely.

Dan picked up the knife with his handkerchief and stepped close, holding it up before her.

"You know this knife killed a man, don't you?"

"Please—don't!"

In her slim white neck a tiny pulse was beating madly; she was breathing fast. Dan had seen a small bird breathe that way as it lay in its captor's hand, looking up with the same fixed terror that was in her gaze.

"Where were you going with all this?" he questioned.

Again she did not answer. Dan caught her arm, shook her, and she made no resistance.

"This is enough to hang you!" he reminded gruffly. "Say something!"

But she only looked at him.

Dan put the gun and knife and gloves in the raincoat, and stowed them all in the brown leather bag.

"This will be pretty tough on Harry," he said as he closed the bag.

That broke her down. Harsh, dry sobs racked her slim figure. Tears rolled down her pale cheeks. She fumbled for a handkerchief, and then forgot to use it.

"D-do you have to tell him?" she wrenched out.

"Certainly. This is a case for the police now. But he'll have to know first. Did you do it?"

Dan shot the last at her suddenly. Her mouth opened involuntarily for a reply, and then closed again before she uttered a word. But it looked as if she had been going to deny it.

"Let's get over to the lot and see Harry before we do anything else," Dan said, picking up the bag.

She came obediently. And it was not until they were halfway to the lot that Dan remembered he had forgotten to get the flashlight. He did not turn back. The matter in hand was more important. Marta White walked silently at his side, head bowed. Now and then a small hand stole up and brushed a handkerchief against her eyes.

Dan counted back.

That evening her act had not gone on at the time of the murder. Had she slipped out of her dressing tent for a few minutes without anyone seeing her? Many things were revolving furiously in his mind. This had been so sudden, so unexpected, that he was confused himself.

THE night was inky black. The wind rushed into their faces, whipped Marta White's skirt about her legs. Now and then little spats of rain fell. But the wind and threat of rain were not keeping the towners away. Already the streets converging on the show lots were filled with automobiles, and crowds of pedestrians were milling about the entrances to the lots.

Finke and Streit had taken a leaf out of Harry's methods of the afternoon, had ticket sellers out in the streets also. But Dan paid little attention to that. He had struck the trail of murder and was conning every angle of it. He suspected there was much more to this than appeared on the surface.

As they came to the lot, Dan suggested: "You go over to the office and find Harry. Tell him about it. I'll be along in a few minutes."

For the first time since leaving the yards Marta White looked up into his face. "You don't think I'll run away?" she asked in a lifeless voice.

"I don't think so," Dan smiled. "You see, there isn't much chance of your getting very far. The best thing you can do is make a clean breast of it to Harry."

"And—and shall I take the bag to him too?"

Dan's smile turned grim. "I'll keep that," he declared.

He turned away, left her to go on toward the portable office. She did, walking faster. Dan waited a few moments, and then followed her. He wanted to see where she went and what she did. Once she looked back, but he was able to step behind a group of towners and keep out of sight.

His eyes narrowed thoughtfully as he trailed her. For instead of turning off and going somewhere else, as he had half expected, Marta White went straight to the office where he had sent her. As soon as she entered and the door closed behind her, Dan made a rapid circle out in the darkness and came up behind the wagon.

There was a small window set in each side and one in the back. Dan pressed his ear close to the boards, shamelessly trying to hear what was being said inside. He got the rapid murmur of voices, but that was all. No words. In a few moments the front door opened, someone hurried out.

Peering around the side cautiously he saw old Twitty hurrying away. Dan smiled grimly, busied himself for a moment with the bag, and then followed the old man. But Twitty had moved faster than Dan expected. He lost him in the gathering crowd.

Dan swore at himself in chagrin when he realized it, and set out to find Harry himself. Luck was with him. The ticket man in the marquee said the boss had passed inside a few minutes before, leaving word he was going back in the yard where the dressing tents were.

He found Harry in the yard, standing beside a litter of bewildering objects—colored tubs and pedestals, queer carts and automobiles, barrels painted red and blue and trimmed with decorations, coaches and wagons of gold and bright red plush. All the paraphernalia to be used in the tournament which opened the show, and the acts that followed.

Harry was talking with Carl Thaller, the equestrian director, who was already dressed in his long-tailed coat, white trousers and high black leather boots. He lifted a hand in greeting and called: "Get my flashlight?"

"No," said Dan. "Got something to tell you."

A last word with the equestrian director, and Harry came over and joined him.

"What's the big secret?" Harry asked,

a hint of apprehension in his tones. "Something wrong?"

Making sure no one could overhear, Dan let Harry have the brutal truth briefly.

The blood drained from Harry's face as he listened. The fingers of his right hand clenched tight. His eyes searched Dan's face, as if trying to find some hint that it was all untrue. But at the finish Harry's shoulders were slumped. He looked like a man who had received a terrible blow.

"You sure there's no doubt about it, Dan?" he begged huskily. His eyes went to the bag Dan carried.

"This was on her berth, Harry."

"It's hers, all right."

Harry brushed a hand across his eyes, as if trying to wipe away the sight. "I can't believe it," he gulped. And the strength surged back into his voice. His jaw snapped tight. "She didn't do that!" he burst out harshly. "I know Marta! She couldn't!"

"I didn't say she did," Dan reminded. "But—she knows—"

"Marta wouldn't do that to me! Why —why, I was going to ask her to marry me. She wouldn't throw me down—see my father attacked—a man slaughtered like that—"

"You'd better go over and talk to her," Dan suggested. "She wouldn't say a thing to me. Perhaps she'll tell you. I think she's told her father. They talked fast before he went out to look for you."

"I haven't seen him, Dan."

"Perhaps he's back by now. You talk to Marta and I'll tackle her father."

THEY walked back to the office together. Harry Brown moved like a man in the grip of a nightmare. Dan's heart went out to him. It was a sickening job for a man to find one he idolized and cherished mixed up in a thing like this.

Marta was sitting listlessly in a chair as Harry opened the office door and stepped in. She looked up at him, and then dropped her eyes. Only by the way her fingers pulled nervously at her small handkerchief did she betray her emotion. Twitty, her father, was not there. He had not returned yet. Dan closed the door behind Harry and left the two together. He shook his head sadly as he turned away.

Twitty was his goal.

And Twitty seemed to have disappeared. Man after man whom Dan questioned denied seeing the stooped leathery figure lately. But finally he struck the trail. The overalled engineer at the light truck raised his voice above the rhythmic rush of the big gasoline engine turning the dynamo.

"Yeah, I seen the old feller 'bout a quarter of an hour ago. He was walkin' over there toward the horse tents."

So Dan walked quickly to the horse tents. A hostler loitering in front of them remembered vaguely seeing Twitty cutting off to the right in the darkness. Dan followed his direction and found a path. He remembered now that the show lot ended in a sharp bluff that dropped down to a little-traveled street below. And near the edge of the bluff was an old unused shed.

Back of him the reflected light from the two great shows so near together cast a yellow murk through the night. The shed loomed up, dark, silent. Dan turned off the path to it.

He walked along the side of the shed toward the edge of the bluff a score of yards away. Perhaps Twitty had scrambled down to the street below.

But Dan never reached that bluff. As he went past the end of the shed his feet struck something on the ground. He tripped, almost fell. And as he regained his balance and turned back, he felt his pulses hammering. That yielding object his foot had stubbed into felt mighty like a body.

And it was. The match he struck cast a pale halo over the ground. Twitty's parchment like face was there, its eyes gazing up in a wide, fixed stare. The stare of death. One clawlike hand was crooked to the side of Twitty's bald, pallid dome. A great ugly bruise and a trickle of blood stood out starkly on the scalp.

Dan dropped the bag he had carried all this time and struck another match, going down to his knees beside Twitty. A close look showed that Twitty was dead from the blow on the head.

And as Dan took that in he became conscious of a faint stir in the darkness behind him. He tried to leap and turn. Too late. Something struck his head a terrific blow. The night dissolved in a glittering burst of fire . . .

Dan's last thought was that death had found him as it had Twitty. And then blackness shrouded his senses as he fell across Twitty's body.

CHAPTER SEVEN

Fire!

A GLARE of light was the first thing Dan knew again. Bright, dazzling light shining into his eyes. And a voice swearing softly over his head. He opened his eyes.

A strong arm under his shoulders lifted him up. The swearing stopped. The voice said: "How do you feel now, partner?"

"Lupe," Dan muttered.

A chuckle greeted that. "Yep. It's me," said Lupe. "You got a head on you, mister, to pick me out that quick in the dark. How are you feelin'?"

Dan's senses were clearing rapidly now. He had a terrific headache. His hand, exploring his scalp, encountered a bloody cut and a big swelling on the back of his head.

The smell of liquor was in his nostrils. His mouth burned with the taste of it. He felt a small flask pressed to his lips.

"Take another swig of this," Lupe advised. "I poured some in your face, but I don't know how much went down. It's raw an' strong, but it'll buck you up."

Dan drank obediently, choking on the fiery drink. But it warmed him, sent strength rushing through him, cleared his head. With Lupe's aid he staggered to his feet.

"All right now?" Lupe asked solicitously.

"I guess so," Dan admitted, feeling his head again and looking around. They were still beside the shed in the darkness. Over there in the night was the circus lot, bright with light. Lupe had a flashlight, and its beam dropped to the ground over Twitty.

"Maybe you can tell me about this," Lupe said soberly. "He's dead."

"Yes," said Dan. "He's a case for the coroner. I found him here, and then someone slipped up from behind and knocked me on the head. It must have been the fellow who killed him."

"*Hmmm*," said Lupe slowly. "Kind of funny place for you two to be."

"I was hunting him, and was told that he had been seen walking this way," Dan explained. "What brought you here? You seem to have a habit of turning up where I am."

"I spotted you slipping over this way an' thought I'd slip along too," Lupe confessed. "I never know when you're goin' to turn up something worth while." Admiration tinged his tone as he said: "You sure did it this time. I mighty near fell over you when I seen you both lying there on the ground. When I seen Twitty was dead and you were breathing I did my best to bring you back. Thought for a few minutes I'd have to leave you here an' run for a doc. But you give a grunt an' started to come around, so I stayed."

"How long have I been out?"

"Can't be long. I wasn't walkin' very far behind you. Guess it took me five minutes anyway to bring you around after I found you."

"Did you see anyone around here?"

"Not a sign," Lupe denied. "But then, it's pretty dark around here an' I snuck up easy. Whoever cracked you could have shinned down the bank over there an' been gone while I was following. I come so easy he probably didn't know I was around. Did he leave that?"

Lupe's flashlight picked up the leather bag Dan had carried. It was resting where he had dropped it, apparently untouched. Dan considered that fact with a frown, and then picked up the bag.

"I brought it," he said briefly. "We've got to notify the police and have this body taken care of. Want to wait here with it?"

"Not me," Lupe assured him hastily. "I never did like dead folks in the dark. They start my teeth chatterin'. Guess it won't hurt any to leave him alone here for a little while."

"Probably not," Dan agreed.

They walked back toward the tents together.

THE police force had detailed several patrolmen on each show lot. Dan saw one near the marquee and went to him.

"There's a dead man over there at the back of this field," he told the copper. "Right beside that old shed. You'd better notify headquarters to take care of the matter. I'm one of the show detectives."

The patrolman was a big awkward-looking man with a weather-beaten face that was not too bright. His jaw dropped as he stared at Dan.

"Dead man?" he gulped.

"Yes. He belongs to the show."

"Uh—all right, mister. There's a couple of plainclothesmen around here. I'll find one of them and tell him." The patrolman hurried away.

"I wonder what I better do?" Lupe said helplessly. "Where's Fletcher? That fellow never is around when you want him."

"Look him up and tell him what's happened. Then get over to Twitty with him. I'm going to notify Harry Brown."

They separated then. Dan hurried to the office wagon and entered. Harry was holding a weeping girl in his arms, trying to comfort her. He looked up helplessly.

"She won't talk, Dan."

Dan nodded soberly. He hesitated, eyeing the girl.

"I'm sorry," he said awkwardly. "Something terrible has happened. It's going to be hard for you, Miss White."

His words seemed to give her strength. "It's—my father?" she asked slowly.

Dan nodded.

"Tell me."

"Something happened to him. He's—"

"Dead?"

"Yes."

Harry caught her hand, and fired at Dan: "What happened?"

Dan told him. And when he finished Marta White wiped her eyes and drew a shuddering breath. "I suppose it's best," she said unsteadily. "The disgrace would have been almost as bad. Harry—that bag was in his compartment. He knew the answer to it."

"And that's why you wouldn't talk?"

She nodded. "Night before last he asked me to carry his bag to the train for him, as I often did. He used it for his raincoat and anything else he wanted to take back and forth to the lot. I gave it back to him at the train. Tonight when I saw it was going to rain I went into his compartment to get his raincoat and take it to him. The door was locked, but I had

his extra key and got in. And—when I looked in his bag I found the knife and gun and gloves. Right away I knew it all had something to do with the trouble the other night. And all I could think of was getting them away somewhere."

"What did your father say when you told him?" Dan asked shrewdly.

Marta White spread her hands hopelessly. "He begged me to be quiet for a while. And then he said he was going to get Harry, and hurried out."

The picture was clear enough—only Twitty had not gone for Harry. He had looked for someone else—and found death.

Who was that person? Why had he killed Twitty.

Dan studied Marta White's face. She seemed to be telling the truth, without holding anything back.

Harry was eyeing him questionly. Dan shrugged.

"The police have been notified. They'll take charge of things. And we're up a tree again. Twitty was the man who could have set us right—and he's dead."

Harry clenched a fist impotently. "Isn't there any way of getting at the bottom of all this?" he burst out helplessly.

"I think there is," Dan said slowly.

"What?"

"Tell you later—if it works out. We're up against someone who has a lot of brains, Harry. He's clever—diabolically clever. There's only one weak spot about him that I can see."

"What?" Harry challenged.

Dan smiled thinly. "He thinks I'm a fool, according to the report he turned into Finke. That is, if it's the same man; and I think it is. A man who makes a snap judgment like that is riding for a fall. He takes chances he wouldn't with a clever man. And I think he has done just that this time."

"What did he do?" Harry asked with

interest. "What have you got up your sleeve?"

"Perhaps nothing," Dan grinned. "Perhaps a lot. We'll see if he takes the bait I'm going to put out—like a fool."

They had to be satisfied with that. Marta refused to see her father, preferring to remember him as she had last seen him. And like a game trouper she insisted on going to her dressing room and getting ready for the night's show. Harry's protests were of no avail.

THE towners were crowding the midway, streaming into the sideshows, buying balloons, popcorn, canes, lemonade and hot dogs. Those who had bought tickets early were beginning to trickle into the menagerie, to stare at the big assortment of wild animals before they went into the big top and found seats.

"We're getting more than our share of the crowd," Harry said to McGrath as together they strolled around the lot.

"Which won't make Finke and Streit feel any better."

"I'm wondering about them."

"So am I," Dan confessed. "If they know what I suspect, they'll not be feeling well right now."

"I wish you'd tell me what you've got up your sleeve. What are you carrying that bag for? Let me see in it."

"Later," Dan grinned. "It's empty."

"Where's the stuff that was in it?"

"The fellow who knocked me down was after it," Dan said.

"Then your evidence is gone?"

"Perhaps." Dan smiled, and Harry had to be satisfied with that.

Fletcher came lumbering up to them. "What's this Lupe tells me about Twitty?" he rumbled.

"It was probably right," Dan said coolly, eyeing Fletcher steadily.

Fletcher scowled at him, and his over-fleshed jowls grew red. "By golly, that killer's still with us!" he exploded.

"He seems to be," Dan said coolly.

Fletcher glared at him, and Harry looked at him curiously. But Fletcher said nothing, and Harry kept silent. They saw lights winking over where Twitty's body lay. Dan and Harry went there, leaving Fletcher behind. Two patrolmen and three plainclothesmen were there, examining the body and searching around in the darkness.

After finding out who they were Dan found himself the target of a barrage of questions laid down by a thin, sharp, suspicious man who had introduced himself as Detective Sergeant Simpson.

Dan told him what had happened.

Simpson listened suspiciously. "We ain't here to solve something what happened outside the county," he said. "But we'll get the fellow who did this if we have to keep the whole show here. You people can't come in this town and start killing each other and get away with it."

"Officer, if you catch the man who did this I'll give you a thousand dollars cash," Harry offered curtly. "Or any man on your force. That's how bad we want him."

There was more talk, but Dan paid little attention to it. His mind was on other things. He had said nothing about the contents of that bag, or Marta White.

An ambulance and the coroner's assistant came, and they were hardly there when Harry suddenly cried angrily: "What's happened to the lights?"

Every light around the lot had suddenly blanked out.

"More trouble!" Dan guessed. "Come on, Harry!" He started for the light truck at a run.

Shouted orders, cries of alarm, shrill whoops and laughter met them as the circus people and the spectators reacted in different ways to the sudden darkness that had fallen over everything.

"Why doesn't O'Malley start the reserve truck, blast him!" Harry swore.

And as they came up, Harry shouted: "O'Malley, where the devil are you?"

There was no reply. The gasoline engine was still running steadily.

An electric torch winked out near them. "Bring that light here!" Harry bawled. And when the man ran over with it Harry threw the light on the truck.

"On the ground!" Dan snapped.

There on the ground by the truck lay the overalled figure of the man in charge. The same one who had told Dan where Twitty had gone. And when they bent over him they saw he was barely breathing. He had been knocked unconscious.

Harry straightened up and ran around to the other side of the truck.

"Here!" he shouted a moment later. "The light cable had been chopped in two! Cut off the switch and splice it quick!"

Other men had come up; other torches were there. Dan couldn't identify them, but one man at least knew how to carry out the order. He started to work. *"Fire!"*

The cry drifted fast on the wind around the great curved side of the big top. Chilling, ominous.

"Fire!"

"Fire!"

Other voices took it up. It was around on the other side by the menagerie tent. A lurid red glare tinted the night.

"My God!" Harry gasped, and ran.

Dan went at his heels.

CHAPTER EIGHT

Showman's Set-up

THE lurid glow intensified rapidly as they raced around the big top. They reached the back of it. A chilling sight burst on their eyes. The back of the menagerie tent was on fire. Long tongues of flame were racing up the dry canvas, fanned by the wind. Leaping, licking tongues of flame threw out long streamers of sparks, which fell on the canvas and started new areas burning.

Men were futilely beating at the bottom of the flames. A section of canvas burned through, fell away in a shower of sparks. They could see the interior of the menagerie tent. Spectators were stampeding toward safety. Lions were roaring, elephants bawling in fear. Monkeys screamed and chattered. Pandemonium reigned in the tent. Women shrieked and others took it up.

"Get the fire truck here!" Harry shouted.

A gong chattered shrilly. That was the portable fire apparatus that accompanied the show and was always ready.

"It will get away from them in this wind!" Harry groaned. "The whole show will go!"

His flashlight stabbing before him, Harry sprang through the bursted sidewall into the interior of the tent. Already the place was filling with hot, stifling smoke. And overhead the flames were racing over the canvas before the wind—swift, deadly.

Dan heard the fire truck clang to a stop outside. A moment later the hiss of chemicals struck the flames. But the fire had too great a start.

Harry's flash swept around the yawning interior of the tent. The last of the towers were scrambling out of the entrance. Harry ran to the great end pole and clawed at a rope fastened there.

"Run for it, Dan!" he shouted.

His hands threw the rope free. His light raced for the king pole and did the same thing, and then to the second end pole. Blocks and tackle screeched as ropes raced fast through the big blocks. And overhead the great flaming canopy bellied down toward the ground.

Dan just made it out behind Harry,

speeded by the rush of wind and sparks as the canvas settled down. And suddenly the leaking pillars of wind-blown flame were on the ground in the center of the tent, burning more slowly. And canvas men and roustabouts were lowering the quarter poles.

In a few short minutes the big menagerie tent was flat on the ground, except where it mounded over the cages. And the stream of chemicals was blotting out the fire.

What had seemed certain destruction had been nipped in the bud by Harry's quick thinking.

The lights flashed on again, showing the surging crowd in the midway. People who had been on the edge of panic began to laugh sheepishly, and crowd in closer where they could see better. The brass band appeared out of the big top and began to play loudly. The circus people began to bring order out of chaos.

"They're a great bunch!" Harry said huskily to Dan.

A roustabout ran up to them, his grimy face sweating. "Somebody pitched gasoline on the tent and tossed a match against it, boss!" he panted.

"Did you see who it was?"

"No. He was gone by the time we got there."

Marta White ran up to them, a dark cape around her gauzy ring costume. "Harry—it's too bad!" she cried impulsively.

"It's all right, honey," Harry said, patting her arm reassuringly.

And then his face went hard as he looked off to the side. "I want to talk to those crooks!" he said savagely. "Come on!"

DAN recognized the two men Harry was making for. One was the tall, smooth, immaculately turned out Finke. The other was a short, fat, unwholesome looking fellow with a fat cigar in his mouth. Finke saw Harry coming and nudged his partner. They turned to Harry.

"I see you're having a little hard luck, Mr. Brown," Finke said smoothly.

"Damn you two!" Harry rapped out, stopping before them with clenched fists.

"Why, what's the matter?" Finke asked in mock surprise, and hurt. "Here we come over to offer you sympathy and any help we can give you and you talk like that. Eh, Streit?"

Streit rolled his cigar to the other corner of his mouth and grinned.

"That's right," he agreed.

"You dirty crooks!" Harry threw at them.

"Now, now," Finke said smoothly.

Detective Sergeant Simpson strode up in time to hear the last interchange of remarks, and after him came Fletcher and his man Lupe.

"What's the matter?" Simpson growled to Dan. "What's crooked around here? Did somebody start that fire?"

"Someone did!" Harry charged quickly, and he indicated Finke and Streit. "And they know a thing or two about it!"

"Be careful what you say!" Finke warned sharply.

Streit took the fat cigar out of his mouth and aimed it like a weapon at Harry.

"When you get to talkin' like that, remember there's such a thing as libel!" he spluttered with virtuous indignation. "You can't talk about us like that!"

"Can't I?" Harry cried. "I'll say that and a lot more! I've got a good idea you know the truth about the attack on my father and the two killings we've had! You wouldn't stop at murder!"

"Watch out, Harry!" Dan warned sharply, laying a hand on his friend's arm.

"Are you accusing these two men of having a hand in that killing tonight?"

Simpson demanded of Harry. "Have you been holding anything back from us?"

"Officer, you were a witness to that statement he made!" Finke said coldly. "The man's out of his head. We own the show across the street and came over here to help. If you've had any other trouble tonight this is the first we've heard about it."

"There was a man killed," Simpson growled.

Finke's face was a study. "Who?" he asked.

"Twitty!" Harry snarled at him. "What have you got to say about that?"

Finke blinked, swallowed, and then shrugged. "I don't know anything about it," he disclaimed.

"I think you all better come down to headquarters and talk this over," Simpson decided angrily. "I've got an idea you people know more about this business than you're saying."

Dan came to a sudden decision. It was time to cast the dice and see what they brought.

"Just a minute," he said to Simpson. "I think I have some evidence that will clear everything up."

"Huh? You have? Why didn't you say so before?"

"I have the weapons used in the killing night before last," Dan told him. "And I have pretty good reason to think that the killer tonight was the same person."

"Why didn't you tell me about this before?" Simpson blustered.

DAN ignored his manner. "These weapons have fingerprints on them," he said. "I suggest you and I go to headquarters and get a fingerprint man and any other experts we want. Then we can come back, take fingerprints of all the possible suspects in the show and compare them with the prints on the blood-covered weapons I have. That will settle everything beyond doubt. That sound all right to you, gentlemen?" He looked at Finke and Streit.

Finke's face was a study. Streit took the cigar from his mouth and stared at Dan with a strange expression.

"Why, yes, I suppose so," Finke muttered. "That is, if you've really got what you say. Where are these weapons?"

Dan smiled innocently. "All safe and sound in by compartment in Mr. Brown's private car. I hid them there a while ago. Are you ready to start, Simpson? We can get a taxi out there in front."

"All right," Simpson agreed.

"Come on, then," Dan said. "Walk out and see us off, Harry. We'll soon be at the bottom of this."

Harry and Marta White fell in beside them. And as they went toward the front of the lot Dan spoke out of the corner of his mouth to Harry.

"I'll do it," Harry answered.

Dan was smiling to himself as they hailed a taxi in front, and got in. They drove off toward the center of town.

Just before they reached the next corner, Dan called to the driver: "Cut around the block and drive back to the edge of the railroad yards."

"Hey, what's the idea?" Simpson protested irritably.

"Just a little smooth work," Dan chuckled.

"What do you mean? We're going to headquarters."

"Presently," Dan reassured him. "Got something else to do first."

Simpson growled, but he sat silent as the taxi took them down a blind street and stopped at the end.

Dan jumped out and gave the driver a dollar bill. "This way," he said.

Beyond the end of the pavement was a patch of weedy bank, a fence, and then the railroad yards with lines of cars standing dark and silent. Dan climbed swiftly over the fence, and the detective followed, muttering to himself. Dan led him at a fast pace in and out of the string of cars and coaches, until suddenly they came out by Harry's private car. A quick swing up over the back platform and they were in the dark interior. Dan turned on no lights.

"I don't get the idea of this," Simpson said irritably.

"You will. Keep quiet."

They had been inside only a few moments when steps scraped on the back platform. The door opened and four figures stepped in. Finke's voice said angrily: "Take that gun out of my back, damn you! I'll see that you're arrested for this!"

And Harry answered soothingly: "Sure. Any time you see fit, after we're through. Step right in my bedroom here."

"And we'll go in with you," Dan said under his breath from the end of the room.

Finke swore. "What are you doing here?"

"Loafing. Shut up. Not another sound out of you. Come in here, Simpson, and keep quiet!"

They all crowded into the pitch blackness of the small room. Dan closed the door to a crack.

Silence fell over them. And as they waited Dan began to doubt. Suppose he was wrong after all? What then? But he refused to dwell on that side of it.

THE minutes dragged by. The wait seemed interminable. Doubts again crept back to Dan. This was a pretty mess if he had guessed wrong.

His thoughts were cut short by the creak of a door hinge. Soft, stealthy

steps came across the sitting room. The intruder bumped into a chair and muttered a low curse, barely audible. Then his steps came on again.

They passed the door where Dan was standing rigid. Went on to the next one, where his things were. The door latch there creaked softly. The intruder was entering. Dan slowly peered out. A thread of light came out into the passage as a flash was used inside.

Softly Dan opened the door and stepped out into the passage. He could hear the rustle of someone looking through his things. And suddenly, without warning, a loud sneeze came from the spot where Finke was standing. The man had given them away.

The thread of light went out. The door flung open. A dark form stepped quickly out into the passage. And Dan hurled himself at it.

His arms went around the intruder. A heavy flashlight clipped past his ear and struck his shoulder.

Something hard jammed into his ribs. He knocked it away, just as a gun roared. Its hot breath drove into his flesh, the bullet raked his ribs.

Dan grabbed the gun hand and held it away in spite of the other's desperate efforts to bring it back to him. They reeled from side to side of the narrow passage. Dan's back crashed into a window glass, shattering it. With a mighty heave he threw his man back against the opposite wall.

The gun roared again as the trigger finger contracted spasmodically. But the bullet missed him entirely this time.

He swung his leg quickly and tripped the other. They crashed hard to the floor, Dan on top. The other struggled feebly, half knocked out by the impact of his head on the floor. Dan got both hands on the revolver and wrenched it away.

And as he did that a flashlight shone over both of them. Simpson dropped down beside him and clapped a pair of handcuffs on the intruder's wrists. Together they jerked the man to his feet. And Simpson threw the flashlight in his face.

It was Lupe!

"Bring him in the sitting room!" Dan panted and when they had Lupe in there Dan switched on the lights. Harry stared in amazement at the captive.

"Good heavens, I didn't think he was the man!" he burst out.

Lupe was a disheveled and dangerous figure as he stood there before them in his ill-fitting clothes. His prominent Adam's Apple was working up and down in his corded neck. His easy good nature was gone. His face was twisting with rage. His eyes glared at them. His teeth worked over his lower lip as if he wanted to rend and tear.

"This is your man," Dan said to Simpson. "He's the killer, and the one who's behind all the trouble we've been having. He had me fooled for a while. Had me thinking it was Fletcher."

"Is Fletcher in on this?" Harry demanded.

"I doubt it," Dan said. "Fletcher's a rather thick-headed wheel horse, running around in circles, not quite sure what it's all about. This man handled him without any trouble. He was damnably clever. Just a little too much so. He gave his hand away tonight when he killed Twitty."

"Did—did he kill my father?" Marta asked in a tight voice.

"Yes," said Dan. "You see, after you talked to your father, he had gone out quick in a panic to get hold of Lupe and let him know. And I imagine Lupe decided he couldn't be trusted now that things were getting hot, and knocked him on the head. And then I came up with the bag your father had just told him about. There was a chance to get all the evidence and put me out of the way. So Lupe knocked me out. But when he looked in the bag he found it was empty. And I was the only man who could lead him to the evidence against him. So he worked over me until I regained consciousness, playing the good samaritan. Lupe," Dan smiled, "you must have thought I was a mighty big fool, or you would have latched the bag when you closed it in a hurry."

LUPE was livid with rage. "Damn you!" he choked. "I don't know what all this is about! I thought you were a sneak thief in the car here and went after you!"

"Without doubt," Dan agreed. "And I wonder what you'll think when your fingerprints are compared with those on the knife that cut the throat of Wolfe, that poor canvas man. I can't understand that killing, Lupe. You seem to have more brains than that. Didn't you think so, Finke? They made a fool out of you Lupe."

"You mean they talked about me?" Lupe choked.

"They're here, aren't they?" Dan said coolly. "They had their hides to save."

"He's lying!" Finke cried angrily.

But the damage had been done. Lupe's face turned pale.

"So you double-crossed me after all, damn you!" he screamed at the two partners. "I took your dirty money while you played safe! And as soon as it got hot you threw me over! But you won't get by with it! You'll take the same dose I do!"

"For God's sake watch out what you're saying!" Finke warned wildly.

But Lupe was beyond all stopping now.

"These two were paying me money!" he raged. "Me and Twitty, who used to work for them. We were to make all the trouble we could, and put old man Brown out of the way if possible. He wouldn't deal with them. Finke had something on Twitty and was making him jump to time when he ordered. Put the old man out of the way, Finke said. So I did! And right after I knocked him over that fool canvas man walked up and threw a light on me. He recognized me and jumped me. I tried to stop him with my knife and he dove into it after he yelled for help. I ducked away and turned the knife and gun I carried over to Twitty. And when Finke didn't get any further with his ideas he told me to shoot the works and burn the tents down, if I had to. Do this and do that, he said. I fired the tents like he asked. And then he threw me down! Let's see if he can talk himself out of it now! He'll never run another show on the road!"

Lupe broke away from Simpson and leaped on Finke, clubbing two-handed with the steel handcuffs. Finke squealed with fright, and then went down heavily, striking his head on the steam pipe against the wall with sickening force. He moaned once, and lay there, still.

That seemed to sober the maddened man. He offered no resistance as Simpson dragged him back. Dan knelt by Finke. His face was grave when he looked up a moment later.

"I think he's dead too," he said. "That pipe has crushed in the back of his skull."

"I don't care," Lupe moaned. "He had it coming to him."

Streit had dissolved into a trembling wretch who cowered back against the wall away from Lupe. Dan glanced at him estimatingly, and then said to Simpson: "Better arrest him, too. They sowed trouble and they've reaped this."

Steps stumbled on the back platform. Fletcher came blundering in.

"Say, Mr. Brown," he called before he was hardly in the door. "I just thought that maybe someone'd try to get in here and get that evidence. You better hide it away before—"

And then Fletcher stopped short inside the door, staring at the scene before him.

"What—what's happened?" he got out in a weak, horrified voice.

Dan had to laugh at the ludicrous surprise and amazement on Fletcher's face.

"You had the same idea that I did, only you're a little late," he told Fletcher. "Better help Simpson here clean up the mess."

Fletcher jerked off his hat. "Lupe!" he got out. "You been doing all this?"

"Shut up, you fool!" Lupe snarled at him.

Fletcher confessed weakly and sheepishly: "I was tryin' hard, Mr. Brown. I even offered to sell out to Finke last night, but he put me off. Had my girl friend, Barbara Price, workin' with me, an' everything. But we didn't suspect anything was wrong with Lupe. He was workin' hard with us all the time. I guess I was only a fool after all."

"Don't let that worry you," Dan said kindly. "I was a fool too. Lupe reported that to Finke. And here I am— and there he is. Harry, I think I'll go back to the lot and get that evidence I hid under your office car. Simpson will want it."

Lupe's head came up. "You—you didn't have anything here?" he asked hoarsely.

"No," said Dan.

"What a fool you made out of me!" Lupe sobbed, burying his face in his manacled hands.

TURN TO PAGE 124 FOR A GREAT SURPRISE ANNOUNCEMENT!

The Death Master

A Vee Brown Story

by
Carroll John Daly

Author of "The Call to Kill," etc.

I closed my fist and
let him have it.

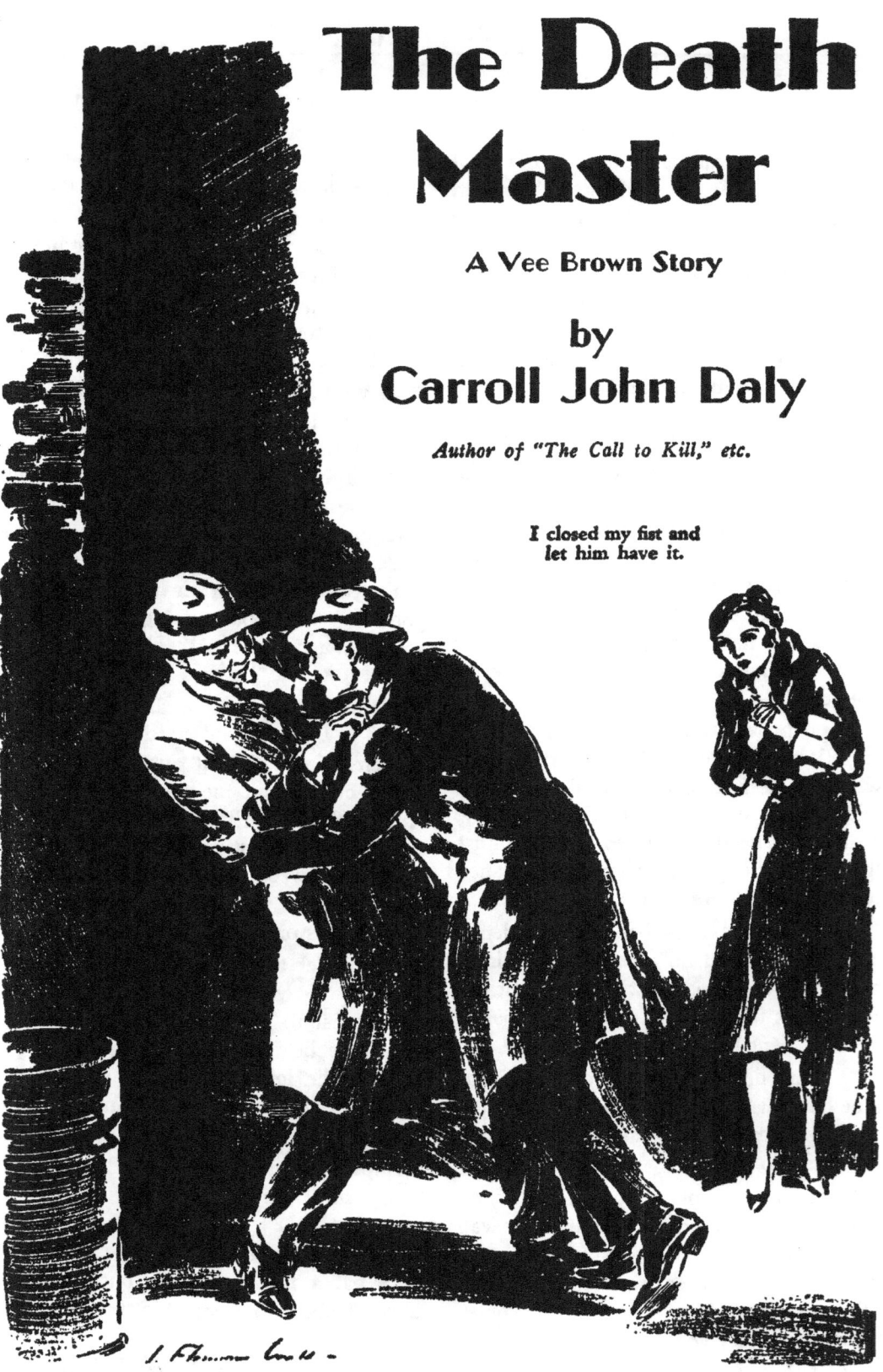

The trap was set and now its jaws began to close. For every entrance to that room was guarded—every corner of it manned with killer kings. And on a couch lay Condon, bound and gagged, human bait to lure Vee Brown to double danger—certain death.

CHAPTER ONE

World of Fear

OLD DOCTOR REISTACH lived alone in a three-story house on a side street in the upper Eighties. He had helped me considerably in the days when my buoyant securities allowed me to go big game hunting in Africa. Now that he had returned, friendless, to the city I visited him every Thursday night.

The doctor was greatly interested in present-day crime, and in Vee Brown, first-grade detective assigned to the district attorney's office.

I had been associated with Vee Brown for some time and was still sharing his luxurious penthouse on top of one of Park Avenue's most pretentious apartment houses. Indeed, the lease was in my name, for no one but myself knew that the small, almost delicate detective, who was feared by all criminals, was also Vivian, the unknown writer of many of our most sentimental song hits, the enormous income from which he kept secret.

"Killer of Men" he was spoken of in the department and the criminal world. "Master of Melodies" he was called in Tin Pan Alley.

It was late when I stood up to leave the doctor, and he was still talking to me about my promise to bring Vee Brown to visit him some time.

"I envy you your association with this Vee Brown, Dean," he said at parting. "I worry about you, of course, but I envy you the very air of danger that you breathe."

"Don't!" I laughed as he held the door

open. "Gunmen, racketeers, murderers—they have no interest in me. It's just Vee Brown they want to kill."

"Yes—certainly." The shrewd old man nodded his head as I went down the stone steps. "But did you ever think that they might try to strike at him through you? Take care of yourself."

That was all. As I reached the bottom step Doctor Reistach closed the door, and I was alone on the deserted street.

And that side street wasn't deserted. I had hardly gone more than a few houses down the block when I heard the whistle, then saw the cab. At least that was my impression afterward—that I had heard a whistle. Just a few bars of a popular song, one of Vee Brown's songs, by the way. But I did see the taxi that turned the corner down the street, directly ahead of me.

It pulled to the curb across the street and a girl got out, paid the driver, looked up and down the block as the taxi jerked from the curb and shot by me. For a moment the girl seemed to hesitate, then, when I was almost opposite her, she swung suddenly on her heels and started back down the street in the same direction she had come.

She saw me all right, for she kept looking over her shoulder and across at me. Hurrying too, making her feet move faster as I increased my speed to keep abreast of her. Why did I increase my speed? I don't know. She just gave me the feeling that she was frightened, watchful, suspecting some sort of danger. Even my presence on the same street seemed to alarm her.

Then, as she turned her head back from watching me and started almost into a run, she stopped dead. I heard plainly the little breathless cry of fear in her throat—fear that was stifled somewhat by surprise, I guess.

A man had stepped from a side alley between two of the houses. A big, broad-shouldered figure with coat collar turned up, slouch hat pulled down. An arm had stretched out and a hand had fastened on the girl's shoulder.

He was talking too, a sort of rumble in his voice. The girl started to scream, I think, but can't be sure. Anyway, the man's other hand shot out and covered her mouth. He was holding her tight, pulling her close to him, dragging her toward the alley from which he had come.

I was out in the street, across it, running toward the girl who now struggled frantically in the man's grip.

THE man didn't see me. Never suspected my presence, I guess, until I clutched him by the arm, tore his hand loose from the girl and swung him viciously around to face me. I'm a strong man, was a bit of an athlete in earlier days, and my outdoor life and wanderings in foreign countries have left me in the pink of condition.

Glaring eyes stared at me; thick lips slipped back and stained teeth showed. But he still held the girl with his left hand, while his right hung at his side, hung there empty.

"No cause for trouble, mister." He sort of shot the words through the side of his mouth. "The little lady and me are friends. She'll tell you that. We had a bit of disagreement. You're a detective, ain't ya?" There was a half warning glance over his shoulder at the girl.

"No," I said, "I'm not. Take your hand off that girl. Now, miss—" I started, but never finished. The man and the girl had both raised their heads, both turned them slightly in the direction I was facing. And I saw what they had heard. Coming

down the street was a black sedan. It was moving slowly, almost furtively, it seemed, in the darkness.

Even in the dim light I felt sure that I saw elation in the man's face, and fear in the girl's. But I was sure of the elation in the man's voice.

"Now, bozo—" He fairly bellowed the words. "You'll find you've stepped into the wrong party." His right hand came up and gripped me tightly by my coat collar, and at that moment the girl jerked herself free. Jerked herself free as I raised my hand, closed my fist and let him have it.

It was a fair blow, delivered rather short and more on the side of the jaw than on the point, for the man had turned his head. But the man's hand dropped from my coat collar; he staggered slightly backward, gave at the knees, and I stepped forward and struck him again. There was nothing wrong with my second blow, nothing "just fair" about it either. It caught him square on the chin as he was staggering. He folded up at once and sank slowly to the pavement.

Someone shouted down the street; the soft purr of the approaching car turned into a sudden roar. A man cursed loudly, and the girl had me by the arm, half dragging me toward the alley by the side of the house. The next instant we were in the alley and running madly down it, across an open court, toward a high wooden fence.

A barrel crashed as I stumbled against it, made a terrific racket as it rolled over on the uneven flags of the court. I drew up sharp by the fence, jerked out my police whistle, had it almost to my mouth when the girl clutched at my arm.

"Don't—don't!" she yelled. "They'll—"

"But they'll hear us—follow us. Why, the car was right on top of us when we made the dash. The police will—"

"The police will send me to jail," she cut in as she jumped, gripped the top of the fence and swung herself up on it.

"Quick!" She caught herself as she almost tumbled to the other side. "What's that? Good God! you're armed. Put that gun away. They might have killed you."

And I was armed. I was standing there against the fence, a heavy police automatic in my hand.

"Come—come!" the girl kept urging me. And hearing nothing in the alley we had left, seeing no running figures in the darkness, I turned, pocketed the gun, swung up on the fence and dropped beside the girl.

"They didn't follow us," I said in some surprise as we ran across the court, out another alley and onto the next street.

"No—no." And after a moment's pause, "They didn't dare. There's a police car that comes down that street at one-fifteen. Regular patrol, lately." And as we reached a small car by the curb, "Get in. They may come around the block, and —I can't leave you to them."

I LOOKED up and down the street before I climbed into the small coupe and sat beside her. Then I patted my gun and sat up a little straighter. If Vee Brown could see me now! I had rescued a woman from a big bruiser of a man; rescued her in the very face of others in that closed car. I glanced at the girl sharply as the car pulled from the curb and started down the street. This had been no ordinary attack. It had been planned in advance. And the girl! Well, she had stood there alone on the sidewalk when I struck the man down, stood there as the car approached—stood there silent when she might have awakened the whole block with her screams. Might have— And I remembered that she did not want the police in it. She was rather tall and rather slim. But she wasn't thin. She had a good profile, though a little sharp perhaps. Her lips! Well, from the side they seemed narrow. And her eyes! But it was later that I found out that her eyes were black, as black as her hair—blacker maybe.

"Where do you live?" she said, and when my mouth opened somewhat in surprise, "You've done a lot for me tonight. I'd feel better if I knew you were safe. I want to drive you home."

"That's very thoughtful of you." There was a touch of sarcasm in my voice. "But don't you think I should see you home? After all, I was doing rather nicely alone on the block when you—"

"Oh, don't be facetious," she ran in as we turned the corner and continued uptown. "You saved me for a while at least. I owe you everything for that. But don't you see—" Then suddenly, "It's over now. I'll drop you off and drop you out of my life." And with a sigh, that might have been resignation, in her voice, "Life is that way, you know—at least, my life."

"Life is what you make it," I told her, without much sense. "Tonight, I think I'll see you home."

She looked at me so sharply, so suddenly and so appraisingly that I added, almost involuntarily, "Of course—if you haven't any objection."

She shrugged her shoulders.

"Only, that I'm not the kind of a girl a man like you should know."

"What do you mean 'a man like me'?" I asked.

"Well," she said. "You're brave, you're refined, and you're just a little foolish."

"Any man would have—"I started.

"*Any* man would not." She put the words almost viciously. "The sort of men I know lately wouldn't. But why do you want to see me home?"

I thought a moment. Then, "You're brave too. And besides, it's customary for a man to see a girl home after he helps her out of an embarrassing situation."

"You can see me home if you wish. But I'm warning you. I'm not your kind of a girl."

"And just what is my kind of a girl?"

"I'm not your people," she said abruptly. "There are two worlds. I'm in the other one."

"The criminal world?"

"I suppose so," she said quickly. "That's as good a name as another."

"You're trying to tell me you're a criminal?" This as we drew up before a walk-up apartment, and I stepped from the car to the sidewalk.

"Just that." She was on the sidewalk, facing me now. "And you don't believe it, of course. Scientists, psychologists, sociologists, criminologists discuss the reasons. Mine is neither hereditary nor environment, just the force of circumstances. A bad break. Good night!" She held out her hand.

I IGNORED the hand and followed her up the stone steps, watched her take the key from her purse and open the door. She blocked my passage then.

"Aren't you nervous or afraid?" I asked.

"I live in a world of fear." She looked right at me when she spoke. "Every night when I enter here I expect to have happen what happened tonight. I expect to find someone lurking in every dark corner of the two flights I climb. I expect to be confronted the moment I enter my apartment."

"Let me see you safely in then. Your own apartment. It may not be just proper, but—"

"Proper!" She laughed mirthlessly, and when I waited for her to explain, "It just struck me funny, that's all. Yes, I'd like you to come up with me. There's comfort in another human being, isn't there? Funny, that! I'd be better off if I'd gone with Ernie Slawson tonight." She looked startled as she pronounced the name, and watched my face for a long moment. "It's like watching someone you love die slowly, I guess. It rips into your very stomach. You know it's going to happen, dread it, fear it. And then you're —well if not exactly glad, you're relieved when it's over. I watched my mother die." She ended abruptly. "Now I'm watching myself—die. Funny, isn't it?"

All her fears about people lurking in her apartment proved groundless. I searched it like a fine tooth comb. If Vee Brown could have only seen me then! My hand in my jacket pocket, caressing a gun, a finger nicely upon the trigger, my thumb upon the safety catch.

The girl had taken off her hat and coat and thrown herself upon the couch in the living room. She was smoking a cigarette when I returned; she motioned toward a box on the table. She was older than I had thought—or was she?

Twenty-two, I had guessed in the car. Now—well, she might be twenty-five, even thirty. As if she read my thoughts, she spoke.

"I'm twenty-three in years, hundreds in living." And suddenly getting to her feet, "I'm going to let you go now. I'm going to do the first decent thing I've done in a long time. You're never going to see me again." She walked past me to the door, and when I would have objected, "No, you'll be the kind who'd respect my wish in that. Now—now get out!"

I was slightly indignant, I'll admit, as I stood there, my hat in my hand. Perhaps I had risked my life, perhaps I hadn't. But I had come to her when she needed help, wanted help—at least, accepted help. And the end of the story was to be—"Get out!"

"Of course," I half bowed, or perhaps nodded somewhat stiffly, "I won't presume on the unfortunate circumstances that shoved me upon you." I opened the door. Then my natural pride melted a bit as I looked at her face, the lines already beginning to mar youth, the thin lips, the lower of which was caught between her teeth. But what decided me, I think, were her eyes. The peculiar haunted look that dulled the brilliance of the black. A look that seemed to come and go against the brightness of her eyes, like the dullness in between the flashes of an electric light sign.

"If you should have any further use for me—Here!" I took out a card and handed it to her. She didn't look at it, simply tossed it on the table.

"Now—go," she said again, and her voice this time was very low.

I stood facing her a long moment—then turned and started down the hall. But I'd hardly put my hand on the bannister of the stairs when she was on me, gripping me by the shoulders, turning me around, shaking me slightly.

"You're a gentleman," she was saying, and her voice was low and tense. "Promise me you won't mention what you did for me tonight, not to a single person."

"I have a friend who might—" I started, thinking of Vee Brown.

"No—no! Promise me. You must, you should! Don't make my meeting with you unfortunate for me. I'm not going to make it unfortunate for you."

"Very well. I won't mention it."

"It's your word," she said. "Now, forget me."

And she was gone, closing the door behind her, putting the chain I had seen into the bolt. I plainly heard it click before I started down those stairs.

When I came out onto the street the car was gone. A man from the garage must have called for it, I thought—that is, if I thought of it at all. But one promise I hadn't made. Not to try to see her again. But would I try? I told myself, indignantly, No. "Get out!" eh? A nice way to treat a man who has saved your life or—— But I was walking home,

whistling to myself. Vee Brown couldn't have made a better job of it. Not half so good, in fact. He'd of—— But I'd show him how unnecessary it is to clutter up the street with dead men. I'd prove my point that it wasn't often necessary. And then I remembered my promise to the girl. I was not to mention my little adventure of the night.

CHAPTER TWO

"I'll Tell Tonight"

VEE BROWN was still up when I reached our penthouse. He was lying off in a big chair, his feet stretched out, a cigarette, long dead, hanging from his lips, a leather-bound volume of Dante upon his knees, slowly but visibly slipping toward the floor.

"New piece go all right?" I jerked a thumb toward the music room.

"Fine." He blinked up at me. "Music always stimulates my mind in a criminal way. Crime stimulates it in a musical or sentimental way. Funny, isn't it? But one sets off the other."

"And Dante?" I nodded at the book.

"The hell that lies between." He laughed. "But seriously, Dean, the thing's been playing on my mind. McCarthy's been dead nearly three weeks. It was a brutal murder. It bothers me day and night."

"The pension fund takes care of the widow and orphans. The police——"

"I wasn't thinking of that." He came to his feet, ignoring the volume that crashed to the floor. "I was thinking—who'd take care of McCarthy?"

"But McCarthy's dead. You're not thinking of vengeance, Vee?"

"McCarthy saved my life once. I'm the law. The law knows no vengeance, only retribution. Besides, while his murderer lives, it interferes with my work —my songs. You can't have murder and young love in your heart—at least, not at the same time." He gave that little twisted smile of his. And after a minute's pause, "McCarthy was shot in the back. He was shot because——"

"Because——" I encouraged.

"Because he was a cop who couldn't be fixed."

"But the police are doing everything possible. Murder will out, you know. Some day you'll find out who did it and——"

"Who did it!" Brown swung on me suddenly. "Why I've known who did it ever since—well before they buried McCarthy."

"And they haven't been able to find him. He's got a hideout that——"

"Yes, a good hideout. Almost impossible to get him because he has the protection of the big interests. Mandozza is behind him, of course. And there's a real criminal for you. He snaps his fingers and judges act. He snaps them again and a man dies. Now he has a job for McCarthy's murderer. Do you know what that job is, Dean?"

"No—" I said, "I don't."

Vee Brown laughed.

"That job," he said, "is to kill me. Noble purpose, eh?" And looking down at his wrist watch, "Doctor Reistach, you tell me, is seventy-five. You gave him a run for his health tonight. Twenty minutes of three!"

I hadn't known it was that late. But those sharp black eyes were on me.

"He hasn't got a granddaughter, now, has he?"

"No," I said, "he hasn't. As a matter of fact, I felt restless and took a long walk." And changing the subject quickly, "What of McCarthy? If the man who killed him is caught, can you convict him?"

"If he is caught in time before witnesses are bought off; spirited out of the country—or murdered, like McCarthy."

"Is this murderer a well-known gunman?"

"Well enough." Vee Brown nodded.

"Then, who is he? Tell me or don't tell me, but don't drag it out."

"It's Ernie Slawson," Vee Brown said slowly. Then, "What's the matter, Dean?"

And there was something the matter. Ernie Slawson, the murderer! He was the man I had struck down that night.

I DON'T know just how I covered my confusion, indeed if I did cover it at all. But I lifted the decanter from the side table, swallowed a generous dose neat and looked at Brown.

"Well—out with it." He smiled.

"Out with what?"

"I'm no mind reader, Dean. I'm not going to pose as a Sherlock Holmes. A ten-year-old child would see the truth in your face. The name of Slawson startled you. Now, let's have it."

"I never heard the name before tonight," I blurted out.

"Before tonight!" Brown picked me right up. "Let's not quibble. What did you hear about him tonight?"

"What would you say, Vee," I did myself another drink and got just a bit chesty. "What would you say if I told you that I knocked Slawson down tonight?"

"I'd say that he was drunk," Vee answered almost without a moment's hesitation. "He's twice your size and has the strength of a lion—and will shoot to kill."

"And if I said he wasn't drunk?"

"Then I'd say that you are." Vee took the decanter from me, eyed it a moment.

"I've got it, Dean," he said, his face lighting up. And raising his right hand he began to hum softly, beating time with the music before he turned and passed into the music room. There was no use to talk to him then. He might be at the piano for an hour and he might be at it until breakfast time. It often struck him suddenly like that, and he'd leave me right in the middle of a conversation.

Thoughts! I had plenty of them, and I didn't need that couple of drinks to stimulate and excite those thoughts. Who was the girl? What did she have to do with Slawson? Would I see her again? Was it possible that she might put me in the way of finding Slawson? It would be a great feather in my cap if I could come to Vee Brown and tell him I had located Slawson for him.

And why not? That the girl feared Slawson was certain. She might very easily be glad to help me convict him of a crime that would rid her of him forever. And such a girl! Why it was impossible to connect her up with criminals, racketeers, gangsters.

Yes, it was hard to believe badly of the girl. Unfortunate? Certainly. That was it. I'd see her again. Unless—unless she suspected just that, and would leave her apartment at once.

And her name! I cursed myself for a fool then. I'd never even thought to look at the little cards above the bells in the outside hall of the apartment building. Well I'd remedy that in the morning. It was a cinch she was hiding out there, hiding from something, from someone. That was why— But I'd see her in the morning. Hunt her up first thing. And I slept.

The next thing I knew it was morning and Vee Brown was standing over me, fully dressed—shaking me. "It's the telephone, Dean," he was saying. "It's important. At least, it's important to the caller."

I got up, slipped on my dressing gown and went sleepily to the phone. Then I was wide awake. It was the girl of the night before.

"You haven't said anything to anyone about last night, have you?" Her words were breathless. "Of course I know you haven't, but I want your promise again. Something has come up—"

"I'll see you for lunch," I told her, and named a well-known hotel.

She wouldn't have it at first, but when I insisted she named a restaurant herself. A little secluded place on a side street. Then she hung up.

"I thought maybe you'd lunch downtown with me today," Vee Brown suggested at breakfast.

"Sorry—I have an engagement." And when he frowned, "Of course, if it's important, has to do with your work, I can arrange—"

"No, no." He shook his head. "No bad news on the phone, I hope."

"Not at all, rather good news. At least I think it is." And when he grinned at me, I lied. "It was Doctor Reistach."

"Charming voice, the doctor's." Vee toyed with his coffee.

"Someone called for the doctor," I explained.

"So—" He made a wry face and went on with his breakfast. He didn't believe me and I didn't care. Besides, what business was it of his? That is, as far as he knew. But I smiled to myself.

"It's just possible," I said as I left the table, "that I may deliver Slawson into your hands—I mean, the hands of the law."

"Great!" He beamed. "But you've more than hinted that the old doctor goes in for criminology. Clues and that sort of thing. Am I to thank him for this?"

But I only smiled and left him.

HER name was Una Coles. At least that was what she told me, though I always doubted the last part of it anyway.

We sat there in a tiny, secluded dining booth, and she told me why she had called.

"I'm in great trouble, Mr. Condon."

She held in her hand my card she had so carelessly tossed upon the table the night before. "No one can help me, so I shan't ask for help. But—" She smiled a tired, wan little smile—"if you can't help me, you wouldn't hurt me?"

"Of course not," I told her. "What put that into your head?"

"Your name." She looked down at the card. "I saw it on the table this morning. At first I didn't place it—and then I did. You're the Dean Condon who's been writing the articles in the paper about Vee Brown, the detective, aren't you?"

And when I admitted that, she added, "You won't ever tell him about me, will you?"

Both her hands stretched across the table and gripped mine. And in her eyes was the fear again, the hunted, even haunted, look.

"I won't tell him, of course, if you wish it that way. But I'll try to convince you that I should tell him. He can help you. He—"

"He's the law." She drew her hand away suddenly. "I can find no help there. I—" And looking straight into my eyes, "Why did I see you again?"

And that was the first of many meetings with Una. I didn't know then and I don't know now if I was actually in love with her or not, the time things came to a head.

And by things "coming to a head," I mean that night in her apartment when I held her in my arms, smoothed back her hair and—well, got her promise to bring Vee Brown into her confidence.

"No, no." She jerked free, almost threw herself across the room onto the couch. "You mustn't touch me. I'm not fit for it. A man—a criminal—has only to stretch out a hand, beckon me back and I must go. I hide away, and fool myself that I am free. Free, because they can't find me—free, because they don't

know where I am! But I'm not free. They have only to open their mouths, drop a hint in the right direction, and every one of the twenty-odd thousand policemen in the city will be watching for me."

"Is that the unfortunate thing that— the bad break you got? What was it, Una?"

"I won't tell you that," she said. "I should have faced it then, but I didn't— I couldn't. Now it's too late. But I'll tell you where Slawson is."

"What do you know about Slawson?" I asked her.

"Enough," she said, "to send him to the chair."

"Una," I said very seriously, "I don't know what you've done. But this I promise you. Slawson killed McCarthy. Vee Brown knows it. Vee Brown will protect you if you'll help him get Slawson."

"I know—I know," she said. "I should have spoken. I've been afraid. He'll kill me. Vee Brown—he's your friend. He'll help me, protect me." And there were more tears and fears, and a trembling little body held close to mine. But I won out.

"Slawson can't hurt you if he's in jail, you know," I told her.

"No, no, he can't. But there's another —his friend. A terrible name in the underworld. Ruthless, cruel. One who protects Slawson and will avenge him. What of him? Will Vee Brown be able to protect me from him. Mandozza?"

"He will," I said. "Don't you see, Una, you have to tell. You've run away; you're hiding out. Sooner or later Slawson will find you again, as he did the other night. He'll be afraid you'll talk and—"

"Yes, yes, I know. I know," she said. "Slawson will kill me finally. I'll tell this Vee Brown. If anyone can protect me, he can. I know about him, know how they all fear him."

SHE seemed very frightened after she had decided to deliver up Slawson. At first it was in my mind to take Slawson myself and show Vee Brown that I could do a bit of real detective work where the department had failed. But she wouldn't hear of that. And I got a kick out of her objections. She was thinking entirely of me.

"No!" She was emphatic. "That would be too dangerous. Slawson is bad. We must leave his capture entirely up to Vee Brown." And with a little shake of her head, "I know what's on your mind. You'd like to do it yourself. I'll tell Vee Brown Slawson's hideout. He can make his own arrangements then. If things break right, Slawson is out of my life. If they don't, and Slawson escapes, then Slawson won't know I—" And again the fear came into her voice. "Dean, Dean," she said suddenly, "I can't go through with it. Slawson will kill me. Slawson will kill me."

But I laughed aside any such idea as that. It took time, but at last I had her promise. Vee Brown was to come and see her. She would tell him all she knew. She made the arrangements for that very night.

"I trust you, Dean, but—but no policeman, no district attorney. Just Vee Brown alone to talk to, until Slawson is safe behind bars. Brown must come here alone, and late at night. He must be careful he isn't followed. Slawson hates him, fears him too, maybe. The only man I ever heard of Slawson fearing! You'll promise me Brown will be careful and that he'll come alone?"

I promised, and told her not to worry.

"Slawson doesn't suspect where you are or he'd have found you by now. As for Vee Brown—he always works alone, independent of instructions. You need fear nothing. I promise you he'll question you only about Slawson and nothing more. Just where is Slawson?" I tried that again.

"I'll tell it all to Vee Brown." She set her thin red lips lightly. "I'll tell. I'll tell him tonight."

CHAPTER THREE

Slawson

I WAS rather cocky that night when I dragged Vee Brown from his music and into the living room.

"You've never done this before, Dean." He looked at me sharply. "You know how I feel about such— It must be very important."

"It is!" I told him, and meant it. "The thing you want most. I'm going to deliver Slawson to you. Don't laugh! You want the murderer of McCarthy for the state. Well you're going to have him."

His eyes brightened, dulled, and brightened again.

"Come, Dean, out with it. Someone's been spoofing you."

And I told him of my adventure that night three weeks before, when I left Doctor Reistach's house.

"It was she who called that morning, Vee. She recognized my name and immediately connected up our association. It's been a hard pull. Mandozza—Slawson! They've got some grip over the girl. You must leave her out of it, Vee, protect her too. She's gotten a bad break some place in life. A mistake, perhaps—"

"Yes, yes, I know." Vee Brown narrowed his sharp black eyes. "Tell me something, Dean. Are you in love with the girl?"

"How absurd!" I was startled. "I've known her only three weeks."

"Of course! But that's not answering the question. Are you in love with her?"

"Well—no," I said, grinned at him, and added, "Not yet. Neither Africa nor you have entirely taken the civilization out of me. There's something in her face that frightens me."

"Yes," he said, with a twisted smile. "I can understand that." And when I would have questioned him, "Did she mention Mandozza?"

"Yes, she did. She's done some wrong, Vee. I don't know what it is. You'll help her, protect her. You'll—"

"Of course." His lips set tightly. "That's part of the police system. A good cop never betrays a stool pigeon."

"Vee—" I stepped back from him. "She's not that. She's—"

"She's selling out," Vee cut in abruptly. "The name doesn't mean anything. There wouldn't be a dick worth his salt who didn't employ a stool pigeon. I have scores of them scattered about the city. And don't look so shocked! They are a necessary evil. In a business way, not in a social one," he added as he laid a hand upon my shoulder. "You're falling for the dame, Dean. That's why I'm so brutal. You're bound to learn things about her later, things that will be hard to stomach. I want to make it easier by preparing you."

I CONTROLLED my temper the best I could and said, somewhat stiffly, "You haven't seen her, haven't talked to her. It's simply the force of circumstances that has placed her where she is. Now, she's not a stool pigeon."

"Now," said Vee Brown, slowly, "things are getting too hot and she wants to get out from under. She's not doing it to serve justice; she's doing it to serve herself. She wants something in return.'"

"She wants only protection." I told him. "She'll get that. I promised her that—from you. You'll give it to her, or you'll never get Slawson through her."

"I appreciate that. And I'll give her protection, if she makes good."

"You'll give her protection whether she makes good or not."

Brown was turning away but he swung back. "You love her!" he said suddenly.

"I don't," I denied hotly. "Vee, I've never seen you act like this. You're— By God! you're jealous that I have succeeded where you have failed. The Crime Machine is very human, after all. Vee—"

And he was laughing at me.

"Good old Dean." He laid a hand affectionately upon my arm. "Here I am with a chance to lay the finger on Slawson, the man who murdered McCarthy, shot him in the back—and a chance, perhaps, for the biggest scoop ever pulled off in the city, Mandozza. And I'm crabbing. Why to get Mandozza I'd go on the stand and lie for the girl if she'd killed her grandmother and five infant sisters. Don't you see, Dean? It's you. I'll protect the girl, I'll spare the girl. But it's you I want to spare. At your time of life a woman hits you hard. And I don't want you tearing your heart out for a girl who's turned yellow and wants to blow the works to save her own hide."

He raised a hand when I would have talked. "This is your first experience. I've seen it a hundred times. Stoolies are part of the system, certainly. But we don't take them into our homes, marry them and—"

"You might wait till you see her, if you do see her."

"But I'm going to see her, Dean. I dare say I'm wrong and she's the model of all the virtues. Let it go at that. But be prepared for the let-down if I'm right."

And when I still sulked, and with good cause, I thought, he went into the plans for the night. Made me go over and over them.

"Good!" he said finally. "You're to go there at twelve-thirty. It's nearly nine now. Half an hour later I'm to pass down the block, alone. If things are right you'll wave a handkerchief to me from the front window. That's one o'clock exactly. I'll be there to see this paragon of all the virtues."

And he turned on his heels, walked back into the music room and slammed the door behind him.

"I THOUGHT you'd never come, half wished you'd never come," the girl told me, even though I appeared at her door ahead of time.

"Well," I told her with a grin, "you took long enough to let me in."

"Yes, I know. I was frightened. I—"

"You mustn't be." I took her by both shoulders and held her steady before me, looking down into those eyes. Black—like Vee Brown's, they were. But the haunted look was still there, the uncertain look of fear, that belied the set lips and the determined tilt of her chin. "It'll be all over soon, once Slawson is taken. Vee acts quickly, Una. Then this thing that is between us, this—"

"Between us?" She put up both her slender hands and tried to push me away from her. "What do you mean, what do you mean?"

"That I love you, Una." I just pulled her to me. "Don't you see? Once the thing is cleared up, then we can—"

"We can't. We can't. We can't!" She struggled in my arms, half pushed me from her. Then, when I released her, she stood swaying there in the middle of the floor, her eyes very wide, her face very pale. And she did it. Suddenly her arms were around me and she was kissing me frantically, holding me to her, crying softly.

I held her. Brown was right. But I don't think I knew it till he told me, or until I saw her again. Now— Stool pigeon, eh? Yellow, eh? No! To me she was—

She was talking, low, fast, hysterically, I thought—as if she had forgotten our plans for the evening.

"Go, then, go. Forget me, and I'll try to remember that for one brief moment I was—was the girl—"

"What are you saying, Una?" I laughed lightly as I pulled her to me again. "You—"

And I stopped talking. Stood still, holding her there. A shadow had crossed the light, crossed her face. I didn't move. I couldn't move. Footsteps had crossed the room, a body was close to mine. I couldn't see it, couldn't feel it; perhaps I heard the man's breathing. But no matter what the sensation, I did know it. Another human body was close to mine.

"What does it mean, Una?" I said, inanely looking straight into her face, a face white and filled with fear. Or was it fear? Horror, perhaps, maybe even loathing. And I knew the truth even before the man spoke. The girl had trapped me.

"I suppose," said the voice behind me, "that you're entitled to a little fun. You're all right, Una. I didn't think you'd—"

And I swung and faced the man. It was the man I had seen that night I first met Una. It was Ernie Slawson.

"There, there." The big man stepped back, knocking up my chin with his gun when I nearly collided with him. "My God! You don't want to kiss me too. And you're a pretty boy. I dare say Una's had her fun, running around with you. She's a cute bag of tricks. Never played up to me much, but then a condemned man like you is entitled to a little recreation. I don't think Mandozza would approve, though. He's fussy about—"

I wasn't listening. I was looking into the man's face. The coarse evil mouth, the blood-shot, dim blue of those eyes. And I was thinking just one thought. Vee Brown was coming. And I'd trapped him to his death.

Then a wild idea. I didn't care about myself. I didn't think about myself. Suppose I was killed there! A shot would disturb others in the building. A shot would be heard on the street, bring in the police. It was a good half hour yet before Vee Brown was coming. I'd chance it. My life to save Vee's life, which I—

My right hand shot to my jacket pocket. The girl screamed, Slawson cursed, and his gun hand moved. My gun caught in my pocket. Not that it would have mattered maybe. I never could have raised it in time but I might have fired a single shot into the floor, that would—

But Slawson's left hand flashed down and held my wrist. His right simply moved up and down, I think. I can't be sure. But there was a thud, as if two objects had come together. My knees sagged; things danced before my eyes. And I knew the truth. Slawson had crashed his heavy automatic down upon my head.

After that, a sensation of sinking—then, blackness.

CHAPTER FOUR

Eyes of the Dead

PEOPLE were talking. I could hear the distant voices. People? It was the girl, Una.

"You promised me that," she was saying. "And, now—what of him?"

The voice of Slawson answered.

"You see how it is, kid. Vee Brown's got to die. You weren't fool enough to believe that I was going to take him away some place and nurse him, like I told you. This guy, Condon! Well—it's just too bad, that's all."

"You're going to kill him, after what you told me, promised me?" Her voice was tense, almost a metallic note in it.

"Maybe we won't have to. Just let him stay there and—"

"That's a lie," the girl said. "He'd

know who killed Brown. If Brown dies, he has to die. You're going to kill him! You're—"

"Now, kid, you know how it is. Why it wouldn't make sense to knock over one and let the other stand up in court and put the finger on us. Be sensible. You've gone through the thing fine. We're all mighty proud of you. We—"

"You needn't be proud of me. I went through it to save my own miserable self. You know that. You made me do it because—"

"Because—" Slawson fairly hurled the words. "Because things are just the same now as they ever were. I still know what I know. Me and Mandozza. You don't want anyone else to know. Have sense! There, get in the bedroom. It'll be over in a minute."

"You're going to murder him before Brown comes! And—"

"Not so loud," Slawson cautioned. "There's the two getaway cars on the street behind. I'd of let you go before, kid, only you squawked so about this punk."

A strange voice suddenly said, "Getting close to one o'clock, boss. Had I better pull the handkerchief trick?"

And I opened my eyes to stark horror.

Horror? Yes. A man lounged against the front window, a cigarette hanging from his lips. Another sat almost directly in the center of the room, facing the door. It was that man—or the thing the man held across his knees—that furnished the horror.

It was a Thompson sub-machine gun, and the nose of it was directed full on the door. On the door that would soon open, on the door that would frame Vee Brown's small slender body. Frame it in a frame of death.

Over by the bedroom door was the back of Slawson, beyond him the girl. I could see only her skirt, but I could hear her voice. The huge body of Slawson blocked her from the room.

As for myself! I was bound hand and foot and stretched upon the couch. I tried to speak.

"All these men for one man—Vee Brown." There was a sneer in my voice, a voice I could not hear, for no words came. I was gagged. If I could slip off that gag I could shriek my warning to Vee Brown. One sudden cry as he turned from those stairs to the door of death. Would he know. Would he understand? And I thought that he wouldn't. Or if he did, he would come on anyway. That would be like Brown. Vee Brown, my friend! The friend I had trapped. For it was I who had trapped him, not the girl.

Why hadn't I seen the hundred and one little things that should have warned me? The blow that I had struck the giant, Slawson, the blow that he had pretended to stagger under. Then the escape! The man in the car hadn't followed us through that alley—across the court behind the house. And the girl's story, that a police car came down the block, to explain our all too easy escape.

AGAIN, her alarm when she saw the gun in my hand, her saying that I might have been killed, and her stopping me from blowing the police whistle. How easily we got into the car and drove away! And all the time she had been in touch with Slawson, planning this. I was a fool, a blithering idiot.

"Hello!" said Slawson, turning around and looking at me. "You're feeling better. Like our little display? Want to kiss the girl friend?" Then to the man at the window, "Benny, it's getting near time. Better gag this punk on the couch. You know!" He turned from the girl and ran a finger across his throat. "Gag

him good, so he won't talk. The kid's going to stay in the bedroom."

"No, no." The girl was by Slawson, jerking herself free from the hand that clutched at her. The man at the window had started toward me when she flung herself between us.

"You can't! Mandozza promised me. Mandozza will—"

"We ain't going to hurt him." The man with the cigarette was putting something that flashed like steel back in his pocket. "Just gag him."

"But he is gagged. He can't move. He can't speak. He can't—"

"We're just going to tighten up the gag a bit and—"

"You're going to kill him. You— Benny. You've got a knife there. I saw it. You— No. No!" She was screeching now, as Slawson crossed the room and laid a huge hand over her mouth.

"Slit his throat and get it over with," Slawson said to the man who had pocketed the knife. "What Mandozza sees in this she devil beats me. If I thought he'd believe my story I'd do for her too." He cursed and jerked his hand from the girl's mouth. There was blood on his palm. He fastened his hand upon her throat. Then the clock struck—just a single gong. But everyone in that room was tense. It was one o'clock. The hour of death!

"All right." Slawson dropped his hand from the girl's throat. "You behave, now, and we won't kill the boy friend. No harm will come to him. You, Benny, pull the handkerchief act. We'll let this bozo live." He winked over the girl's head at Benny.

Benny nodded, raised his eyebrows and winked back. The man with the machine gun looked over his shoulder, caught the wink, looked at me, then nodded.

And Una! She was across the room,

on her knees beside me, her head close to mine. Tears streaked her face.

"I didn't know, I didn't know," she said over and over. "But they shan't harm you. They—"

She drew back slightly, as if I had struck her—and I guess I had mentally. I saw the man by the window waving the handkerchief. Vee Brown was even now coming to his death. And I— It was not she he had trusted. It was I. But my eyes must have told her the truth.

"Don't! Don't look at me like that." She put her hands, one on either side of my face.

This time, when she half straightened, she must have read something in my face. But she didn't read it correctly. The horror in my eyes was not for what she had done—not then. For I wasn't looking at her. I was looking beyond her, over her shoulder. The horror in my eyes was for her. There, behind her, was Slawson, an evil smirk on his face. In his hand was a gun and it was raised above her head.

Now, it was sweeping down! nearer, closer to that black bobbed head. She half turned her head, or started to turn her head as I tried to pitch myself from the couch and hurl her aside.

She never saw it, never knew what struck her. There was just a dull thud. Mechanically, or at least, involuntarily— my eyes closed. Something sank upon my chest, soft hair swept my cheek.

WHEN I opened my eyes again Slawson was dragging the girl from the room. I saw him pitch her inert form into the bedroom, pull the door partly closed and face the door again. The hall door. The door through which Vee Brown must pass.

Then Benny spoke.

"You should'a smacked her down long

ago," he said. "Will I do the handkerchief trick again?"

The man with the machine gun spoke for the first time.

"The dame would'a been all right if you hadn't kept her here. She did her trick and you should'a thrown her out. It ain't no place for a girl."

"Yeah?" Slawson said. "Well, I didn't like her last act with the punk. I thought she was going soft." And to Benny, "Did you see anyone on the street?"

"No—" said Benny, "I didn't. That wasn't part of the show, was it? I didn't stick my mug to the window. Vee Brown has sharp eyes. You're sure you'll get him, 'Gunner?'"

The man with the gun spat on the floor and grinned.

"They'll be picking lead out of him for a couple of days. When the cops try to lift him to carry him to the wagon they'll think he's nailed to the floor." And then he added, as if he dared anyone to disprove it. "The girl did her trick. This ain't like a simple knockover. Dames can't stomach seeing guys blasted out. You should'a chucked her out. Now, she may remember too much." He added the last sentence thoughtfully.

"And the punk?" said Benny, clicking the blade from an especially wicked looking knife handle. "Will I give it to him now?"

"Now!" said the gunner. "We move fast after the racket. Tommy, here, will damn near tear the side out of the building." He patted the machine gun.

"The getaway is a cinch," said Slawson. "Down the stairs, out the back, over the fence, and the car is behind. It'll be ten minutes before the cops get here. As for the sleepers, you'll take care of them, Gunner. I'll cart the girl, if she can't waddle. I didn't crack her none too hard."

"Yeah," said the Gunner. "It'll be

just too bad if the tenants act up. Better give it to the punk. And if I were you, Slawson, I'd let the girl lie there when we leave."

"To squawk to the cops when they come?"

"Well—" said the Gunner, in a whisper, as he seemed to listen for steps in the hall, "I'd put something in her to keep her down and silent."

"Yeah." Slawson stroked his chin with his left hand, caressing the gun with his right. "I think, maybe, you said something." He half turned toward the bedroom door.

"Better give it to the punk first." The Gunner nodded his head toward me.

"O. K.," said Slawson. "All right, Benny, make it quiet. Make it quiet and make it quick. Brown ought to be up any minute now. I'll be ready to throw the door open. Ready, Gunner!"

He walked to the door and stood beside it, close to the light switch.

Benny came softly over to me. There was something in his movements like a cat, something feline in his face, too. The quiver of his lips, the soft cruelness of his green eyes. I was going to die. I won't say that the man seemed to like the job of killing me, but I will say that he didn't especially dislike it. He just— Well my thought, then, was that it didn't interest him one way or the other. It was a job that had to be done. And somehow I felt that Benny would do it well.

Benny's left hand pulled at my collar. Like an executioner preparing to carry out the sentence of the court! Up to that time I was in more or less of a dream. It hadn't all seemed real. Now those malignant green eyes, the sharp nose and the cruel twisted lips! The knife—the cold steel blade a few inches from my throat. Good God! he was going to cut my throat. Cut my throat as I lay there facing the window, looking through the glass against the whiteness of a tan shade. Beyond was the sky, the stars—the city with its millions of citizens; its twenty thousands of police, honest, fearless and— God! I was to be butchered; my throat cut because I had listened to a woman. A woman who had wanted to save me at the last.

I told myself that. I told myself— And the knife! I struggled frantically, broke the man's grip upon my coat; twisted myself nearly off the couch. Then I was flat on my back on it again, a knee was on my chest. My tongue was trying to lick at dry lips but the gag held it back in my throat. The knife! It was in the air now, poised, ready! I tried to close my eyes but I couldn't. The lids refused to obey the order from my brain. And the knife started down! Yes, started down. I could see—could see— could— And, mercifully, my eyes closed.

I heard the shot, and in a dull way thought Vee Brown has come and Vee Brown is dead. But it was a single shot only. And the knife had not—

I opened my eyes and shrieked, yes, shrieked beneath the gag. Benny was still there, his knee still upon my chest, his hand still raised in the air, the sharp steel still glittering above me. And his eyes! His eyes were what made me shriek beneath the gag. They were no longer malignant and cruel. The eyes were glassy and staring, staring at nothing. Sightless—that was it. And I knew. Somehow I knew that I was looking into the eyes of a dead man.

CHAPTER FIVE

On a Split Second

BENNY'S body swayed slightly. His head was dropping forward on his chest, his fingers were opening—and I twisted my body to avoid the falling knife. Benny seemed to straighten, to sit up almost straight; his head lolled back; his mouth hung open, and turning grotesquely he crashed to the floor.

All this happened in a few seconds, a single second, maybe even a split second. The Gunner cursed, glass crashed, the shade was torn from the window—and I was looking straight into the face of Vee Brown. The fighting face of Vee Brown, the killer face of Vee Brown. For Vee Brown with a gun in his hand and death in his heart was a different person. But he had crashed through that front window and dropped to the floor.

I tried to cry out a warning as the Gunner swung and his Tommy gun started to play its tune of death. Started—that was all. He was firing it as he turned. And I saw in his face what Vee Brown said was in the faces of most murderers when it came their time to take it. Surprise—then uncertainty. Then fear—abject terror. Then death.

Vee Brown simply jerked up his gun before that Tommy gun was fully around. I didn't even hear the report of the shot. No doubt it was drowned out in that furious *rat-tat* of the machine gun. The *rat-tat* that died suddenly, leaving the room deadly quiet—and the Gunner lying on the floor.

The lights went out, a board creaked. Then silence! Burnt powder was in my nostrils, back in my throat, cutting, biting, choking.

A door slammed, a key turned in a lock, and the lights went on. Two men lay dead on the floor. The bedroom door was closed. Vee Brown was moving toward it stealthily, his gun raised, his eyes two points of glittering blackness. And I! My eyes were bulging, my tongue parched. I could not breathe. The fumes were strangling me. I was dying. With a frantic effort I swung my body free of the couch, plunged to the floor, rolled sideways and luckily braced my shoulders against the couch, my feet resting on something soft and yielding. It was Benny. But I was choking to death, things were going black. And Vee Brown turned his head and saw me—and knew the truth.

He took two quick steps and swept the dead Benny's knife from the floor. I felt it across my cheek, the coldness of it, as he cut the gag. The warmness too, as if blood trickled down my face.

I gasped in the air, air foul with smoke, gun powder, sickening fumes. But it seemed like pure oxygen to my bursting lungs. In a dim distant way I saw Vee cross to the bathroom, return with a glass of water and put it to my swollen lips. He let me gulp some of it down, splashed the rest across my face. Then he hacked at the tight, strong rope as he talked.

"Poor old Dean." There was that twisted smile to the corner of his mouth. "You couldn't see it, of course. That's why I thought you must love the girl. Slawson knocked about—Slawson not drawing a gun or following you! The girl attacked on a dark side street by Slawson, a street that you visited every Thursday night and left each time at about the same hour! Quite a coincidence, that, Dean. In fiction—yes. But in real life—no. Didn't you think that maybe they'd strike at me through you?"

"That," I coughed, "is just what Doctor Reistach said."

"Of course, shrewd old doctor. You neglected him, after that, for the girl."

"When did you first suspect——?" I pulled myself onto the couch. Not because I felt stronger or sought more comfort, but because of the thing beneath my legs, beneath my knees. The soft yielding thing that had been Benny.

"I suspected as soon as you told me. I wasn't sure, of course, Dean. But fairly sure. I shouldn't have let you come. But then, I wanted Slawson. I couldn't tell you, though God knows I hinted. Your face would have warned Slawson at once." He shrugged his shoulders. "Your sweet girl friend traps me to my supposed death through you, and I miss her and Slawson while I stop to save your life!"

"It's a wonder he—Slawson—didn't kill you when he had the chance, before the light went out."

VEE BROWN laughed. "He didn't have the chance, Dean, and he knew it. I was watching him when I killed—" He looked down at the dead man with the machine gun. "I thought so. Gunner Platz."

"What did you mean, Slawson didn't have a chance? You shot Benny and saved me. You shot Gunner Platz, and Slawson had a gun in his hand."

"Right!" said Vee. "In his hand, at his side. Benny died before they even knew I was on the fire-escape. Gunner swung his typewriter when I crashed the window. But Slawson only turned his head, not his gun. I was watching him, marking him, and he knew it."

"But why didn't you—" I paused. It wasn't like Vee Brown to spare a man, a man like Slawson, for any reason. He considered the killing of a murderer his duty to the state.

"Mandozza," he said, shaking his head. "Slawson might prove a rat, and squeal. That's why he didn't raise his gun—and die, Dean. He was thinking what I was thinking. I'd like to know about Mandozza, and dead men don't talk. His other hand was behind him, on the light button. I didn't know that then, I couldn't see the button. I suppose he was ready to pitch the place in darkness as soon as they dynamited me out."

"But he might have fired in the dark and—"

"Not him. Slawson isn't as easily scared into shooting as that. I moved quickly when the light went out. He guessed that. And if he had fired, I'd of spotted the flash of the gun and got him sure. No, he didn't know I came alone, and he wasn't anxious to force me into killing him."

He paused a moment and tossed the knife into a corner of the room. "Life is like that, Dean. You sometimes look too far into the future and miss the opportunities of the present. I should have killed him and let Mendozza go for the time being. McCarthy would have liked it better that way. I think too much of the masses and not enough of the individual. It—"

He paused and straightened. A woman screamed, but it was not from behind that bedroom door. A man was shouting, then a police whistle rang shrilly in the night.

Vee Brown smiled when I sat erect and looked at him.

"Surely you're not surprised, Dean. A gun shot or two may not disturb a public that is used to violence. But a machine gun in your own apartment house—Well, even murder in our city has its limitations."

"But," I stammered, pointing to the bedroom door, "Slawson went in there." Then in sudden thought I staggered to my feet and clutched Vee by the arm. "You've got him. He can't escape. The fire-escape was on the front window, the only door there." I pointed to the hall door. "There isn't any rear or servants' entrance to these walk-up apartments. He's trapped, for you—there."

"You think so?" Vee looked at me. "Well, it's quite possible of course. Gunmen are morons or they wouldn't be gunmen. That is, common ones, not boys like Slawson. But suppose he is there, and is trapped! If I break the door down he'll put a few bullets in me while I'm doing it. If I fire through the door it will be a waste of the department's money on bullets. Slawson won't be apt to stand in front of the door."

"What do you intend to do?"

"The place will be filthy with the police in a minute or two, and I like to work alone. My guess, Dean, is that Slawson is not there. Suppose I didn't come alone but brought a few cops with me! Surely the front door or the fire-escape would not be a safe retreat for Slawson. No, the thing has been more carefully thought out than that. As you say, there is no servants' entrance. But I pride myself that the fine Italian hand of Mandozza was in the planning of my death. Wouldn't it be wisdom to hire the apartment behind this, knock a hole in the wall and have a means of escape. No, Mr. Slawson is down another fire-escape and through the back court, or perhaps up the fire-escape or the stairs, and over the roof."

There were loud voices in the hall. A shrill feminine voice cried out, "It was murder."

Other throats were raised in angry protest, and a final high rough voice of authority.

"Our brave public has recovered." Vee smiled. "Quiet before, that of fear. Now confidence has returned. Courage and the love of justice beats again in good citizens' breasts. There's a reason for it, Dean. The police have arrived."

VEE BROWN walked to the door and threw it open. A uniformed policeman was coming heavily down the hall; frightened, bewildered and angry people followed him. They were in all forms of dress—or undress. The cop was talking to them over his shoulder, telling them in a loud voice to stand back.

And they did stand back, jarred against one another as Vee suddenly opened that door and stood in the light. The cop's gun came up as Vee Brown spoke.

"Detective Vee Brown, from the district attorney's office," he said sharply. "I was trapped here, with my friend." He swept a hand toward the body as the cop stood in the doorway. "I had to defend myself."

"I've seen your picture," the cop was saying without lowering his gun. "You look like it, and—" he looked toward the bodies—"you act like Vee Brown." Then turning to the little crowd of people pushing toward the doorway, "Back, now, all of ya. There's been murder done." The door closed and the officer faced us again, looked steadily at Vee Brown, walked over to the bodies, stared down at the hole in Gunner's forehead, looked at the other hole in Benny's neck, and scratched his head.

"I've heard tell of you often, Vee Brown, and read about you too." And glancing at the bodies once more, "I thought the stories were mostly lies, but I guess not."

"Did anybody telephone headquarters?"

"Sure," the cop answered. "I let Mulligan do that. He heard the shots, and a couple of half-dressed women outside gave us directions. Mulligan dropped into an apartment below. He'll—"

The door flew open and another cop came in. It was Mulligan.

"I put the call through and— Hello, Brown. Your work?" He jerked a thumb at the lifeless figures.

Vee Brown nodded to Mulligan, and half introduced me. His story of the shooting was crisp and correct, though he ignored my part in it. Just that I went there and he followed, pointing to the broken glass to show his entrance. But he made no mention of the girl, Una.

"You don't look cut up none." Mulligan looked at the window.

"No—" said Brown. "Had a coat over my arm." He pointed to his top coat on the floor.

"Looks like a woman lived here." Mulligan was looking at Una's hat and coat on the costumer to the right of the door.

"Maybe." Vee shrugged. But he looked at me. Did he wink? I wasn't sure, but I was sure he was going to spare me the real story of the night.

"Huh!" said Mulligan, going to the bed room door and shaking it. "Locked! No key outside. Maybe—" he pounded his weight against the door. It groaned.

"There was another man here," said Vee Brown. "He went that way. He probably had an out, but if he's still in there—" And when Mulligan just looked at him, preparing for another thrust of his huge right shoulder, "His name is Slawson."

"Cripes!" Mulligan side stepped quickly from the door. "Ernie Slawson?"

"Yes—" Brown grinned. "But he's gone now. Else that first thrust against the door would have brought some lead."

"Yeah," said Mulligan, eyeing Brown belligerently. "Yeah."

A ND all this time had I forgotten about the girl? No, I hadn't. She was continually on my mind. Should I tell Brown? Should I let her make her escape. Or would silence cause her death? Had Slawson taken her with him to kill her?

Brown was talking to the policeman, giving him orders. Explaining his theory of Slawson's escape; the entrance to the apartment in the rear, that he suspected.

"I'll be here." He jerked his head toward the bedroom door. "You better go together. Slawson is really bad. If you can't get in with the janitor's key there'll be a special lock. Break the door

in. No, I don't think you'll find him, but you may. Or I may be wrong, and the apartment behind occupied, in which case—"

There was more, and the cops were gone. The door was closed and Brown was talking to me.

"Now, Dean, the whole story. What they did. How the girl cleared out. And mostly, exactly what she looked like. We may be able to—"

"Vee," I said to him suddenly, "she didn't know they planned to kill you, even kill me. At the last moment she tried to save us. She thought—"

"My God!" Vee cut in on me. "I spare you all— Well, you like to write up my cases for the newspaper. How about the full details of this one? You're not— Dean, I knew it. You're in love with that girl."

"I'm not. I'm not!" I yelled. "I never—" and I stopped dead. "Well, I realize the truth now. You're right, of course, but at the end—"

"I know, I know." His facetiousness was worse than if he condemned me bitterly for the whole thing. "She's too sweet and innocent to enter into a machine-gun trap. A forty-four in the stomach, now or a knife in your heart would be more suitable for her gentle, womanly feelings." And when I just sulked, "Come, Dean, be a man. Take it on the chin and be done with it. I'm only asking you what became of the girl."

Should I tell him? Of course I should. But would I—

I looked toward the bedroom door. Metal had clicked against metal. A key had spun in the lock. The door knob was turning slowly. Vee Brown's gun was in his hand, covering that door, a finger of his left hand to his lips, cautioning me to silence.

The door opened slowly, a figure was

framed in the blackness—and Brown spoke.

"Hands up and empty, Slawson, if you want to live. I—" A sudden intake of Vee's breath, and then, "It's the woman of all the virtues."

And it was the woman—the girl, Una. White, but for that part of her face that was streaked with already drying blood from an ugly cut well up on her forehead, almost hidden by her jet black hair.

Two steps forward she took, and stood swaying on her feet. Her black eyes were dull and lifeless as she stared at me, rubbed a hand across them and stared again. I don't think she saw Vee Brown. I don't think she even saw the dead bodies upon the floor. Then she swayed again, as if about to fall, took two lurching steps forward—and was in my arms.

"Dean, Dean!" she was crying. "They didn't— You're alive. You're not dead. Tell me you're not dead."

"Oblige the lady, Dean." There was a sneer in Brown's voice. "Tell her you're not dead." And when I glared at him over the girl's shoulder he added with a grin, "Except from the neck up."

"Brown," I said, "she's badly hurt. It was Slawson who did it. Now, she—"

"Now she's trapped, caught in the net of her own making, and she wants to play with the winners. At least, for a bit. Come!" He jerked the girl from me and twisted her around.

I TOOK a step forward and stopped dead, a hand half outstretched. I remembered the Gunner, who sat with the machine gun across his knee waiting for Vee Brown; Benny, the man who had placed a knee upon my chest and held a knife close to my throat.

"Where's Slawson?" Vee Brown asked the girl.

"He went through that room." The girl spoke mechanically. "When he threw me in there I—" she ran a hand across her head. "I think there were shots, and I crawled into the closet. The closet door was partly open. Slawson came into the room and went into the next apartment. There's a hole in the wall, behind a curtain."

Brown nodded at me, bit his lower lip and said: "Sister, you're in a jam—on a tough spot. You made a fool out of Dean Condon. He's my friend and you're going to pay for it. Where did Slawson go?"

"I don't know. I don't know." She swayed slightly and I gripped her arm.

"Well, where does he live, where's his hideout? You know that!" His lips curved. "You were going to tell me tonight. Now, do you tell me or the cops? I'm no flatfoot. I don't abuse women. But they'll have ways of making you talk all right." He stopped and listened. "They'll be through in a minute. I'm going to turn you in."

"No, no!" she shrieked, swung herself free and was in my arms again.

"She's dazed, Vee," I told him as I held her. "Slawson hit her and—" I gulped. "Must you turn her in?"

"You haven't read the police manual," Vee snapped. "And that'll be the boys!" He stepped to the bedroom door quickly and closed it as voices and the distant pounding of feet reached us. "Quick!" Vee grabbed the girl's hat and coat from the costumer by the hall door, thrust the hat on her head, pulled it down so the cut was hidden, and threw the coat over her shoulders.

"No time to wash her up. Do the best you can with her face on the stairs; have her hold her head down." He was pushing us toward the door, the girl trembling, leaning against me.

"You're—you're going to let her go, Vee?"

"Go? Hell, no! Keep her down stairs

until I come. There don't be a sap all the time, Dean. I'm going to take her home and talk with her. I work alone. She's going to deliver Slawson to me, going to deliver him this morning, or take the rap."

Mulligan cursed with elation from the bedroom. He had found the entrance then. His heavy feet were pounding on the floor and Una and I were out the door, Brown's final instructions in my ears.

"There'll be a swarm of police here in a few minutes. Mix with the tenants. They are down the hall now. Get below, and say you're waiting for me. I'll be along shortly. Nothing else for me here."

CHAPTER SIX

Getaway Car

THE door closed and I was helping the girl along the hall. No one seemed to notice us—at least, suspiciously. Twice we were spoken to. Once a man in pajamas offered me a drink, and a fat lady in a faded pink bathrobe of many dirty squares said—

"It's been a respectable house and a respectable neighborhood. Why, they couldn't—" and stopped dead.

The long drawn out wail of a police siren shrieked somewhere from the street below.

"Clean your face," I said abruptly to Una as we started down the stairs, bumping into several people who were standing there. Once a boy of about twelve wanted to know if it was true that a whole family of ten had been wiped out. His eyes shone brightly, eagerly, and he kept saying, "Oh, Gee! Oh, Gee!" while a woman on the ground floor was calling in a cracked voice. "Robert!"

The police came. In a few minutes the building was full of them. People were herded together, questioned quickly and pushed into their apartments. And I got a break. Sergeant Dryer came and saved me much embarrassment.

"Vee Brown's here," I said to him quickly. "The young lady is a friend of his."

"Brown, eh?" The sergeant glanced once at the girl, who now held a handkerchief over her face. "There's been real shooting then."

"Two dead," I told him listlessly. "Brown's all right."

"You look washed out, Condon. Better go home and sleep it off."

"I know," I said. "I was in it. Brown too."

"Oh, it's all right for Brown." He nodded. "Killings, and stiffs, and holes in men's heads. Cripes! I'd like to know how he does it, but most of all, how he gets away with it." And there was admiration as well as envy in his voice. I always liked Sergeant Dryer.

"Brophy—" Sergeant Dryer called to a big red-faced officer he had left with two others by the entrance, "this here's a right guy, playmate of Vee Brown." And as Brophy waved a hand in a half salute and grunted something, Dryer turned to me again.

"What's the racket? Who was behind it?"

"I don't know, exactly. Slawson—I think," I replied.

"Yeah?" Sergeant Dryer's face lighted up. "What a break! Brown swore he'd get Slawson, and—"

"He didn't get him," I said. "Not yet." And I leaned against the wall, close to the girl. The air from the open door was good. In a dreamy way I watched Sergeant Dryer bound up those stairs, watched others follow him. I felt sick, down deep in the stomach. Maybe I'd never get used to death—death by violence—dead so sudden and so sure. May-

be it was the gag, the fumes. A policeman was talking. Brophy, the officer by
the door.

"You can't go outside, miss. I know—
I know. If you need the air go hang out
a window. Hang out of it, not climb out
of it, mind you. There's cops in the
alley, and more—"

I straightened and shook my head,
cleared it and looked at Brophy and the
girl he was talking to. It was Una. I
saw her and recognized her too, before I
was fully aware that I no longer had her
by the arm.

SHE came to me as I walked toward
the door. Her face was very white
but the blood was gone. Just a streak
here and there, where her handkerchief
had smeared it out rather than cleaned it
away. But it was not noticeable—that is,
not recognizable as blood.

"Dean, Dean!" She dragged me to the
darkness by the side of the stairs. "Let
me go. The policeman will let me go if
you say so. The sergeant, he knew you
and told the one at the door you were all
right."

"I can't, Una, I can't. You ask me
that, after—"

"But it means my life, Dean. You
said you loved me, tonight. I wanted to
turn back. I didn't want to go through
with it when I knew— Don't you see?
I love you too."

Was she lying? I didn't know. I
didn't care. I didn't— But I was thinking that she had fought for my life, that
she had—

"Dean, Dean!" She was clutching at
my coat. "Let me go. If you knew
what it meant! I'd rather die than—
I'll even— But not this, not arrest—
not—"

"You know where Slawson is?"

"I—how could I?" And suddenly, "I
won't lie to you. I do not know where

he is—at least, where he will go, must
go, and report failure. I—"

"Then tell Vee, and he'll—"

"I can't do that. I can't do that. I told
you once that I made a mistake. All this
is the result. They'll find out who I am
if I'm arrested, and if I— Please, Dean!"
She threw up her head, looked straight
into my eyes. There in the semi-darkness
I could catch again that haunted—that
terrible look of fear. "Take me out in
the air anyway. I—"

People were coming down the stairs,
arguing with the police. A door of an
apartment opened and someone looked
out. The girl was clinging to my jacket
again, shaking me, rocking back and forth
on her heels. At least, I told myself that
was the reason I agreed to take her out in
the air. Maybe it was the reason. Maybe
it wasn't. Maybe, just as Brown said, I
was a sap. Somehow, when I looked into
her eyes—

But enough of that. I took her to the
door, grinned at Brophy and muttered
something about waiting outside for Vee
Brown.

"O. K.!" He looked hard at the girl.
"Lady sick?" he asked.

"Slightly. It's been rather trying." I
thought that was a safe one.

Brophy called to a uniformed officer on
the sidewalk that we were "all right," then
whispered to me.

"They say it's Vee Brown again, and
he knocked off two loo-loos. That one of
them was Gunner Platz. Is that right?"

"That's right." I took the girl by the
arm and passed out into the night.

"Great guy, Brown," said Officer
Brophy. And Una and I were on the sidewalk.

Little groups of people were forming.
Another police car had drawn up. A man
with a camera passed us on the way in, a
gray-haired man with a bag was whistling

softly as he nodded to different officers who saluted him.

There were half a dozen taxis, the drivers leaning eagerly from the cabs but ready to move on if a cop should order them away.

WE edged down from the building, twice policemen spoke to me. I held the girl's arm tightly now.

She was at it again.

"You can say I jumped out on you," she pleaded, as she looked longingly at one taxi that stayed despite police warnings to move on. "It means my life—my life. You wouldn't kill me! You—"

But I held her arm as she tried to move across the sidewalk.

"I can't do it, Una," I told her huskily. "Not after tonight, not after what happened. I was just a fool before. Vee Brown will understand that. Now you want me to deliberately double-cross Vee, my friend, send you out to maybe plan his death again."

"No, no, no!" she said almost frantically, looking back at the apartment entrance. "I swear I'll protect him after this. I'll warn you if they—if Slawson plans anything." And suddenly, "You say you love me."

"I said it," I told her. "But I don't know now. I'll use all my influence with Brown for you, even after what you've done. I'll—"

"Will you let me go in that taxi? Yes or no?" There was a peculiar note in her voice, so different now. Almost a warning, almost a threat too, I thought.

But I looked her straight in the eyes and said, "No!"

"All right. Now take me to that cab. I'm sorry, Dean, but I'm not fooling. I have people who don't know what I've done—what I've become. I've got to do it for them. I—"

And my mouth was hanging open. I didn't see the gun at first, but I felt it. Felt it tightly against my ribs. I didn't speak. I didn't move. I couldn't. I was dumbfounded.

"Come!" Her lips were set in one straight line. "I'll press the trigger if you make one move—one cry."

The haunted look had gone from her eyes for a moment. A dangerous, determined light was there.

Did I think she'd shoot? I didn't know. Was I glad of the excuse to let her go? Among my disordered, jerky thoughts was one single dominating thought. I was not breaking faith with Vee Brown. He had sent me below with the girl—a girl who associated with criminals—even murderers, and she was armed. It was his fault as much as mine.

I was moving toward the cab. The girl was nodding at the driver. He was leaning back, opening the door.

"Drive up Broadway," the girl was saying to the driver as she backed into the cab. And to me, low and soft as she leaned close to me, the gun hard against my stomach now: "I could take you with me, Dean, but that wouldn't help you any. Say you were dizzy and I skipped out, and I'll pay you back. I'll help Vee Brown and you. Don't call the police when I'm gone. It'll mean my death. I won't be taken alive tonight. Good-by!" She leaned forward quickly and kissed me on the lips, then backed into the car.

What should I do? There I stood, like a dummy, on the sidewalk. Should I—

And no more thoughts.

THE girl screamed once and was silent. A man laughed from inside the cab. A voice said, "Climb in, Dean, and join the party. The little lady has changed her mind about traveling alone. And if you're alarmed about firearms—why I have the gun."

"Vee—Vee Brown!" I stammered. "How did you get here?"

"If I can climb up a fire-escape, surely I can climb down one too."

I got into the cab, Vee Brown jerked the door closed and the car shot away.

"You see, Dean, I didn't especially fancy explaining too much to the police just yet. The real story is not such a good one. So I left word with Mulligan that I was going after Ernie Slawson, then ducked down the fire-escape to avoid too much notoriety. Of course the police were curious, but then I play rather a lone hand."

I fell back in the seat beside him and looked over at the girl in the far corner. Just the whiteness of her face, the set lips, but she was breathing heavily.

"Brown," I said suddenly, "that's not true. You went down that fire-escape to head me off. You thought—" And in great indignation, "you didn't trust me."

Brown looked at me sharply.

"And if I didn't, would that be surprising?" Then gripping me by the arm, "But you made good, Dean. It took some time for her to get you out. I was almost going to send in for you. Then the eyes, and the pleading. It was quite a study, watching you. Women have done for the biggest men, Dean. But you're all right, fundamentally sound, and with that loyalty. But it's over now." And he started humming.

Silence from me, silence from the girl. Then suddenly from Vee Brown right in the middle of a note: "Death is funny, Dean. Benny, of course, was a coward at heart. But he died with a surprised, sort of hurt look in his eyes. It was Gunner Platz who knew fear. Slawson, I imagine, will take it with hatred and—"

"Vee—Vee," I cut in. "The thing is terrible, nauseating. I— How can you talk like that of those you— Don't you ever have regrets?"

"Good old Dean." He patted me on the back. "Those sort of humans have to die so others can live. Regrets!" He snapped the word out with real sincerity. "Yes, I have a regret tonight, a real regret. I'm thinking of McCarthy. I regret that I didn't drop Ernie Slawson across the body of Gunner Platz."

"What are you going to do with the girl?" I whispered that. But his answer was loud and clear.

"I'm going to listen to her talk. I'm going to give her a photograph of McCarthy's widow and the kids. And I'm going to give her a chance to clean the blood off her soul like she cleaned it off her face. I'm—"

"I'll tell where Slawson is," the girl said suddenly.

And the taxi drew up to the curb before the apartment.

"You'll let her go then, Dean?" I started.

"We'll see." His face was cold and hard when he climbed from the cab, took the girl by the arm and told me to pay the driver. I heard them walk toward the entrance.

I turned from the cab and stood frozen to the sidewalk. Vee Brown and the girl were almost at the entrance. They were waiting, their backs to me. But I wasn't looking at them. I was looking at the figure that stood against the fancy iron railing before the apartment. His slouch hat was pulled well down, his coat collar turned well up. I had seen him like that once before. The night I first met the girl. But this time in his hand he held a snub-nosed bit of blue steel, and he was extending his arm toward Vee Brown and the girl.

IT WAS Ernie Slawson. His shot would be drowned by the motor of the taxi, which was already pulling from the curb. And I stood there, my mouth hanging open. I was unarmed. All this, of course, happened in a flash.

And Una turned, cried out almost the same instant that I jumped forward. Then she threw her arms about Vee Brown.

There was the roar of a gun, the sudden spurt of orange blue flame as I clutched for that gun of Slawson's and missed. I heard Vee Brown's shout, clear and steady.

"Back, Dean!"

Then the sudden burn, as if a hot poker had been pulled across my arm—and numbness as my arm dropped to my side.

I think that Vee Brown's hand jerked up from around the girl. I didn't see any flame, but I did hear the roar of a gun. His gun? Or was it the second shot from Ernie Slawson's gun? Ernie Slawson! And I was looking right at him. Looking right at those eyes that were barely visible, and the whiteness across the bridge of his nose, between them—a whiteness that was no longer a whiteness, but a peculiar purple. A purple that, with a little gasp, I realized was not purple but a hole; a hole that was widening and becoming red—a vivid red. And Ernie Slawson suddenly straightened and crashed to the pavement.

Something flashed by me, I think. Vee Brown was at my side. A motor roared on the avenue. I turned as Vee Brown turned.

A car was passing, slowing down. A figure was running toward it. The figure reached the car, was gripping the handle of the rear door, had climbed onto the running board, was crouched there on the side as the car gathered speed. It was Una.

"Slawson's getaway car!" Vee Brown jerked up his gun, and I flung myself upon him, knocking up his arm.

A gun roared, glass crashed in a window of the car. The car swerved dangerously, then turned the corner.

"Vee—Vee!" I yelled out to him. "She tried to save your life, threw herself before you to protect you."

"That's your story. She did it to prevent my shot."

"But, why? Slawson wanted to kill her too. I heard him say—"

"Slawson would never shoot at the girl while I was there. I have too much pride to believe that. Men don't press gun triggers more than once even when my back is turned. But you, Dean, did he get you?"

"I was right," Vee said later in our apartment, after he had dressed my arm. "There was hate in Slawson's eyes—it stayed there when he died. He guessed I'd bring the girl here and question her. He knew I worked independent of the police. He hoped to get both of us. In a way, he had guts to come. But I think it was mostly fear. Fear of facing Mandozza with a failure, fear of what the girl might tell me. There, Dean." He laid a hand upon my shoulder. "I don't blame you for knocking up my gun. In a way I thank you. It wouldn't be pleasant to kill a woman."

"But you wouldn't have—really. You were shooting at the driver, just trying to stop the car. You wouldn't shoot a woman!"

"Dean," Vee Brown said very solemnly, "there is no sex in crime." A moment's pause while he paced the room, snuffed out a half-smoked cigarette in an onyx ash tray and lit another. Then, "Would I kill a woman? I hope not. But you saved me from definitely answering that question tonight."

SEE PAGE 124 FOR A REAL THRILL-SPECIAL SURPRISE!

Murder stalked the shores of Lasker Lake and terror rode the icy storm. For somewhere there a killer lurked, ready to loose red messengers of death— loose them against the dick who sought to cleave the flake-white curtain which wrapped those lumberlands in crime.

"Give me another shot, Doc—" A bullet found him and he crumpled up.

RED BULLETS

by
Edward Parrish Ware

Author of "The Skull of Judgment," etc.

CHAPTER ONE

White Bullets—And Black

WHEN a sleuth is all fed up with poking into the crimes of the ordinary crook, it's actually refreshing to stack up against one that's different. I did just that, a short time back. The bird I have in mind stood out from the herd like a black stump in a snow storm.

I'll tell you about him.

As a matter of fact, the case really began to break in a snow storm. One of those blanket-thick deluges, with flakes big and sleety, fired down from invisible clouds like billions of white bullets from hidden guns. Visibility was limited by a twenty-foot circle, and beyond that the inscrutable blanket.

I was out in it. Moreover, I was riding a skittish horse up a rugged trail into a country I had never traveled before. The Lasker Lake region of the Missouri Ozarks, to be exact. Hills, hollows, trees, and then more hills, hollows and trees, with human habitations few and far between. Rough going at best, but absolutely hellish in a storm like that.

Cougar Creek, then only a ten-foot span of water which followed the devious windings of Cougar Hollow, was reached and crossed, and I faced a long slope ahead which would put me on top of a hill again, where the wind-driven flakes would show no mercy. Five miles more would bring me to Lasker Lake, and the big hardwood mill Casper Hammett had sent me to investigate.

We had topped the rise, and I was bending as low as possible against the wind when my mount suddenly snorted and leaped forward. Something snarled past the back of my head, and from the brush on the left came the crack of a rifle. Instantly, I threw myself low over the right side of my horse, clutching the horn with my left hand, while with my right I quirted hard.

Wham! Zinngg!

Once more the rifle cracked, and once more potential death sang its sinister song above me. The horse, terrified, stung by the thongs of the quirt, leaped madly forward into the concealing blanket. I swung back into the saddle, let him have his head for a quarter of a mile, then gentled him down to a walk a quarter farther on.

But I went no farther then. Swinging down into the ankle-deep snow, I tied the reins to a tree limb at the side of the trail, then slipped into the brush on the right and swiftly back-tracked on my course.

If only that bushwhacker would believe he had hit me the first time—my plunge over the right side of the horse might easily convince him—he would almost certainly trail the horse. That would prove a costly mistake for him, whoever he was.

I had covered perhaps half a quarter on the back-track when I caught a vague glimpse of something moving swiftly along the trail. A sixgun in hand, I crouched in the brush and waited. The moving object took form, became a human being—and when the human being came opposite me I stepped out.

"Steady where you are!" I called. "Drop that rifle, and elevate your paws! Quick, damn you!"

The first order was instantly obeyed. The trailer seemed to freeze solid, becoming as motionless as a shaft of black ice. A slender shaft, and not very tall. I stepped nearer, amazement gripping me. A mere lad, this bushwhacker, and young for such a job as he had tackled. Still, mountain boys are generally men, or so regarded, by the time they reach fifteen. Shoot straight, too.

"Hey, buddy!" I shouted against the

wind. "What the hell is the big idea? Didn't you know better than to trail me in the open?"

"I—I was afeard you was hurted!" came the explanation. "Never thought you'd be back-trackin' like you was!"

I thrust my sixgun back into its holster. The trailer was a girl!

"Darned if I get this," I said, approaching her, "and it's up to you, sister, to come plumb clean. You surely didn't shoot at me from the brush a while ago, did you?"

"O cou'se I never!" Came instant denial.

"But you know who did?"

She was silent, merely staring at me out of big, fear-hunted brown eyes, eyes that somehow or other got under my skin.

"Don't want to answer?" I queried. "Afraid to, maybe?"

She nodded her head quickly, and I noticed that her body was trembling, regardless of the fact that it was well protected against the cold.

"You realize, don't you, that I could take you down to the county-seat and put you in jail?" I asked. "Make you tell what you know—and maybe not let you out again for a long, long time?"

"No, suh," she assured me calmly. "You couldn't never git away with nothin' like that. You'd be waylaid ag'in—an' mebbe that time you would stop some lead. I ain't none afeared of you, an' whut you threat me with. I'm powerful afeared, though, of somebody else. You better be afeared of him, too, 'cause he's after you like a hongry pan'ter after a lamb!"

THAT panther simile might be correct enough, I thought, but I felt like laughing when she likened me to a lamb. A lamb! Think of that! Nobody had ever called "Spot" Murphy a lamb before!

"You've called my bluff, sister," I acknowledged. "Never had any intention of taking you anywhere against your will. Certainly I don't want you to get into trouble on my account. So I'm going to let you go—on one condition. You're to tell me your name, where you live, and then take that muffler down from your lower features so I'll be able to recognize you again. Willing to do that?"

For answer, she pulled down the concealing muffler, and exposed her face entirely. I got a start when I saw it. The girl was more than pretty she was beautiful. I must have shown my thoughts in my manner, for her face, now flushed a trifle, was quickly covered again.

"My name," she said, accepting the condition in its entirety, "is Nan Pollard, an' I live on th' south shore of Lasker Lake. Anybody kin tell you where at Leach Pollard's cabin is. He's my pappy."

"I'm taking your word for that," I told her. "Now get along, before something busts loose around here and gets you into deep trouble. You got a horse somewhere close?"

"I'm walkin'," she informed me. "But I ain't goin' nary step, until you tells me whut you aims to do when I'm out th' way. You goin' huntin' trouble?"

"Exactly," I told her. "But the trouble may be all the other fellow's. If you just have to know, I'm going to pick up that bushwhacking hombre's trail while the trailing is still good."

"No!" she said, and in her voice was a plea. "Please don't! You won't have no luck trailin' him, an' you prob'ly would git kilt. Let him go—"

"Is he your sweetheart, brother, cousin maybe?" I interrupted.

"No!" She almost screamed, and I saw her face working in anger. "He's not no kinfolks of mine! Please go back to your hoss, an' git on your way!"

"And maybe get shot at again," I said. "How do I know, sister, that you and the bushwhacking gent are not framing me? He may have circled ahead and found another convenient cover. I'm beginning to believe you really meant it, when you called me a lamb a while ago. Forget it, sis. I may be a lot of other things, but I'm no baby ba-ba."

No, old Casper Hammet, general manager of Ozark Mills, Incorporated, had not wished that tough job onto me because he thought I had fleece on my back. Old Man Cas knew me well enough, and because he did he elected to stack me up against whatever it was in the Lasker Lake country that was keeping him awake at night. He didn't know what was ailing things himself, so it followed that I didn't know either. What I didn't know, however, it was my job to find out.

But why tell the little mountain girl that? She had never heard of Spot Murphy, of the Murphy Detective Agency, and didn't know me from a side of salt-horse. All I wanted from her then was a set of boot-tracks in the snow—and leading away from me, too.

"You'd better hustle on, sis," I advised. "You're walking, and these white bullets are getting bigger and harder right along. Beat it, like a good girl."

She looked at me questioningly for an instant, then suddenly got what I meant by white bullets. She held out a small brown hand and caught a few, crunched them into powder and let the powder sift through her fingers.

"Nobody need be afeared of them white bullets," she said contemptuously. Then her voice became earnest. "But there's another kind of bullets that's threatenin' you, Mr. Murphy. Lot's of 'em, if more'n one air needed. Black bullets. Bullets that'll put you in yore grave!"

It was almost as bad as stopping one of those black bullets, her calling my name that way! It staggered me. Nobody was supposed to know about my trip except Casper Hammet, yet this mountain girl knew my name—and very likely knew what had brought me there.

"Say," I asked, not hoping very high for an answer, "how does it happen that you know me? Who told you my name—"

"Listen!" she interrupted, and pointed back of me toward the opaque curtain that wrapped us in.

I listened. The snow-muffled padding of hoofs came to me faintly, and almost before I had identified them a horse plunged out of the blanket. My own mount, but answering to reins in the hands of a strange rider. And the rider was coming on top of us, hell-bent-for-leather!

"Jump!" I shouted warningly to the girl, and leaped backward myself.

Spurting flame slashed the snow-curtain, and lead whined in the wind. The strange rider, just a black smear in my eyes, was leaning low in the saddle, firing a sixgun as rapidly as he could thumb the hammer.

My gun came out when I leaped, and I fired as he dashed past me. He snapped erect when the gun cracked, so erect he almost went over backward. Then the horse and rider were lost in the storm.

I looked around quickly for the girl. She was gone!

CHAPTER TWO

Blood On the Snow

FRAMED! I'd had the right hunch to go with. That bushwhacker had circled through the timber and gotten ahead of me. Finding my horse, he had tumbled to my back-tracking stunt. And the girl—

Had she held me in conversation in order to give the bushwhacker a chance?

If so, then what about that fleecy lamb business? If I had fallen for a thing like that—well, maybe I was that way.

All this ran through my mind as I plowed down the trail in pursuit of horse and rider. I was confident that my lead had reached him, and that it hadn't done him any good. There's something about the actions of a man when vitally hit that an experienced eye cannot mistake. I expected to find something interesting beside the trail—and I did.

I found him a quarter of a mile away, where he had fallen from the saddle into a snow-bank. He was dead. Of my horse the only signs were far-spaced tracks in the snow. That animal would never stop short of his home stable, ten miles down the trail.

I stood there looking down at the dead bushwhacker, wondering what was back of it all. A young man, he had been. Not over twenty-five at most, he nevertheless had a hard, lined face. His pockets held nothing of interest to me, and, under the circumstances, I had no hesitancy in leaving the body where it had fallen. Let the coroner figure things out when he should get to it.

Heartless? Hardly that. I was a-foot in a wilderness, a storm raging about me, beset by dangers of which I knew nothing whatever. Even a sleuth is entitled to avail himself of that first law of Nature which concerns itself with the important matter of self-preservation. I observed it then, and had no qualms about it.

Certain that the man in the snow-bank was beyond help, I set out swiftly up the trail, came to where the girl had been standing when I glimpsed her last, and took observations. She had eluded me, in so far as her person was concerned, but she couldn't hide or cover her trail. It stretched away into the timber in the otherwise untrodden snow, and I pounced on it, determined to follow wherever it led.

Miss Nan Pollard, if that were really her name, had a key that would turn the bolts in a lock which absorbed me completely, and I meant to get that key. In other words, granting I found her, I'd have the facts of that trail-side shooting out of her. That she was wise to it I knew, and fleecy lamb or not, what she knew, I damned well meant to learn.

The trail led through brush and trees, down a slope into a hollow, up along a path which followed a bench—and on the bench I first saw the red spots on the snow.

Blood on the snow!

The girl, then, was wounded. Only her small boot-tracks were there, so no other conclusion was tennable. I hurried faster, and despite the state of my feelings over the way I had been tricked, anxiety was gnawing at me. The blood spots became larger and more numerous as the trail unfolded.

Down into a gulch it led me, and along the bottom which grew thick with brush and briers. But I followed on. Followed until I broke from cover where the gulch began widening out and found her crouching in the snow, her face pale as death, brown eyes filled with agony.

I dropped down beside her, pulled her hands aside, and located the wound. She had been shot through the calf of the left leg, but had gone on until loss of blood brought her down exhausted.

"Is there a house near?" I asked.

She pointed up the gulch. "Half a mile," came in a gasp from her blue lips.

I PARKED her rifle in the thick foliage of a nearby juniper, picked her up from the snow and struck out. From the amount of blood she had lost, I judged her condition to be serious. She had to have help, and that quickly.

I'm husky, standing above six feet in my socks, and weighing around a hundred and eighty-five. Moreover, I've got the strength to go with it. But just try carrying a dead weight of a hundred and ten or fifteen pounds through unbroken snow, with sleety flakes beating in your face, and you'll know what I was up against. Yes, I was carrying a dead weight, because the girl had promptly fainted.

When I had gone up the gulch some distance, I placed her on the snow and managed to revive her. Had to, for I had found no house and only she could tell me where to look. After a glance around, she directed me.

"When you come to that fire-blackened stump yonder, turn off to the left," she said. "Go straight ahead, two hundred yards. The cabin is there against the wall of the gulch. Hard to find, but you can't miss it."

I picked her up again, followed directions, and finally stood before a small cabin of logs which backed close against the south wall of the gulch. It looked deserted, and nobody came in answer to my call. But calling got me something, for it aroused the girl.

"Push the door open and go in," she bade me.

I did so, and found myself in a crudely furnished room with a fireplace at one end. There was a bunk in a corner, furnished with blankets, a cupboard set against the back wall, and by the hearth was stacked a quantity of dry wood.

As far as I could see we were not much better off then we had been. I say we, because I had definitely put in with the girl, even though I suspected her of treacherously attempting to do away with me. So I set about doing what I could for her.

After laying her in the bunk, I built a good fire, set a tea-kettle where it would heat, then returned to tackle the job of uncovering the wound and determining just how much damage had been done.

The girl had somewhat recovered from her semicoma and watched anxiously while I loosened the laces of her boot; slowly and as easily as possible I drew it off. When I had removed her stocking and bared the wound, I saw at a glance that the lead had passed through the calf in a straight course, leaving a clean hole which, barring complications, would prove more painful than actually serious.

"Does this place boast any sheets, rags, or anything clean enough to use for a bandage?" I asked, getting up from my knees.

"Look on the cupboard shelves," she suggested.

A pile of clean muslin, tea-towels perhaps, provided plenty of bandage. I did the best possible job of cleansing the wound that could have been done under such conditions, applied the bandage, and was heartened to see the girl resting easier. I left her in the bunk, and began scouting about for something to eat. The larder was fairly well stocked, and I proceeded to help myself.

I gave the girl some coffee, and later got her to take some soup which came out of a can. Then I fed myself. While I was eating, the showdown came between us.

"Whut you-all aim to do next?" The girl broke a long silence with the query.

"Listen, sister," I chided, laying down the fragment of hoecake I had in my hand, "can the innocent mountain-gal lingo, and get down to business. When you were lying there in the snow you used as good American as I do—and maybe better. Now you're stronger, feeling safe, you go trying to cover up again.

Come clean, because you won't be able to fool me now."

SHE looked at me steadily for a moment, then countered.

"Why should you care whether I use dialect or not?" she asked.

"I don't care, not even a small damn," I assured her. "Just so you quit stalling and tell me what I want to know. You can spill it in any style that pleases you. Set it to music if you are talented that way. The only condition I make is that you use words that I can understand."

"And you feel you are in a position to impose conditions?" The sarcasm didn't miss me, but I never let it register.

"You spar like a country-raised diplomat," I accused her. "Well, maybe I can bring you out of it. I'll trade you information for information. I have no doubt you'd be interested in knowing what became of that bushwhacker partner of yours—eh?"

She sat up suddenly, her big eyes round with concern, and I knew I had hit.

"Tell me—" she began.

"Trade you," I insisted. "And since you have already proved to be such a smooth little liar, you'll show your goods first. Shoot when ready, sister. I'm all ears."

The girl's face flushed hotly, and she trembled on the verge of flaying me with words. She reconsidered that, however.

"What do you want to know?" she asked in a resigned voice.

"Who shot at me on the trail?"

"Gid Hailey."

"Yeah. And who is Gid Hailey?"

"A woodspilot from the Ozark Mills."

"Why did Gid want to muss me up?"

"Because you are Spot Murphy, a detective sent in here by Mr. Casper Hammet."

"How did Gid find that out?"

"I do not know."

"How did you find it out?"

"John Hammet, Casper Hammet's nephew, told me you were coming."

"John's sure got a loose tongue," I commented. "Know of anybody else beside John, and Gid and yourself that knew I was coming?"

"I suppose Mr. Lampkin, the superintendent of the mills, knew of it."

"Yeah. And I'm beginning to think nearly everybody in this neck of the woods had the information," I said disgustedly. "You put in with this Gid," I went on accusingly. "Why?"

Her eyes expressed astonishment, but whether she was acting or not I could not determine.

"I was out there to try and save you from being murdered!" she protested. "Gid Hailey did not even know I was there! How dare you make such a charge!"

My come-back to that would have been more or less caustic, had I come-back at all. I didn't. For at that instant the door crashed open, and on the sill stood a man who almost filled the frame. A regular giant, he was, and his thick red beard, beaded with ice, seemed to bristle like so many rusted spikes. He glared at me out of eyes like icy pools, and when he spoke his voice reminded me of the bellow of an ox.

"Yeah," the big man boomed, "suppose yuh tell us th' answer to that question? Howcome yuh to make sich a charge?"

He moved inside, and another man took his place on the sill. A smaller chap, compared to the other, but big and husky for all that. He was clean-shaved, dark-skinned, and had blue eyes that were difficult to fathom. A woodsman, by his looks.

"Well," I snapped, not moving from my chair, "why in hell don't you hombres come in and close the door? Want to blow all my fire up the chimney?"

I heard something that sounded suspiciously like a giggle, and turned to look behind me. The girl had her face turned away, and when I looked back toward my callers I began to get it good and proper that this was serious business.

The big man had me covered with a gun!

CHAPTER THREE

"He Was Murdered!"

"**B**EN LASKER, put that gun up!" It was the girl speaking, and there was confident command in her voice. I shot her a glance and observed that anger had reddened her cheeks, made her eyes bright. The big man, Lasker, hesitated for an instant, gave me a hard look, then pocketed his weapon.

"Mebbe yuh know whut yuh air about, Nan Pollard," he said grudgingly. "But, frum th' looks of things, I taken it yuh war up against somethin' that called fur action."

"I am not, however," Nan Pollard denied emphatically. "How came you here?" she demanded.

The young man spoke up then.

"You didn't report for work this morning, Miss Pollard," he explained, "and I got uneasy. The storm, and all that. So I crossed the lake to your house, learned from your father that you had gone out with your rifle, and I guessed that you would come here. I ran across Lasker a short while later, and he came along. That's how we came to be here."

"Now that you are here, Mr. Hammet," the girl said, "you might as well become acquainted with Mr. Spot Murphy, the detective your uncle sent in. Then I'll have something to say that should clear things up a little."

The young man stared at me for a moment, then came across and offered his hand. We shook, and then the giant took a grip on me. After that we sat down, and Miss Pollard told what had happened on the trail.

But that was all she told. Never a word about how she came to know that Gid Hailey was going to slug me, or any other particular of importance. She dodged every issue I was interested in, and did a neat job of it, too. When she had finished, John Hammet spoke.

"I have no idea what induced Hailey to try and kill you, Murphy," he assured me earnestly. "When I saw him last, early this morning, he was walking away from the mill, going toward the west. He and Mr. Lampkin were to trekk to one of the logging fronts today."

He paused there, drew a deep breath, and went on.

"At nine o'clock this morning," he said and his voice sounded strained, "the body of Mr. Lampkin was found in the snow, where he had evidently slipped and fallen. Unfortunately, he struck his head on a log nearby and his neck was broken. Hailey was nowhere to be seen, and the snow had concealed all tracks in the vicinity."

Nan Pollard cried out sharply when she heard of Lampkin's death. Just one cry expressing horror, and then she merely sat and stared. Stared past John Hammet to where Lasker stood with his back against the front wall. It was as if she queried him silently, although that may have been just a notion in my own mind.

Lasker spoke, his words grunted out like they were too precious to spill liberally.

"Somethin' dead up th' creek," he declared jerkily. "Hailey must of give Lampkin his'n, then lit a shuck to do th' same for Murphy. Sound reasonable to you, Murphy?"

"Say on," I suggested. "I'm listening."

"Well," Lasker said heavily, "somebody give them orders to Hailey. Somebody he didn't dare not to obey. Somebody that war intrusted in gittin' Lampkin outten th' way, an' stoppin' yuh, Murphy, frum comin' in. That's th' way it looks to me."

"Good reasoning, Lasker," I applauded. "What's your job up here?"

"Mine?" The giant spoke as though I should certainly have known about him. There was surprise in his voice. "Well, neighbor, I'm th' Law, up here in th' Lasker Lake section. Th' onliest Law thar is, in fact. I'm th' deppity sheriff of this here deestrick."

"Didn't Uncle Casper tell you about conditions up here, Murphy?" The young man asked. "Surely he must have given you a general idea about the personnel of the mill, and wised you how to contact with the deputy, Mr. Lasker, in case you needed aid?"

I LOOKED at him sharply, trying to make him out. But that bird was not so easy to make. It struck me that he was rather resentful toward me, or perhaps toward his uncle for sending for me. I marked that down for future thought.

I knew a little about young Hammet. He was Casper's heir, and had been trained for the job of assistant superintendent of the big operation on Lasker Lake. Groomed for the superintendency, in fact, which would be his when he had had seasoning enough. Well, he was in a good place to acquire all the seasoning he needed, and no mistake about that.

"Casper didn't tell me much," I replied to Hammet's query. "He didn't want to send me in here with a prejudiced mind, perhaps. What interests me above anything else, however, is this— How did it happen that everybody and his brother knew about Mr. Hammet sending me up here? We were to keep that secret, and nobody here was to know until such time as I saw fit to hand Lampkin a letter from him which would introduce me, define my purpose in being on the ground, and make me solid. How did it leak out?"

"Yuh mentioned it to me, John," Lasker reminded the young man.

"So I did," John acknowledged. "No one told me it was to be kept secret from you."

I turned to the girl. "How did you find it out, Miss Pollard?" I queried.

"I'm telegraph operator at the mill," she told me. "A message came in yesterday morning, instructing me to inform Mr. Lampkin that you were on your way, and should arrive at the lake today. I was out of the office at the time, and Mr. Hammet took the message off the wire. He told me of it later."

"Do you know who sent the message?" I asked Hammet.

"It was supposed to come from Casper Hammet. His name was signed," John answered.

"Anybody can sign a name by telegraph," I commented. "From what point was the message relayed to you?"

"White Oak, the county-seat. Our wire goes no farther than there."

"Something crooked in the main office," I offered. "A leak of some kind. You acquainted with anybody there who might not be playing the game square with the Old Man?" I asked John.

"Uncle Casper is a harsh man in all his contacts," the young man stated. "If there is treachery in his office, he can blame himself for it. Let me point out to you, Murphy," he went on, scowling slightly, "that if the news was sent to Lampkin by somebody besides my uncle, that suggests guilt of some sort on Lampkin's part. You surely have no such suspicion in your mind?"

"All I was told about Lampkin," I answered, "was that he had been superintendent of operations up here for the past three years. I don't believe Casper Hammet has any definite suspicion about anybody."

"Then what the devil did he send you up here for?" John Hammet demanded heatedly.

"That's what I'm cravin' to know," Lasker seconded.

"Well," I said, "there's no secret about it, men. Casper wanted to know how it happened that thirty thousand dollars worth of drying lumber caught fire on the kiln, and burned to ashes. That was a couple of months ago. He is also concerned over the fact that the Ozark Mills plant at Lasker earned forty thousand dollars less last year than it had done for several years back. Finally, he'd give a bit extra to find out the origin of the fire that destroyed the new mill before it ever started operating, and made junk out of about one hundred thousand dollars worth of machinery. Naturally, Casper is interested in all that, so he sent me up to check things over. That's all."

"And his sending you to do that was an insult to Mr. Lampkin and myself!" John Hammet exclaimed wrathfully.

"Yeah? Well, judging by what happened on the trail this morning, I'm thinking my presence is more of a menace than an insult—to somebody, at any rate. The effort to rub me out, Hammet, smells a lot like there really is something rotten around here. That's the slant I take at it, if you're interested in knowing."

"I am interested in knowing!" he exclaimed. "Unless the reason is uncovered, you and Uncle Casper are certain to draw a wrong conclusion. I am going to make it my business to learn all about it!"

"Same here," grunted the deputy sheriff.

"Make it three," I added. "I'm somewhat inclined to dig that thing out myself. By the way," I queried, "how do things stand at the mill now? Who steps up into Lampkin's place?"

"I do," John replied. "I'm superintendent for the time at least. Uncle will probably remove me, but until he does I'm in charge."

"So I figured. And who takes your vacancy?"

"Frank Lasker, who has been woods superintendent for the past two years," John answered. "Frank is Ben's son, and a thoroughly competent man for any position in either woods or mill."

"You're fortunate in having him," I commented. "And now, if you gents agree, we'd better consider ways and means of getting Miss Pollard home. She'll need the attention of a doctor, I'm thinking. Did you hombres walk in or ride?"

BEFORE anybody could answer, we had another interruption. The door swung open and another caller appeared. A tall man, wearing a mackinaw which was covered with snow. As he advanced into the room, shaking the flakes from his cap, I clicked to him. Only a couple of sizes smaller than Ben, and a bit less rugged of visage, he was clearly the deputy's son. Frank Lasker, for a ten-spot.

"Hope I'm not horning in on any secret conference," the young man said, cold, slate-gray eyes sizing up each of us in turn. "If I am, I'll vamoose, just as soon as I can give you the news I came to give."

"How did you know where to find us, Frank?" Hammet asked crisply.

"I trailed your horses, after Pollard told me you had headed this way," Frank replied. "But I had a good reason for it. Dan," he went on, speaking to the deputy, "you're wanted across the lake. Doc McKibbe has cut loose with his verdict—

and it's not what we thought it would be."

"Hell!" Ben Lasker exclaimed, startled. "Yuh mean Doc has finally said his say about Lampkin?"

"Just that. Lampkin, he declares, did not die an accidental death. He was murdered!"

John Hammet, Ben Lasker and the girl all stared at the newsbringer in silent astonishment. Maybe they felt that way. I didn't. That case had begun to develop more angles than a country road and was just as jolty.

"Let's go," I said, getting up and reaching for my leather coat. "While we're sticking around here, things are happening across the lake. I've got a hunch to step on it."

"I agree!" young Lasker snapped. Then to me, "I take it you're Murphy, the cop Cas Hammet wished onto us?"

"No use denying it," I told him. "I've been discovered—in several different places. Did you ride here or walk?"

"Rode. Nan can have my mount, and you and I can trot along and keep her company."

"What about us?" Hammet demanded. "Are we excluded?"

"Not at all," Frank Lasker assured him. "I naturally supposed you and dad would hurry on ahead, and leave somebody else to bring in the wounded. And, by the way, how came the wound?"

"No time to discuss that," Nan told him. "Bring up your horse, Frank. I want to go."

"What about that bird Hailey?" I asked. "Hadn't you better take him in, Mr. Deputy?"

"Gawdamighty!" Ben Lasker almost shouted. "I'd do it in a hurry, if I knew where to find him!"

"That's easy," I said, for the first time disclosing the fate of the bushwhacker. "He's lying in a snow-bank beside the trail, about a quarter south of where Miss Pollard and I stood talking. You'll need a wagon or a pack-horse, because he's dead—"

"Dead!" Ben Lasker broke in, his eyes narrowing. "Who kilt him?"

"I did," I answered. "Got him as he rode past me, but too late to prevent him from slugging Miss Pollard. What would you expect me to do? Stand there like a snow-man, and let him get away?"

"Sure not," the deputy said. "I was just surprised, is all. Yuh hadn't spilt nothin' about killin' him."

"As a matter of fact, I'd forgotten about it," I told him, just for the pleasure of witnessing his reaction. "I never bother about the small potatoes, sheriff, and this Hailey was just that, I'm thinking. Now, with your permission, I'll step along and see if I can't uncover a hill with a big spud in it. You can find me easy enough, if you want to ask me any questions."

"I hardly think there will be any questions, Mr. Murphy," Miss Pollard said, as she drew on her mackinaw. "I saw what happened, and my word is good—even with Ben Lasker."

Ben's face flushed, and he turned away without a word.

WE followed the gulch for about a mile, turned left along a small hollow and trekked two miles, then came out on the south shore of Lasker. The lake is a mile wide and five miles long, as clear and beautiful a body of water as can be found in the Ozarks.

On the north shore of the lake, the mill buildings stood, but they were invisible from where I was because of the snow-fall. Here and there along the south shore were dwellings occupied by the old-timers in the section. Among them was the comfortable four-room log house in which lived Leach Pollard and his daughter.

Our trip had begun in silence, so far as conversation was concerned, and it ended in silence—until old man Pollard heard the story. Then there was plenty of talk. He was a small man, sixty years old and with hair as white as the snow outside, but he more than made the well known welkin ring!

We corraled him just as he was filling his pockets with ammunition, and declaring he aimed to kill every Hailey in the hills. In his younger days, old Leach Pollard must have been a true hellion. And he was far from tame at sixty.

After he had quieted down and promised to let things ride as they were for a while, Frank Lasker and I crossed the lake in one of the company's motorboats, and I found myself, after certain vicissitudes and deviations, at the place I had headed for at daybreak that morning.

"You will want to view Lampkin's body," Frank Lasker said when we were ashore, "and talk with Dr. McKibbe. So you'd better go to Doc's house at once, for he'll be on his way to dress that wound of Miss Pollard's very shortly."

We found Dr. McKibbe in the three-room shack which served him as bachelor quarters and office. He was the only sawbones in that neck of the woods, and had been imported by the milling company. I liked the lank, red-faced Scotch-American the minute I laid eyes on him.

"Come in, Murphy," he invited, "and let's talk."

And there was another one who knew I was coming!

I followed the doc into a sitting room back of the office, and young Lasker departed. I promised to look him up at the mill office when I had finished at the doctor's.

"There's a job for you across the lake, Doc," I told McKibbe, and gave him the details. "Just let me examine Lampkin's body, and we'll talk things over after you

return. That suits you all right doesn't it?"

"Right!" he exclaimed, getting into his storm coat and snatching up his satchel. "But I'm more interested in that girl across the lake, I'll confess, than I am in anything else right now. A good chance for a bad infection, you know. Come with me to the shack where Lampkin is laid out, and examine him all you want to. I'd be interested in having your opinion, formed during my absence. Maybe you and I won't see things eye to eye, but I have a notion we will."

He conducted me to a small shack which stood off to itself, informing me as he unlocked the door that the place served the mill village as an undertaking parlor. I went in, snapped on all the lights there were, and prepared to get busy.

Pulling back a sheet that covered the body which lay on a long table, I exposed the features of the dead man.

Herbert Lampkin had been a fine-looking man in life, and there was something distinguished-looking about him even then. Perhaps it was his gray hair and the Vandyke beard he affected, as well as his finely chiseled features, that set him apart. At any rate, Lampkin had been a most personable type of man.

I soon forgot the man, however, and set in on the wound which he had received at the back of his head. Then I carefully examined the snapped vertebra which was supposed to have caused his death. His clothing came next under my eyes, and when I got through searching each article I made a thorough job of it. The only definite result gained by my examination of the clothing was this—

The inside breast-pocket of the lumberjack Lampkin had worn, and which had been on him when he was found dead, was slightly smeared with what appeared to be fresh oil. Moreover, the pocket sagged somewhat, and one side had recently been ripped at the seam.

When the doc returned, just at lamp-light, I was ready for him.

CHAPTER FOUR

Some Bits of Bark

I WAS smoking a pipe in McKibbe's office when he came in. "Simple matter, that bullet hole," he said briskly. "She'll be walking again in a day or two. Now, granting you think I'm worthy of your confidence, suppose you spill what's on your mind?"

"A question or two first," I returned. "Did you view Lampkin's body before it was brought in?"

"I did."

"How far from the log was the body?"

"Right at it. Close enough to bear out the theory that he had struck his head on it when he fell."

"What was the condition of the snow around the spot?"

"It showed the tracks of the trapper That sound reasonable?"
who found the body, and reported it to the office. Old-timer named Brown, nick-named 'Reckless,' but I'd stake a lot on his word."

"You found nothing in the way of clues on the spot?"

"Not a thing," McKibbe answered, eyeing me keenly.

"Now," I went on, "we'll talk about that wound in the back of Lampkin's head. You surely didn't fall for any bunk about a blow against a log smashing his skull like that?"

"Not at all," McKibbe answered instantly.

"Done with a club, perhaps?"

"What makes you think it was a club?" McKibbe countered.

For answer, I took out an envelope, inverted it and spilled three small fragments on the table top.

"Bark," I said. "I picked the fragments out of the wound. Did you, by any chance, notice what kind of a log it was beside which Lampkin was lying?"

"I did. It was oak. Red oak."

"Absolutely certain, are you?" I insisted.

"Of course. I know trees, Murphy."

"Well, Doc," I said, "let me call your attention to the fact that those fragments on the table are bits of hickory bark."

Doc looked at me steadily for an instant, then bent over the bits on the table. "You're right," he agreed, straightening up. "They're hickory. What puzzles me, Murphy, is how you surmised the log might have been of a different character. Mind telling me how you arrived at that conclusion?"

"Not a bit. The hickory in this section is scarce, and does not grow big enough to be called timber, hardly. Oak and pine, with a scattering of gum, is about all you find up here. So I thought it likely the log would be either oak, pine or gum."

"I see you know trees, too," McKibbe grinned. "And I reckon those bits of hickory bark cinch the fact that Lampkin was murdered."

"Still, Doc," I argued, "it might be possible for a man to injure his skull and break his neck in the manner Lampkin appeared to have done, isn't it?"

"Possible, but damned unlikely. And there is the hickory bark, Murphy, you picked from the wound. Don't forget that."

"I'm not forgetting it. And here is something I want you to think over. On the lining of the inside breast-pocket of Lampkin's mackinaw, there are signs of fresh oil. The pocket sags pretty much. Lampkin evidently carried a gun in that pocket."

McKibbe sat up straighter, and his eyes had the glint of deep interest in them.

"Go on," he said. "Spring it."

"Sure. That fresh oil suggests that Lampkin had a gun in his pocket when he left the mill this morning," I offered. "Among the articles in the undertaking shack, all personal effects taken from the pockets of the corpse, I found no revolver. How about it?"

"There was none," McKibbe answered. "Lampkin had no weapon on him when I searched his body."

"I guessed as much," I told him. "You see, Mac, one side of the pocket is ripped pretty badly. Reckon, maybe, the damage was done by somebody snatching that gun by force?"

"Very likely. And that would be, if true, further evidence of murder. Come clean, Murphy. You think Lampkin was murdered, don't you?"

"No question about it," I said. "And now that we have fixed that fact, suppose you do a little confiding yourself. You've got suspicions. Spill 'em."

DOC was silent for the space of a minute, then he raised his clear eyes to mine and spoke quietly.

"There has been a lot of underhand business going on here during the past year," he stated. "Old man Biggers, the regular kiln-man, was laid off for a time, two months ago. And while he was off a kiln of lumber went up in smoke, thirty thousand dollars shot to hell. A month later, a new mill just completed and equipped was also burned. A hundred thousand dollars worth of new machinery became junk.

"Now, Murphy," he went on earnestly, "I've got a feeling that those two destructive fires didn't happen by chance.

"Suppose, now, that Lampkin had been doing some quiet investigating, and had uncovered facts that would damage somebody? Suppose that person, or those persons, as the case may be, learned of his activities, and bumped him off to protect the secret?"

I had followed McKibbe's theory closely, and at the end I nodded. It was plausible. Still, I did not exactly endorse it. Never like to form hard and fast opinions on somebody else's deductions.

"That's one out," I conceded. "Now, Doc, suppose you unlimber a trifle more, and tell me who, if anybody, you suspect?"

I could see that he hated to do that, and it looked for a moment or two like he was going to refuse. Finally, however, he came through.

"Here's a bit of history that may wise you up some, Murphy," he said, careful to keep his voice low. "Old Jake Lasker, father of Ben, bought one hundred thousand acres of land in this section from a concern doing business as the Ozark Land Improvement Company. That was many years ago, and land and timber up here had practically no value. He bought the immense tract very cheaply. The company got it in a grant from the government, and the grant was allowed in return for certain improvements, settlements and the like, that the company agreed to make.

"Well, to cut it short, the improvement company failed to do anything except grab all the jack it could, then went broke. The government vacated all their deeds and contracts, repossessed the land they had sold, and finally reimbursed the innocent buyers whom the company had victimized. Later on, five years ago in fact, Casper Hammet quietly bought up the former Lasker tract, and is now milling the trees and getting rich off the lumber. Some of the Lasker family—and they are numerous hereabouts—bitterly resent what they call the steal old Casper put over on them. They actually claim the land and timber, they're that ignorant and strong-headed."

He stopped speaking, and waited for me to comment. I did.

"You are telling me that you think the Lasker bunch is back of the trouble up here," I said. "Any other suspect in mind?"

"I'm not saying I suspect anybody at all," Doc reminded me. "I have just given you a bit of local history, and you can chew on it until you find something more to your taste—if you do. The Lasker connections are far reaching, and they are a rough-and-tumble set. I'd not like to have any of them after me. So don't quote me, please."

"Don't lose any sleep over that," I told him. "Can you get into Lampkin's quarters without attracting attention?"

"I have been already," was the answer.

"Any weapon there?"

"None. And I went over things thoroughly. Neither is his gun in his office. Take it from me, Murphy, Lampkin left here with that gun in his pocket."

"Yeah, so I'm thinking," I agreed. "And he had oiled it recently. Would you recognize the gun if you should see it?"

"I ought to," he said. "I bought the gun for Lampkin a bit over a year ago, when I was on a trip to Springfield. As you probably know, you must have a permit to buy a revolver in this state, so I had to buy it in my name." He pulled open a drawer of his desk, fished out a printed form and passed it to me. "There's a copy of the permit, and you'll find the make, caliber, and number on it."

"Doc," I said, pocketing the permit after I had looked it over, "if I could tie up with a bird like you every time I tackled a case, my job would be a pipe. Got any more information?"

DOC grinned and shook his head. "I'm plumb dry now, Murphy," he said. "And I only hope what I've told you will help."

"It will," I assured him, picking up my hat. "Guess I'll go over to the office and chin with young Lasker. He's expecting me. See you later, Doc—and thank you a heap."

When I stepped outside, I collided with something that felt like a huge chunk of pig-iron, but it wasn't. It was Ben Lasker, representative of the law in the lake region.

"Looking for somebody?" I asked, after we had righted ourselves.

"Yeah," Ben Lasker grunted. "Lookin' fur you."

"All right. Shoot."

"Yuh walk along to my office with me, young feller," he ordered. "I got somethin' I wants to wise yuh to."

"Fair enough, Ben," I agreed, falling into step beside him. "But make it short and sweet, because I promised to see your son at the office before he leaves."

"He done left half an hour ago," Ben informed me. "Got tired waitin' fur yuh. But that's aside from whut I'm wishful to say to yuh. It air this—I'm th' Law up here, an' I don't aim to allow no outside cop to come in an' crowd me plum' outter things. If yuh do any investigatin' in th' Lasker Lake section, yuh does it in th' open. Yuh gits me?"

"Now, Ben," I said, "that's right plain. Of course I get you. What puzzles me is that you'd think I meant to work without you. Ain't you the deputy up here?"

"I shore am!" Ben declared. "An' whut I says goes."

"It does with me. Now that we understand each other, suppose you spill anything important you may have on your mind?"

"Suppose, fust, yuh tells me whut yuh an' th' Doc had to say to each other," he countered, as we entered his office in a shack not far from the mill headquarters.

We sat down, Ben lit a pipe and I rolled a cigarette. He was so intent upon bully-

ing me that he did not take into consideration what effect his antagonistic attitude
might have on me. Maybe he didn't care,
feeling strong enough to get away with
whatever he chose to put over.

"Doc and I didn't get very far," I told
him. "His reason for thinking that
Lampkin was murdered is based on the
character of the wound in the skull. A
mere fall against a log wouldn't have made
such a fracture. We did a lot of speculat-
ing, but got no further than that."

Ben's icy eyes remained expressionless,
as did his heavy face. I wondered just
how long he had been at the door of Doc's
office, and what he had heard.

"I looked clost at Lampkin's head, when
we taken Hailey's corp in," he informed
me. "Didn't seem reasonable that a fall
would of cracked it up that bad. More
like a club or a sixgun bar'l. An', speakin'
of Hailey, yuh ain't heered th' last of that
killin', young feller—not by a long shot.
Thar's quite a scatterin' of Haileys left in
th' country, an' sum of 'em is plumb bad.
I'm warnin' yuh."

"Thanks,' I said. "Right kind of you,
Ben. That's twice I've been warned since
I hit this section. I was told to beware of
a lot of black bullets that might come my
way. It so happens, however, that I am
not afraid of black bullets."

BEN stared hard at me. "Howcome yuh
ain't?" he demanded.

I grinned. "Well, Ben," I offered, "so
long as a bullet is black it doesn't hurt
anybody. It's when it gets red that it does
the damage. It's red bullets, old-timer,
that fill up the graveyards."

"Huh!" he snorted. "That's one way of
lookin' at it!"

"Well, I'll prove it, Ben," I argued.
"Hailey sent a lot of black bullets my way
this morning, and they didn't do any harm
at all. One red bullet, though, crippled

Miss Pollard up considerable. You get
me, now?"

Ben nodded. "Yuh means that bullets
that's got blood on 'em counts," he
grunted, "an' them as hasn't, don't count.
Yeah, I gits yuh. Now," he went on,
"supposin' yuh tells me whut Nan Pollard
was doin' out on Five Mile Hill this
mawnin'?"

"She was hunting rabbits," I replied
promptly.

"Like hell she was!" he exclaimed angrily. "Rabbit huntin' in sich a storm as
that! Plumb rediculous!"

"Well, if she wasn't hunting rabbits,"
I asked, "what was she hunting?"

"I don't know, but aims to find out.
Whutever she was huntin' fur, she got one
of them red bullets yuh been talkin' about,
an' maybe she won't be so brash frum
now on. She ain't got no call to go buttin'
into things as don't concern her!"

"Was that what she was doing on Five
Mile?" I queried innocently.

"How in hell do I know—!"

Ben broke off, his huge body suddenly
stiffening. From somewhere outside had
come the high, angry crack of a rifle. It
sounded as though it had come from above
the mill office, though the snowfall ren-
dered accuracy of judgment difficult. Ben
was on his feet the next instant, snatching
at his mackinaw which hung on a nail in
the back wall. He jerked it down, hustled
into it, and dashed for the door.

"Come on!" he bellowed. "I may need
yuh!"

But I wasn't ready to go quite yet. Not
until I investigated something that interested me deeply. When Lasker jerked his
mackinaw from the nail, something shiny
had fallen from a pocket—something that
would have made considerable noise, had
it not fallen into a half-filled waste-basket
directly under the coat. I was at that
basket on the jump.

I plunged a hand into the basket and

brought up a nickelplated, thirty-eight caliber, S & W revolver. One swift glance, and I read the number.

It was unquestionably the gun that Doc McKibbe had bought for Lampkin!

I dropped the weapon back into the basket, and leaped out after Ben, overtaking him before he had noticed my tardiness. He was lumbering along through the snow with surprising speed, considering his bulk, and he had an ugly looking hog-leg gripped in his right hand.

As we neared the big mill office, somebody ran around from back of it.

"Halt!" Ben yelled.

The runner stopped in his tracks, and the next moment we recognized him. Bare-headed, in his shirt sleeves, and evidently thoroughly enraged, John Hammet stood there in the snow before us. His right hand held a long-barreled Colt, and he looked like he wanted to use it.

"Whut done happened?" Ben demanded. "Who done that shootin', John?"

"Come in!" John yelled sharply. "You can see, better than I can tell you!"

We followed him along a passage into a lighted office at the rear, and he pointed toward a window. One pane had been shattered, and slivers of glass lay on the floor.

"I was working on some records and tally-sheets," the young super said, his voice still edged with rage, "when somebody took a shot at me through the window. He missed and I didn't give him another chance. My gun was handy, and I beat it out through the back door," he went on, indicating a door that gave onto the back premises, "but of course he had beat it by then. It's a damned outrage, Lasker, all this undercover shooting! It's up to you to do something!"

"I shorely aims to, John!" Ben declared. "That was a rifle shot I heerd, an' I'm bettin' th' feller that shot was somewhere in th' old burnt mill. It's clost enough,

an' would give him jist th' cover he needed —blast him!"

"Well, if he hid there," I offered, "and has gone, he must have left a trail in the snow. How about taking a look?"

"Too many tracks around th' old frame," Ben said. "Besides, if we done that, whut's to keep him frum pottin' us frum some other some other cover?"

"I agree with Lasker," Hammet said coldly. "As a matter of fact, Murphy," he went on, "you were sent in here to check up on certain things pertaining to the mill, and not to usurp the authority of constituted law. Just bear that in mind, will you?"

"Jist whut I was tellin' him awhile ago!" Ben applauded.

I laughed, then walked over and, using the point of my knife, dug a 30-30 rifle bullet out of a side wall and handed it to the deputy.

"Another black one, Ben," I pointed out, grinning. "Just as harmless as if it had never been fired."

"Yuh—yuh go plumb to hell!" Ben snarled, taking the slug from my hand.

"Not tonight," I said, going toward the front. "Instead I'm going to bed. See you in the morning, gents—if you're afoot early enough."

I had been assigned to a room in the make-shift hotel maintained by the company, and when I hit the hay it was to sleep. I never solve my cases while lying in bed.

CHAPTER FIVE

Clues

I WAS up and out at daybreak, despite Sheriff Lasker's warning not to sneak around. Above the office stood the fire-blackened frame of the new mill that had been destroyed, and I got inside it without encountering anybody.

I had an idea that there would be a 30-30 rifle hidden somewhere there, for it stood to reason that the pot-shooter would not be bold enough to take the weapon out with him after he had shot through the office window.

The more I poked about among the ruined machines, the more interested I became.

An hour passed, and just as I was on the point of giving up looking for the rifle, I came upon a heap of charred lumber that looked like it had recently been disturbed. Under the lumber I found what I sought.

A 30-30 rifle, its magazine filled with cartridges, the barrel slightly fouled by powder. It was unquestionably the weapon in use the night before. And, now that I had it, the problem was what to do with it. I solved that by doing what the pot-shooter might have done, had he thought of it. I shoved the barrel down inside my left trouser-leg, slipped the butt snugly under my arm, buttoned my leather coat up, and walked out. A few minutes later, after I had put the gun safely away in my room, I sat down to breakfast in the dining room.

Hammet came in shortly thereafter, gave me a curt nod, and took a seat as far from me as possible. He ate in silence, and only toyed with his food. I was still filling up when he finished. On the way out he paused beside my chair.

"If you are not going to be too busy this morning," he suggested, making no attempt to conceal his dislike, "I would like to have a talk with you in my office. Make it as soon as possible."

"I'll be right on your heels, old-timer," I told him. "Just have patience while I finish this final sausage, and I'll come a-jumping."

He left me abruptly—and left me fed up with something other than the food I'd consumed. I was completely fed up

with the whole damned outfit, and meant for them to know it very soon.

John Hammet, I thought, disliked me because he resented Casper's sending me in to investigate the business at the mill. I could understand that he'd feel hot over the lack of confidence his uncle had shown in him. But that was no reason for him to harpoon me every time he had a chance.

I FOUND John Hammet in his office, the one with the bullet-shattered window, and he seemed to have gotten rid of some of his grouch. We discussed the shooting of the night before for a time, and then John said—

"I've a right to some small items of information, I think, and I hope you'll agree with me. After all, I'm in a responsible as well as trying position here, and if you can help me, I think you'd be serving Uncle Casper's interests to do so. What do you say?"

"I'll be glad to help you any way I can," I assured him, lighting the good cigar he offered. "And, in return, maybe you'll give me a little information that may help me get started on my job. How about that?"

"Willingly," Hammet replied. "First, I'd like a few answers. What, for instance, do you intend to do about this investigation business?"

"I've done that already," I answered, and watched the light of surprise leap into his eyes. "I mean that I know enough about this mill trouble to enable me to make a satisfactory report to Casper. And, in that connection, may I ask who made the deal for the machinery with which to equip the mill that was burned?"

"Lampkin did, of course," John replied without hesitation. "He went to St. Louis and got it. Had it shipped to White Oak, then brought in over our dummy-line. A special crew came along to set it up. We never turned a wheel over there, however, for the fire got the new plant before it was put into operation."

I could have told him that it was a mighty good thing they didn't try to turn a wheel in that new plant, but didn't just then. I asked another question.

"Where were you when the machinery was brought in and set up?"

"I was in Memphis. Uncle sent for me on business, and I left here the day after Lampkin returned from St. Louis."

"And how long after your return was it that the new mill burned?"

"Two days before I returned," he answered.

"Who acted as assistant during your absence?"

"Nobody. Lampkin got along well enough alone."

"Where was Frank Lasker, during that time?"

"Out on the logging-fronts. Lasker has spent very little time here at the mill. He has been woods superintendant, and a good one, even if I don't like him personally—not a little bit."

"Now, John," I said, "you had some questions to ask. Shoot 'em."

"One thing I want to know is how Miss Pollard happened to be out on Five Mile Hill yesterday morning," he said. "What took her there, do you know?"

"Haven't the faintest idea," I replied. "She had just shown up in the trail when Hailey came galloping along on my horse and let her have that slug."

"And did you accompany her to that hunting-camp of Frank Lasker's?"

"So that is Frank's layout, eh? Well, to answer your query, I didn't accompany her there. I trailed her to where she had fallen in the snow, and carried her on to the cabin."

"Did she, er—well, did she tell you anything she had surmised about the attack on you?"

"She didn't. In fact, she seemed to go dumb every time I tried to question her. Really, Hammet, I don't think she knew that attack was to be made."

He looked at me speculatively, trying to make out whether or not I was evading. Well, I was—but my mug didn't tell him anything.

"Sorry I showed so much resentment toward you at first, Murphy," he said finally. "If I can aid you in any way, tell me about it."

"There's one thing I'd like to do," I said, after a moment's thought, "and that is to examine Lampkin's private papers. Begin in his office, and maybe finish up in his living quarters. Any objection to that?"

"Not in the least. Come, I'll show you the office."

LAMPKIN had occupied a room adjoining that of Hammet, and presently I stood before the door of a big safe. It was locked.

"Has it been opened since Lampkin's death was reported?" I ask Hammet.

"No," he replied. "I thought it best to open it in the presence of a second party."

"Well, I'm a second party," I reminded him. "Suppose you open it. Got the combination?"

He nodded, hesitated briefly, then began to whirl the dials. A few minutes sufficed to open the safe, and another few minutes was enough to convince me that there was not a thing there to interest me.

However, I was interested in something that had been there, but was no longer. The bottom of the interior was covered, as is usual, with a square of carpet, and in the nap of the carpet were four distinct impressions that caught my attention. I examined them, then turned to Hammet.

"Lampkin kept a small hand-satchel in the safe,"> I said, indicating the indentations caused by the knobs on the corners of the satchel. "Know what it contained?"

"It was usually empty," Hammet informed me, a frown on his face. "It was used for carrying the payroll out from White Oak. Had a strap on it that buckled over the shoulder, and nobody ever carried it but Lampkin."

"Know where the satchel is now?"

"Of course I don't. Never knew it was gone until this moment."

"Let's have a search for it," I suggested.

It could not be found in the office, or anywhere in the building, nor did a subsequent search of Lampkin's quarters reveal it. The satchel was gone, and that was that.

"Have you got any notions about what became of the satchel, Murphy?" Young Hammet queried anxiously, when we had given up finding it.

"Sure I have," I told him. "Lampkin carried it with him when he left here before daylight yesterday morning. The question is, why did he carry it, and, above all—what did he have in it?"

Hammet's face suddenly became hard and grim, and his gray eyes looked glassy.

"Do you think Lampkin has been putting over something crooked here?" he demanded. "That he has cheated Uncle Casper?"

"I wouldn't be a damned bit surprised to learn for certain that he was," I returned soberly. "By the way, how was payment made for that machinery bought in St. Louis?"

"Lampkin drew drafts on Uncle Casper to meet the cost," John informed me. "That, of course, was according to Uncle's instructions."

"And it's likewise where Casper made a fool of himself," I said sharply.

"How do you mean?" John demanded, bristling up.

"I mean, John, that had Casper gone to St. Louis and purchased that machinery himself, there would have been no fire at the big mill directly after it was set."

John stared at me with clouded eyes for a moment, then declared:

"Damned if I get you, Murphy! Why don't you come clean?"

"Maybe I will—later," I answered, taking up my hat. "But, right now, I've got important matters to look after. See you later, John, and maybe you can figure some of these things out while I'm gone."

After all, John Hammet might not be so innocent as he acted, and it would have been poor business to tell him that the machinery bought in St. Louis, at a cost of one hundred grand, had been junk before it ever left the city.

WHEN I reached the front office on my way out, I found a sallow-faced, skinny man of thirty bending over some tally-sheets at a desk. I had not seen him before, so I went over and got acquainted.

"What's your job here, neighbor?" I queried, after I'd introduced myself.

The clerk looked at me for a moment as though sizing me up, then answered shortly.

"I'm the head log- and lumber-checker," he told me.

"Important job, that," I commented. "You keep the books, too?"

"Yes."

Evidently, here was another hombre who resented me.

"I don't believe I quite got your name," I insinuated.

"Hailey. Tom Hailey," he said, his

eyes flaring. "Anything else you want to know?"

"That'll be all today, Tom," I said easily, and took the air.

A relative of Gid's, no doubt, and that would account for his antagonism. Well, it began to look like Spot Murphy was entirely surrounded by enemies, for a fact. Such being the case, I'd just as well start something and have done with it. So I strolled down to Ben Lasker's office. He was in.

"I've come to ask you a few questions, hombre," I stated, giving him hard look for hard look. "And if you think you can continue to ride me, old-timer, you've got another think coming. What the hell are you trying to cover up, anyhow?"

"Nothing!" Ben snapped.

"You're a liar!" I snapped back. "You tried to cover up something last night. The gun that Lampkin carried when he left here in the morning. I saw it fall from your coat into the waste-basket, and I'm betting it's there yet. You've been wondering, worrying a lot, about how you happened to lose it, no doubt. Well, hombre, I'm telling you."

Ben reared his bulk out of the chair, went to the waste-basket, dug the revolver out from under the crumpled papers, and came slowly back and sat down.

"An' yuh figger I was coverin' it up, huh?" he asked.

"Exactly. Why else did you have Lampkin's gun in your pocket?"

"Well," he drawled slowly, "I put it there when I found it under Gid's body, buried in th' snow. Gid must of had it in his pocket when he tumbled frum th' hoss. I reckoned it was his weapon, an' ain't shore it wasn't now, fur that matter. Whut makes yuh think it was Lampkin's?"

"Because I checked the number," I told him. "That's Lampkin's gun, and he took it with him when he left camp yes-

terday morning. Your explanation sounds plausible, and clicks with a theory of mine. Before I wise you to the theory, though, I want to know if you are acquainted with anybody hereabouts who owns a 30-30 caliber, late model Savage. Are you?"

For once I got some expression from the stolid countenance. A shadow of intense interest passed over Ben's mug. He started to speak, but held his tongue.

"The rifle I'm speaking about," I explained, "is now in my room at the hotel. Want to look at it?"

"I'd admire to," Ben rumbled, getting up. "Le's go."

In the room, Ben carefully examined the rifle, looked at the number.

"Whar at did yuh git this rifle?" he asked.

"From under a pile of charred lumber in the burnt mill," I told him. "It's the weapon used in that shooting last night. Know who owns it?"

BEN simply stared at me, his lips closed in a straight line.

"Want me to inquire about the camp, Ben, and identify the owner, or will you come through?" I asked.

"No use puttin' yuh to that much trouble," the big man said. "Ever'body hereabouts knows it belongs to my son, Frank. But Frank didn't use it last night —an' I kin damned well prove he didn't. He kept it in a closet in his office, an' some skunk snuck it out an' tried to kill Hammet through th' winder. That's whut happened."

"How can you prove that Frank had no hand in it?" I demanded.

"Because he went across th' lake to see Nan Pollard, half an hour before I met yuh at Doc's office," was the answer. "I heered him leave in his motorboat, an' Nan an' Leach Pollard kin testify to when he got there, an' how long he stayed. Yuh aim to check up on him, or do yuh want me to do it?"

"I'll do it," I told him. "What's your grudge against Nan Pollard? It's pretty clear your son is in love with her, and I wouldn't be surprised if she's in love with him. What's wrong between you and her?"

"Th' Laskers an' th' Pollards ain't never mixed none," Ben informed me, his face reddening. "We folks has been enemies fur years. Then my boy goes an' falls in love with a Pollard—dad burn him! Now yuh knows th' reason I am ag'in him marryin' her."

"Well," I told him, "that's not my business, of course. So I'm going to attend to something that is. In the meantime, you can do something that may let a little light into that skullbound mind of yours, Ben. Get up to the mill office, take a look at the floor in young Hammet's room, and determine whether or not I saw some tracks there last night. Wet and black, they were, and led from the door into the room. If you see them too, then think about them, Ben, until you see me again. So long, old-timer."

I left him at the hotel door, his heavy jaw sagging, a look of perplexity in his eyes.

Dr. McKibbe was in his office, and I went right to the point of my business with him.

"Did you know that Tom Hailey, the head checker, is a dope?"

"Damn it all, Murphy!" he exclaimed. "Does nothing escape your eyes?"

"Plenty, Doc," I replied. "But that didn't. He is a dope, isn't he?"

"Yes. Has been for a long time. Why?"

"Because," I answered, watching him closely when I sprung it, "I want you to stage a kidnaping for me, Doc, with Tom as the kidnapee. In the interests of justice, are you game to do it?"

McKibbe stared at me in amazement, choked a time or two.

"That's a hell of a thing to ask a reputable doctor to do!" he blurted. "But go ahead, though, and explain your proposal—damn your hide!"

I grinned. "Want to make Tom talk," I told him. "He's bound to know a lot I want to hear, him being head checker and bookkeeper too. If we take him somewhere, keep the dope away from him—he'll talk."

"What good is a dope-head's word?" Doc demanded.

"Never mind about that," I told him. "When Tom disappears, and it leaks out that I've got him hid somewhere, that will bring somebody out in the open, and he'll be the man I want. Going to put in with me?"

"Might as well," Doc grunted. "But damned if I'd do it except for the fact that I believe you're going to clean up a dirty mess here, and I want to see it done. Leave it to me. When is it to be?"

"Tonight."

"I'll get a couple of native friends to pull it, and take him to the cabin of 'Reckless' Brown, another friend. You must have this case just about in the bag," he ended.

"I have," I agreed, taking up my hat. "Not exactly in the bag, but nearly ready to go in. So long, Doc—and thanks."

CHAPTER SIX

Red Bullets

MUCH to my surprise, Nan Pollard came across the lake next morning and resumed work. She was a trifle pale, and limped considerable, but otherwise appeared all right. I was glad she came, for if she had not I'd have had to cross over and see her.

Nan had some explaining to do, and I wanted to give her a chance. At noon I did. She appeared promptly at twelve, and went toward the hotel for lunch, and I joined her at the table.

"Tell me, Miss Pollard, in words of one syllable, what the devil caused you to act up like you did day before yesterday," was the way I opened the subject.

Miss Pollard smiled, then her face sobered a bit. The next thing I knew she was spilling the works.

"On the day the telegram came," she said, "I was kept late at my desk on some work, but, as it happened, nobody else knew I was in my room. I heard loud voices from Mr. Lampkin's office, and couldn't help hearing something of what was said. Mr. Lampkin was talking, and he was apparently very angry. I heard him say—

" 'If Murphy comes, we're caught!' "

"Someone spoke in a voice too low for me to recognize it, and then Mr. Lampkin flared up again. I heard him quite plainly.

" 'Get him on top of Five Mile Hill! He must never reach the mill!' he said.

"I got up then and opened my door a crack. The voices were then coming in lower tones, and I could make nothing of what was said. Presently the door of Lampkin's office opened, and the last man in the world I expected to see there came out. It was Frank Lasker.

"Frank's face was red and angry, and he slammed the door behind him. Imagine how I felt, Mr. Murphy, if you can. Frank Lasker—well, Frank and I had about decided to get married. And I had just heard him take orders to prevent a man from coming here to investigate the company! Perhaps to kill him! I tried to find Frank that night, but couldn't. So I went out early the next morning, hoping to warn you, else find Frank and make him listen to reason. But the shooting took place before I reached the top of the hill. It was not until I saw Gid Hailey on the horse that I realized Frank was not there at all."

"Why did you stall me with that dialect?" I asked, merely curious about it.

"I had some notion of fooling you, keeping you from discovering who I was," she answered. "But when you made me show my face I knew it was hopeless. You'd be bound to recognize me later. Besides, being a hill-raised woman, dialect comes more easily to me than good English."

"Now, what about Frank? He wasn't in this thing, of course. Tell me how you found it out."

"Frank was at our place last night," she explained, "and told me about it. He had come into the office building through the back door of Hammet's room, and had gone into Lampkin's room to see him. Lampkin was engaged with somebody, Frank wouldn't say who it was, and bawled him out for coming in. That was why he looked so angry when he came into the corridor. Now, Mr. Murphy, do you understand?"

WELL, that was that. A girl's mistake but it almost got an innocent man in bad. We parted shortly thereafter, and I had another stretch of hours to kill. But they passed in time, and as evening came on I still had that feeling that soon some black bullets were due to get red.

Just after dark, Doc McKibbe and I set out down the lake shore.

An hour later, we arrived at a two-roomed log cabin standing alone in a clearing, about three miles from the mill.

We pushed the door open and entered, to be confronted by a tall, raw-boned, bewhiskered native in middle life.

"Hello, Reckless!" the doctor greeted heartily. "How's the patient?"

"How air he?" Reckless repeated sarcastically. "Why th' damned scalawag done made a old man outter me! Old an' reckless! I could git ongodly drunk, only I ain't got nuthin' to do it on!"

"Doctor!" shrieked a voice from a bunk. "Thank God you've come at last! Damn your eyes, have a heart and give me a shot!"

"You had no heart when you helped Lampkin to rob the men who employed you," Doc reminded him.

"That's a lie! I don't know anything about it!"

"Doctor," I queried, "you brought out quite a large supply of morphine—"

"For God's sake give me a little! Just a little!" the crazed man interrupted.

—"did you not?" I finished.

"Well, I did, yes," McKibbe replied. "Figured Tom would act decently, and I'd see he had enough to get him through."

"But he hasn't acted decently," I said. "Now, Doctor, take all the morphine you have about you, every single tablet, and throw it in the fire—when I say the word."

Hailey swore at that, but the doctor got ready to obey orders.

"Now, Tom," I said, sitting down in a chair beside the bed, "I know it all anyhow, so why torture yourself longer? I know that you tampered with the books, so Lampkin could sell logs and pocket the money. I know also that he had that kiln burned after he had sold probably twenty-five thousand dollars worth of the lumber. I know that a fire was set that burned the new mill in order to cover the fact that the mill had been equipped with old, worn-out machinery, all painted up, for which Lampkin paid about two-thousand and pocketed nearly a hundred thousand—"

"Well, I'll be damned if I know how you found out about the machinery!" the doctor broke in, amazed. "That job looked natural enough, I'll say!"

"Yes, it was newly painted, and Lampkin went so far as to remove the old serial numbers and stencil new ones more up to date," I agreed. "But the condition of the axle-bearings gave the snap away. They were all concealed by boxings, and

the whole shebang would soon be junk. So he saw no necessity for going to the expense of molding new bearings for the axles. They would never be seen. Some of the bearings I found today were actually burned past going. That settled that. Now, Tom, do you tell the truth and get your shot, or do you go to prison as an accomplice, where not a bit of dope is ever allowed?"

"A shot!" Hailey screamed the words. "I'll talk!"

"A shot," I told him, "after you talk." And Hailey talked.

"Lampkin began looting the company over a year ago," Hailey groaned. "Made me help him by doctoring tally-sheets and the books. Sold logs to other mills, and pocketed the money. He got me dope when I wanted it, and he could make me do what he pleased. He had the kiln of lumber burned, and set the mill on fire— just like Murphy says. That machinery was all junk to go with. Then somebody in the Memphis office tipped him off that a detective was coming in to investigate the plant, and he got cold feet. He decided to beat it out of the country, and take his plunder with him in that satchel. But—"

HAILEY stopped short, and looked at me out of wild eyes. His lips trembled, but from them came no sounds.

"Hit a snag, didn't you Tom?" I queried. "I thought you would. You've been hoping to put all the blame on a dead man, and protect one that is still alive. Come clean, else you'll lay here another night—"

"No! No!" he shrieked. "It was that damned Hammet, the cruelest fiend alive, that was at the bottom of it all! He got Lampkin into it, and forced me to help. That's the truth, so help me God!"

"You knew that already!" McKibbe accused.

"Not until I saw him walk across the office floor on the night he pretended somebody shot at him," I said. "He did the shooting himself, in order to throw dust in my eyes. Wanted me to think that he was being attacked by whoever was doing the deviltry hereabouts. But his footprints on the floor revealed the fact that he had been walking in charcoal, and I knew he had been in the mill. Also, it was impossible for Lampkin to cheat without the knowledge of his assistant—John Hammet."

Hailey, anxious for his shot began spilling the rest.

"Hammet owned my cousin, Gid Hailey, too. So he ordered Gid to kill Lampkin so it would look like an accident, and then hide the satchel Lampkin was trying to get away with. It held nearly one hundred thousand dollars, his share of the loot. Then Gid was to waylay Murphy on Five Mile Hill and kill him. That's all I know. For God's sake, give me that shot!"

Hardly had Hailey had his shot when I heard a hail from outside. I opened the door, just as somebody came galloping up on a hill-bronc. Then I stared in astonishment, for the rider was Nan Pollard!

"I rode as fast as I could!" she gasped out as I helped her from her saddle. "John Hammet found out where you are holding Tom Hailey, and he has gathered some of the Hailey men and a lot of toughs and is on the way here now!"

At that moment another hill bronc galoped up, and Frank Lasker flung himself out of the saddle.

"Frank!" Nan cried. "How did you happen to come here?"

"I followed you," he said simply. "You see, I had my ears open, too. There's a crowd headed here, Murphy," he went on, addressing me. "If you'll trust me that far, I'll help all I can."

"Come in, both of you," I ordered.

They had hardly entered when we got a hail from outside.

"Hello, Reckless!" It was Hammet.

"Hello yoreself!" the native shouted back.

"You've got a couple of kidnapers in there, old man!" Hammet shouted. "And one of them is a killer! He shot Gid Hailey to death without cause. Going to send them out to us and save trouble?"

"Gents," Reckless whined back, while he loaded the magazine of his rifle, "that air would be plumb inhorspitable! I jist kain't do hit!"

I hastily covered the fire with ashes, making the interior as dark as possible, and thrust Nan into the lean-to. Then a volley came from the outside.

Reckless fired, and a man dropped. The doctor got the next. Then Hailey got up, he having been unstrapped when trouble began, and started hunting the doctor.

"Give me another shot, Doc—"

He never finished, for a bullet found him through a chinkhole and he crumpled up dead on the floor.

Then I got a man who showed too much of himself back of a juniper bush, and saw two others throw down their empty rifles and run toward the lake.

The doctor shot another just then, leaving only Hammet outside—if, indeed, he had not gone to cover too.

I threw open the door and ran toward where I had last seen the crook—and found him, back against a juniper bush, sixgun in hand.

"Just as well die here, as on the gallows!" he yelled, and raised his weapon.

"Better think again, Hammet!" I called. "There's been enough red bullets taking toll tonight. Drop that gun—!"

He laughed sarcastically, and I beat him to the shot by a fraction.

John Hammet, one of the smoothest crooks I ever stacked up against, died there in the snow.

TURN TO PAGE 124 FOR THE GREATEST THRILL IN MONTHS!

The
Screeching Skull

by
J. Allan Dunn

Author of "The Fire Fiend," etc.

Impaled in the dead branches of its tree it grinned with fleshless jaws by day—gibbered and shrieked by night with fiendish glee. Why was it there? What dread tale did that bony, sun-baked maw seek to make known to those who listened horror-eared?

Trent lunged blindly as the blow descended.

CHAPTER ONE

Loot

AT the annual masquerade balls of the exclusive Marina Club of Palm Beach, the costumes were more elaborate and costly each successive season; especially those of the women. The designs were invariably of a type which would be set off by the display of jewels.

There was no estimate given out to the press and public as to the total value of the gems that would be worn. That would not be good form, but the amount would certainly run into the millions.

Naturally every precaution was taken to protect the jewels and their wearers. The manager and his assistants checked off the staff. There were twenty chosen plainclothesmen from private agencies who this night wore fancy clothes, and mingled unobtrusively with the guests. Jim Trent, ex-secret-service man, now a private investigator, had been persuaded by a big fee to oversee the protective forces. All the gems were insured against robbery but the dance committee was taking no chances. Perhaps the recollection that the uncrowned monarch of crookdom owned an island residence at another Floridan resort stimulated them.

Trent was a guest, ostensibly. He had a card to the Marina and mingled freely with the club members. He had consented to oversee the protection of the ball not merely for his fee, but because he had a hint that an attempt might be made to despoil the guests by some bold stroke of banditry.

Trent was one investigator who did not believe in the use of stool pigeons. But he had a vast insight into human nature, studied all walks of life, and mingled in all its phases as one of whatever type he might be studying. And he got tips from all kinds of sources, from one of which, he had gleaned an inkling of the activities of an organization known as the O. & U. A. He had even heard of a certain Mr. S. and knew him for a superman of crime.

It was through an assistant mortician, a source from which clues often came, that Trent had got his hint of the secret hideout of the O. & U. A. in the Everglades. He did not as yet know the significance of the initials of the organization but he was not far from guessing them. What he did believe was that the mysterious disappearances from time to time of avowed criminals or undercover crooks, might be accounted for, if this human cache could be unmasked.

Without a doubt S. made this pay. He was a sort of super blackmail. A raven despoiling crows; a sea eagle levying on fish-hawks. From the Everglades a man could be shipped to Venezuela, or flown there. There is no extradition in Venezuela and it is the refuge of many high-life racketeers who have come to the showdown. No doubt S. and the O. & U. A. guaranteed a safe escape.

No doubt many of those in this swampy hideout were what most police considered amateurs. But there were others among them who were experts in crime, badly wanted, for the penitentiary or the chair, and their presence in the neighborhood was a menace.

THEREFORE Trent was very diligent about his precautions at the Marina Masquerade. There was a man at every entrance, at every approach to the main building and grounds, by land and water.

He knew the number of guests and their names for the elaborately engraved invitation and admission cards were numbered. The main entrance was covered by two armed detectives and he had posted other armed guards at various vantage points. At midnight, when the Grand March and judgment of prizes was to take place, the wrought-iron gates of the entry through an archway to the patio and orangery were closed and guarded. The photographers and pressmen were required to identify themselves.

There were as many precautions, cleverly veiled, as would be needed at a royal function. And from the standpoint of the value of the gems, it was indeed a regal affair. Also, in a measure that he respected, Trent's own reputation was at stake.

At midnight he knew that everything was functioning properly. Everyone was assembling for the Grand March and the review by the judges who would then award the prizes.

Trent sat in the manager's office checking up the invitation cards on which the necessary lettering was engraved in a blank provided by the etcher who had made the plate—an elaborate depiction of a Spanish Carnival. The motif for this affair was supposed to be Spanish—though of no particular period—and the costumes varied from those of medieval splendor down to the twentieth century.

There were infantas and queens, courtiers, matadors and bandits, serenaders and señoritas. There were grand inquisitors and capitans in body armor, hidalgos and peasants. Many came as pirates of the Spanish Main.

The orchestra, imported from Havana as the chief musical feature—there were three orchestras in all—swung into the Grand March.

Trent went over the cards. Two hundred and fourteen acknowledged members and guests. Two hundred and *fifteen* cards. There had been two hundred and fifty struck off. He asked the manager for the overs. There were exactly thirty-six, kept in the safe. No one had stayed away. Trent went through the stacks

again. He sorted the numbers set on each card—and found two numbered 113. Swiftly he compared them, already assured of a clever forgery, or of an extra printing smuggled through somehow.

One card was rough under his sensitive fingertip, a true etching; the other too smooth. A replica photographed and engraved on zinc or copper, but not a true etching.

He rose, snatching his gun from its shoulder holster. At this moment all the dancers, with all their jewels, were in the big ballroom, without exception. And there was an outsider among them. It was an ideal time for a raid. But he was sure there was only one man, one pseudo guest, unaccounted for.

Trent blew his whistle to bring the guards closing in. Then he ran, uncostumed, in regular evening dress, to the ballroom with the manager.

There seemed little cause for alarm. The orchestra played the march as the couples formed, filing before the platform beneath a balcony where the judges sat. Everyone had dined and wined but they were not boisterous.

Trent saw the detectives ranging themselves, drifting in, making themselves part of the pageant.

One man marched without a partner. He was a conquistador who seemed to lack, or scorn, company. He wore a closed helmet, its vizor down, and he had armor over his leather jerkin. Below were trunks, tights ending in leather boots. A long sword swanked at his side. He wore a baldric that held pistols and at one hip there was a pouch. Over his left arm he carried a capa. A plume waved from his helmet. He was well in character as some follower of Cortez, perhaps the bold explorer himself.

Once the glittering and glamorous procession circled the room and, in obedience to the judges, continued. The conquistador fell out. His long sword had slipped somehow, embarassing him, and he fiddled with it while the photographers took temporary charge and herded everyone beneath the balcony, directing them with the supreme confidence and impudence of cameramen who make the news—and also make or unmake social aspirants. They posed them by the dais and were ready for the take. Only the conquistador was out of the picture. One of them called to him.

"Come on, Balboa!"

He made a gesture with a sweeping bow. Then he took his place on the center of the now vacant floor. He postured. Some expected a stunt, a surprise on the program. Some thought him drunk, others considered him merely trying for the limelight.

He bowed again, tossed aside his capa and Trent saw a sort of bag suspended on his arm—canvas, anachronistic.

A voice came hollow from the helmet, muffled and deep. "Here are offerings to the Queen of Beauty! Behold!"

He thrust his hand into the canvas receptacle and even Trent considered him, despite that odd number on the invitation cards, only as some eccentric.

And then it was *too late*.

THE conquistador tossed, one after another, with calm precision about the room, fragile containers of glass that gave out a white mist that speedily set all eyes watering to blindness and all throats to irritant coughing. It was a malignant mixture of tear gas with some other vapor, instantaneously and powerfully effective.

Behind his visor the man was protected with a mask. All the others were exposed, gasping and groping. Trent himself had seen the doors closed and now he was crippled with the rest; seeing—guessing rather than visualizing—the conquistador going among the dan-

cers, gathering loot, from helpless women and men bereft of all power to defend them.

Pearls, diamonds, rubies, emeralds. Bracelets, necklaces, deftly unfastened while their owners choked, blinded. Rings here and there, where they came off easily. Five minutes, perhaps, of expert gleaning with the irritant gas accumulating in its energy.

Trent battled against his stinging, flooded eyes, his contracted throat. The stuff was in his lungs, robbing him of power and action. The despoiled masqueraders milled like stampeding cattle. At last there came a whiff of fresh air. The lone looter was opening doors and Trent broke stumbling through the mob and fired at the figure he could see so vaguely. The man whirled and came for him, the canvas bag on his arm now filled with glittering spoils. Through the scalding veil of water forced from his tear ducts, Trent shot again. He heard the lead strike on the corselet and trusted it was only thin metal. He hoped that his first shot had scored, snap as it had been, and thwarted by the gas.

Women were screaming. Trent lunged blindly toward the open door, both to defend it and get more oxygen into his tortured lungs. A blow descended on top of his skull and he dropped, blackjacked, while the bandit leaped outside with a muffled laugh closing the doors behind him.

They had ventilation going when Trent got off the floor. The tears had stopped, the tortured lungs relieved themselves, for the gas was irritant rather than poison. But the Marina Masquerade was a fiasco.

The lone bandit had outplayed all precautions. Trent's emergency summons had left ways open for escape, through the orangery perhaps, over the golf links. He had got away with at least five million dollars in jewels. Trent felt himself discredited. The gems were insured but not his reputation.

His head throbbing, he directed the search and found the only clue. The man on guard over the launches in the canal that served club members had not left his post on the whistle. He would have been wiser if he had. He had seen the costumed figure running toward him and had hesitated, bewildered, thinking this was surely a duly bidden guest and therefore beyond suspicion. He paid for his mistake with a viciously fractured skull. He revived under powerful stimulant and spoke a few words describing what he knew, then lapsed into a coma, dying within twenty-four hours.

It was murder now, as well as robbery. A launch was missing, a small, fast cruiser. Trent found a smear of blood on the string-piece of the landing stage. It gave no definite fingerprints but it showed that the man was wounded.

The next day Trent himself dropped out of sight. The insurance detectives and other officers found no further clues. The description of the launch was broadcast, with a brief story of the robbery and murder, and promises of ample reward, but there was no satisfactory response. The bandit had several hours of night in which to complete his getaway. The countryside was sparsely inhabited. There were plenty of rumors and conflicting reports but no results. The story blazed in scareheads over the nation for one day, dropped to single-column stuff on the second, died out on the third, supplanted by more up-to-date sensations.

And Trent was gone!

CHAPTER TWO

Craneo Cay

IT WAS dawn—Florida dawn. A flush of pink on the low horizon, roseate as the plumage of the flamingoes that flocked in stately, winged procession, blended into the purple flood of passing night.

This was the Everglades, the western side of that great stretch of savage fenland with its maze of sluggish waterways, half choked with water hyacinth, lotus, arrowhead, wampi and water barley. Close enough to the coast for tidal water to ebb and flow, for seafish to venture on the flood.

The flush of pink had changed. It was orange now, with brilliant lemon where the sun was lifting; green above, blending into deepest blue. In that blue, as yet invisible, but heard—like the humming of a swarm of bees—an airplane came from the north. It seemed to hover up there in the blue as if seeking some spot to descend in the swampy wilderness.

The pilot could see, as visibility increased, the scattered cays of the Ten Thousand Islands, the shine of the dawnlight on the steel rails that ran, with only one insignficant stop at Deep Lake in fifty miles, down to the little-used terminus at Everglades.

Now the plane was lowering, almost vertically. Its supporting blades spun horizontally on their flexible axis, its propeller was idling. The machine was somewhat of a novelty, an autogyro equipped with pontoons.

The pilot was studying a map compiled from aerial photographs for it was his first trip on this expedition. His predecessor had been killed suddenly, though not in a crash. It was a hazardous, adventurous job that was well paid, as were all jobs with the organization known to its intimates—not yet suspected by the police under that title—as the O. & U. A.

That name was a joke on the part of its promoter, its sole controller, the mysterious and sinister Mr. S. To initiates it meant "Overhead and Undercover Association" and it was just what the title might imply to the man outside the law. It was a flourishing and excellently devised machine, with northern headquarters in a deserted spot in the foothills of the Berkshires—and its southern lair here in the fastness of the Florida Cays, on one of which, impaled upon the branches of a dead tree, there was a ghastly object.

It was a skull and the name of the islet it marked was Craneo Cay—Skull Isle. It marked also the entrance to the small laguna which the pilot sought but which showed no passage at water level, so closely grew the semi-tropical bush, unless one knew the token, the sign of the skull.

The cranium shone in the brightening glare of day. Its jaws were open as if in a continuous, sardonic grin, the secret smile of one who has left life behind and knows what lies beyond. The eyes were still socketed in shadow, save for a gleam that reached the inner cavities through a temple suture.

To the flyer, peering from the cockpit, it would be only a white spot, like a lone egg in an eagle's nest and he wanted to make sure of it. Mistakes were not popular with the man known as S.

That symbol might have stood for "Serpent." Perhaps it did. For he had the proverbial subtle wisdom of the serpent, his strike sudden and deadly, and the S on the signet ring, carved deeply in a square emerald, took a serpent's shape, even to the delicately engraved scales and forked tongue flickering from the fanged and open jaws.

The flyer's orders were to deliver sealed communications, on alighting in the laguna, to get a receipt for the same, to answer no questions and return to northern headquarters. But not without being quite sure of his surroundings,

without receiving the proper signal. Also the trip was to acquaint him with the route.

"STUMPY SAM" came yawning from the low, long house that the mangroves masked. His nickname came from the obtruding fact of his left arm, that ended at the elbow. Sam, hailing from Haiti, black as blacking, would tell you it had been bitten off by an alligator, by a shark, lopped off with a caneknife; according to his mood. But he was not afraid of alligators, or of sharks, and he could slash through a young pine at one stroke with the machete he always carried.

He could have lopped off a man's leg with that machete for he kept it razor sharp with grinding. Strong as an ox, superstitious, simple-minded, strenuous in love and liquor, a mean man in a tussle; that was Stumpy Sam, cook to the outfit on Craneo Cay in the place maintained by S as sanctuary for outlaws and refugees.

A wind had sprung up as if summoned by the sun. It rustled in the glossy leaves of the mangroves and the palmetto fronds, it waved the banners of Spanish moss. It was slowly growing in force, blowing from the sea, a cool, stiff wind.

Sam heard the drone of the plane and ran back to the house, returning with a red flag that he used to signal. From the hooded flyer in the autogyro three heavy but small scraps of rock splashed into the water at varying intervals. Sam rolled up his flag like a train brakeman and stuck it under the stump of his arm. He watched the gyro sit down on the laguna like a great seagull with its lifting vanes drooping, and then he got into a shallow dugout of cypress and, wielding the paddle one-handed, fetched the flyer ashore together with a mooring line.

"You'll hab breakfas'?" asked Sam.

"Won't be long. Reckon you got a long ride ahead of you. Mus' make you hungry flyin'?"

"I've got no time to waste," said the flyer, a lean, hawk-faced, hawk-eyed man. "Where's Pell?" he asked. "I deliver to Pell and he gives me a receipt."

"You'll see him at breakfast," said Sam. "He'll git up now he knows you've come. Usual he wallers with his squaw until noon. They take things easy on this cay when they ain't fightin'. Git kind of fed up with each other, those white men. And they ain't enough wimmen to go round. Can't git Injun squaws no mo'. Them Injuns done moved away from heah. But the wimmen we got, stayed. Yessuh. I got me one of those Seminoles myse'f."

A gust of wind ruffled the laguna surface and the gyro swung to its mooring line. An eerie screech, inhuman, eldritch, rising in pitch until it split the air and pierced the ear painfully, made the flyer start.

"What's that?" he asked.

"That's the skull screechin'," said Sam. "Some say it's tryin' to tell where treasure is buried, cause there's blood on the gold and the man who wore that skull, who was a pirate, stays in hell until it's found and restored. Some say it's gyardin' that treasure. Some say when it yells like that it's time fo' some man who hears it to die. Plenty folk died heah, I reckon," he added solemnly. "Some in my time. They quarrel but not with me; I's sort of handy in a quarrel if I have only got one arm. Yessuh. I killed me my man but he shuah had it comin'! An' I got me a conjuh chahm I wear agen that pirate skull."

SAM led the way to the long, low house of coral blocks, washed white with coral lime. Its roof was wattled and thatched, vine covered; trees shaded it. The flyer had not seen it from above. No one, coming by plane or water would think there was a house on Craneo Cay. On the long veranda hammocks swung, and men sprawled in them, drowsing, snoring, awakening, some unshaven and unkempt, others in trim pajamas, clean of face. The porch was screened. The laugh of a woman came that ended in a yelp after the sound of a blow and a curse. Two Seminole squaws came round the house and went down to the laguna, perhaps to wash, or watch the plane. They were short, squat and full breasted, wearing only a yard or so of gaudy print cloth twisted about their hips; their hair hung down their backs, unkempt.

They were what those on the cay facetiously termed their "guests." They had not been invited but kidnaped. Now they were either willing or resigned. They said that the tribe would kill them if they ever tried to rejoin it.

The man named Pell came out, a cringing squaw following him until he fiercely ordered her away, whereupon she slunk off and hunkered down by a tree, submissive but still savage, hate smoldering in her.

Pell was tall and fierce of face and manner. He had a pointed beard and trimmed mustache; his eyes were the color of dishwater with tiny pupils, eyes cruel as those of a shark. He had his choice of Craneo Cay or the "chair," and preferred the former though he chafed at its constraint. He hoped to get away to South America but his passion was gambling and his luck was never in. It cost money to get away from Craneo Cay. Once there you were marooned.

"I'm Pell," he said. "You got a message? What's your name?"

The flyer eyed him coldly. "The name," he said slowly, "ain't been decided on yet. You get the message and I get a receipt."

Pell nodded, held out his hand for the

sealed envelope inside a waterproof oil-skin wrapper. Sam had gone inside. Others of the men were rousing out. They assembled at the breakfast table, leaving the squaws outside. They were a hard-bitten lot, seared by evil and there was little love lost between them.

Pell opened the letter read the short message aloud.

"Expect Fenwick within week. Will give credentials and present satisfactory contribution.   S."

Pell laughed sardonically. The "contributions" were the price of admission to the sanctuary, in money or loot. S. kept a strict accounting. He held them all in the hollow of his hand. The maze of the morass was all about them, the only craft they possessed was the little dugout. Outside, the hounds of the law were waiting to pick up their scent.

"I'll give you a receipt for this after breakfast," he told the flyer.

"I'll take it now," returned the other. "I didn't keep you waiting."

Pell snarled something but the flyer was unmoved. He was as hard as any of them. They were like a pack of dogs under-exercised, their appetites restrained, liberty denied; ready at any moment to turn on each other once a fight was started. Only Stumpy Sam was serene. He and his "woman" got along well. He was paid wages. The rest of them were nearly all broke. Some had lost what they had gambling, and there was no credit from the winners.

The flyer eyed Pell who scrawled a receipt with ill grace. He ate a good meal and went down to the laguna. The wind was still blowing. Sam came out to paddle him off.

The skull was screeching. A fishcrow alighted on it, with flapping wings for balance, cawing. The wind worked at the plane and the flyer revved up. The lifting blades and propeller became a blur of speed. The wind sent the gyro over the water fast and then it lifted, flying north.

Stumpy Sam watched it admiringly before he returned to where his woman was washing the dishes. Then he went to inspect the mash from which he was making pot whisky from corn. The skull kept up its eerie screeching but they were used to it. It was their safeguard as it pitched in the stiff branches of the dead tree like the figurehead of a ship.

CHAPTER THREE

Satan's Sanctuary

THE mysterious Mr. S. had promised Fenwick safety on stiff terms. Fenwick had been driven to seek sanctuary and ultimate arrival in Venezuela or some place immune from the police, by what he considered an unfortunate incident. So did the families of the two men he had been forced to kill before he could get away with the swag from a millionaire's house on Long Island. Only, the families had a harsher phrase for it. The search for him drove him into temporary cover from which he got in touch with S.

S. promised to send down word to Craneo Cay and gave Fenwick credentials he must present for a welcome. Fenwick was broke but he had an idea in his mind—always a fertile one where jewels were concerned—an idea taken from a clipping telling of the forthcoming masquerade in Palm Beach.

"It's on the way to this hideout of yours," he told S. "I ought to be able to turn up something there without any trouble. May not be able to fence it because I don't want to waste any time getting to your place, but I can turn in the ice or whatever I get to the value of the fifty grand you're asking, which is a damn stiff price, if you ask me, for a few days board and a trip to South America."

S. stroked his narrow mustachios and gave Fenwick his inscrutable, Mephistophelean smile.

"You rate high, Fenwick," he told his visitor. "I'll accept your suggestion. Turn over jewels worth fifty thousand dollars to a man named Pell you'll meet at the cay. He's in charge down there. He'll take care of them. But don't show up without the gems, Fenwick, and don't lose the credentials. Or you might find the climate of Craneo Cay unhealthy."

"That's O. K. with me," replied Fenwick. "I can take care of myself and I'll deliver the goods."

He had carefully gone into the details of his proposed robbery when he reached Palm Beach. He had found an empty house on Lake Okeechobee. It had water frontage and he discovered a canoe in a boathouse. There he cached some provisions. A canal ran straight from Palm Beach to the lake.

His raid had staggered even him by the magnitude of its result. He had a hundred times the fifty thousand that S. wanted. In South America he could sell the rest for a fortune and live like a king.

He bothered a little as to how the second man he had slugged would come out of it but he was wounded himself and savage about the hurt. He wished he had hit Trent the harder blow. But now he was busied with his getaway.

He had a map that S. had given him. It was an aerial chart, the duplicate of the one used by the flyer of the autogyro, far more useful from the air than to a man in a canoe. But there were certain salient features he believed he could be sure of, notably that his main course was west, that he must cross a railroad,

that he would know when he was nearing the coast by the presence of mangroves and that there was a secret entrance to the inner laguna of Craneo Cay which was marked by a skull set in a tree.

He sent the launch speeding along the canal and made Lake Okeechobee unobserved. In the early dawn he sank the launch in a small inlet, took the canoe, loaded it and went out into the smaller Hicpoochee. There he went into the Everglades, swallowed up in its watery wilderness. It had been eighty miles from Palm Beach to where he had sunk the launch. He had made twenty knots right along. Now he had another eighty miles to go but it was by tortuous routes, baffling and conflicting.

HE did not dare to travel by day, for there were planes scouting for him within twenty-four hours like hawks searching covert. There would be big rewards out and these flyers had found a new sport that promised easy money. If he had killed that watchman the rewards would read "Dead or Alive." He had no illusions about what those flyers would do if they spotted him.

Therefore, during the daytime, he lay hidden on some wooded hummock, hauling out the canoe, stung by mosquitoes, his wound bothering him considerably. He did not dare to light a fire but ate cold victuals.

Trent's second bullet had gone clear through the phony corselet Fenwick had worn. It was metal but not practical armor. He had a broken rib from that with a flesh wound above it that refused to heal, what with sweat and friction and lack of antiseptics. Trent had got him in the left arm, the one that had the loot bag on it, but that had been only a surface gouge.

He considered also that the Seminoles

might be hunting him, after the reward. Thought of pursuit and the rapid diminishment and spoiling of his stores in the heat spurred him on. He was not an expert paddler and it was a hard task working through choked runs only to find they led nowhere. The water gave him dysentery and some wild figs he ate did not seem to help matters. He was weakening but he held on steadily though he ran a fever nightly and he did not get much rest.

Finally the planes disappeared and he ventured into the open by daylight, making better time. At last he won through to where the railroad line broke through the Everglades. Exhausted, he back-paddled into rushes as he heard the whistle of a train. Curious eyes might see him and report. He watched the accommodation train for both passenger and freight pass, heard it whistle for a station. That would be Deep Lake but he did not dare reveal himself even to obtain food. He did not know what was back of him. They might have found the launch, discovered the canoe was stolen.

He threw a scanty shadow of what he had been over a week ago, when at last he feebly sent the canoe down the final reach and saw the white skull shining in the sun. It was almost noon, the air was breathless and hot as the exhaust of an oven when a door is opened.

Feebly he parted vines and hauled himself down a waterway into the laguna. He saw half-naked women washing clothes, a negro with half an arm peeling vegetables. He fought off collapse desperately for he was nearly spent. And there were five millions dollars worth of jewels in a canvas haversack, wrapped inside shirts and underwear. The necklace for his contribution he carried separately. But he had to stiffen up, and, though his sun-baked skin cracked and his festered lips ran pus, he essayed

a smile and managed an air of jauntiness as he hailed Stumpy Sam.

"Fenwick," he said. "I'm expected."

"You been expected fo' a week an' mo'," said Sam. "Look like you come a long, ha'd way."

"It turned out long," said Fenwick. "For God's sake get me something to drink—and eat."

"Suah will, boss. While I fix the grub, s'pose you clean up some. I kin give you a razor an I kin even trim yo' hair. I'm the chief cook, bottlewasher and barber round here."

PELL stopped them on the long porch, with others of the colony standing by. There was a sly look about all of them as if they appreciated a hidden joke soon to be revealed. Pell had a grim twitch to his mouth but his manner was cordial. Fenwick had anticipated the type of men he saw; they were of his own kidney—most of them were careless of their appearance, unshaven, their clothing wrinkled and spotted, seldom sober.

But Pell, in spotless Palm Beach attire, was different though Fenwick saw plainly the bulge of a shoulder holster and gun. He carried one himself and he did not doubt that the others had weapons handy.

"You've got credentials and a contribution, I understand," said Pell ceremoniously. "It's the custom to present them immediately."

Fenwick brought from his wallet an envelope that contained a square of thick gray paper that bore no writing but the imprint in scarlet wax of the famous signet ring with the S. in the shape of a scaled serpent with fangs and forked tongue. Pell looked at it and passed it on. It was barely glanced at as Fenwick drew from his inner pocket a string of diamonds that flashed and sparkled in the sunlight and made their eyes shine. Pell took it and let it slide over one palm, appraising it.

"I take it that's all you have to show us?" he said half inquiringly. "This goes into the treasury until S. takes it over. We are rather expecting him. Do you want a receipt?" he added sardonically, with an accent that made Fenwick look at all of them, standing watching the necklace and him like a band of wolves, mentally slavering.

Fenwick grinned easily enough. "That ought to be enough," he said. "It should fetch fifty grand. I understood it included board and lodging, among other things. I'm dry as an old bone and I'm famished."

"Of course," said Pell. "The food's good, the rest of the accommodation not so good. There is no private room or bath for you, or any of us. We use the laguna and risk the alligators. You can have a hammock to sleep in. Sam'll fix you up. Have you got a change of clothes?"

"I've got all I want in here," said Fenwick and touched the bag carelessly with his foot. "I don't expect to be here long."

He picked up the bag and again the men followed him with their eyes as he trailed Sam into the kitchen. He liked Sam. The negro was a rascal or he would not be there but he seemed to be honest compared to the rest. And Fenwick had a keen notion that he was going to need a friend.

The others followed Pell back into the house, through the main living room, to Pell's own chamber. A steel safe of modern make stood there and Pell opened it, the only one among them to know the combination which S. had provided. There was a cot, two chairs, a curtain hung across a corner for wardrobe, one window and strips of matting on the floor. Pell drew down a blind through which the sunshine poured transparently making a dancing rainbow heap of the necklace before he put it in the safe. He turned from it laughing.

"The poor sucker," he said. "We'll check the rest over before twenty-four hours. S. is due inside of two days. It ought to see us all in the clear."

"By God, if it don't we'll talk turkey to S." blustered one of them, bloodshot of eyes and blackly bearded.

"Don't be a damned fool," said Pell curtly. "We can't get away without him. And we can't hold out on him. He'll be covered. If we get out it'll be two or three at a time. This is a windfall. Fenwick thinks that necklace will pay his way but he's not as well acquainted with S. as we are. I know him better than any of you. I've known him longer. I'm not afraid of any of you," he added contemptuously, "and you know it. But I'm not trying to get the best of S. Let's have a drink."

"Let's see that paper again," another asked, as Pell produced a demijohn of Sam's brew, with glasses.

PELL took from the table drawer the last message that had come from S. by autogyro. There were no written instructions but there was more than a hint in the folded newspaper that gave a full account of the robbery and a precise list of the jewelry stolen, including the names of the owners and the valuation of the gems. The necklace now in the safe was set down as belonging to Mrs. Hamilton Irwin. It was appraised at sixty-five thousand dollars. The report stated that a well-known detective, acting for the various insurance companies and celebrated in such matters, was handling the affair with hope of restoration.

"S. won't be such a fool as to deal with him," said Pell. "He'll unset and sell abroad. Europe and South America and the Orient."

They listened to him a bit moodily. The rereading of that vast haul whetted their appetites for lusts too long denied. But they deferred to Pell. He was a natural leader. He knew more than they did about the best disposition of stolen jewels and he was closer to S. Right too, about the fact that S. had them under control. They could only go out through means of his contriving, perhaps a series of plane flights to Venezuela or shorter trips to some vessel that would lie out in the Gulf and take them there.

There was not one among them who did not conjure up some vague idea of how he could get a lion's share. Not one of them trusted the other.

Fenwick had guessed that S. would bleed him, above the fifty thousand, and he could spare it, for to him, occupied in desperate flight, nothing but escape mattered. For the time the jewels were so many pebbles.

Now, he saw that they suspected him of holding out and he meant to protect himself. He ate and drank, shaved and put on clean clothes. Sam had produced a professional looking comb, scissors and clippers. Presently he was going to trim Fenwick's somewhat unkempt locks.

Fenwick had preferred to shave himself, because his face was tender from the sun. He used the razor before a mirror which was on a small porch back of Sam's kitchen, with a bench for the water and soap, and a clean towel. He looked at himself in the glass, then fondly regarded the flat automatic on the bench.

"They are a bunch of cutthroats," he told his reflection, inaudibly," and that gee Pell is a tough bird. The rest ain't so congenial either."

He pondered about precautions. He had his blackjack, as well as his gun.

Sleeping in a hammock had its advantages and disadvantages.

He took the mirror off the nail and held it as if to closer scrutinize his features. It enabled him to look two ways at once.

He heard laughter some way off, the clink of glasses and bottles. The jungle came up close to the porch. It was dense but a man could get through it, find some hiding place for the jewels.

Fenwick moved swiftly and silently. He peered into the kitchen and then took the shirt in which five million dollars in precious stones were swathed, and darted into the tangle. In a few minutes he came back, panting a little, regained the porch, closed the zipper and fastened it with a stout little padlock that opened to a letter combination. It would not be any obstacle to determined robbery but it would keep out pilferers. He was not sure how far they might go. They would be afraid of S. and, as Fenwick saw it, they could not possibly do anything but guess that he had more than the one necklace. There were no papers delivered on Craneo Cay. Still they got provisions somehow—they might have got the news at Deep Lake.

SAM came to the door, asking if he was ready and Fenwick gave himself over to his ministrations. Sam settled him in a chair. The Indian woman brought hot towels. Sam handled him deftly and the hot towels helped.

"She's a good squaw," said Sam. "She don't talk much English but she's mighty useful. She kin wash clothes fo' you. Most of 'em don't bother much about that, 'ceptin' Pell. He's finicky."

He went on, garrulous as any barber.

"She's Seminole. She ain't fancy but we get erlong fine. You see, some of the rist of them Injun gals had to be sorter persuaded to stop. Their bucks didn't take it so good but they couldn't do much agen this outfit. But she took a shine to me, probably becos' I'm cullud an' I don't slap her down—much. There you is. I reckon you feel better. You sho' look it."

Pell proposed a game of poker when Fenwick joined them. Five of them made up a game of stud and Fenwick did fairly well. Pell was the big winner. But, all the time, Fenwick felt them eyeing him as cats might watch at a mousehole. They drank steadily and Fenwick poured small. Sam served a plain but abundant supper. The wind came up as usual with sunset. They went out on the screened porch where the hammocks hung and Fenwick carelessly tossed into his the gripsack, knowing he was observed.

Suddenly an eerie, bloodcurdling screech sounded, rising in harsh volume, dying away to increase once more. Fenwick was a bit jumpy.

"What in hell is that?" he asked. "It's not a puma."

The rest laughed jeeringly.

"It's the skull up in the tree by the channel to the laguna," said Pell. "Said to be the skull of a pirate named Dominic. He wouldn't tell where he had hid the loot and so they scragged him and put up his dome for a warning. It wasn't a skull then, but the fishcrows got to it and then it bleached out. Some say the treasure was buried under the tree. But it ain't. I looked. And they say whenever it screeches like that someone who hears it dies before morning. The squaws told us that. They believe it. This place ain't too healthy. Men have died on it, some quicker than others. Mostly their own fault."

He twisted his mustache and tugged lightly at his beard, his shark eyes regarding Fenwick.

"We get along all right so long as nobody holds out on anybody else. Want to tell us how you got that string of ice?"

he asked and Fenwick could feel them listening, holding their breaths.

"I cracked an icebox at Palm Beach," he said briefly. "It was an easy job."

"Pays your passage," said Pell carelessly. "Plenty more where that came from, too, I suppose."

"Palm Beach is a good lay," Fenwick replied, yawning.

They were watching him now—would watch him for a day or so. But he had got the jewels hidden, in a good place. He hoped the damned skull wouldn't screech in the night. It made him gooseflesh. He was sleepy and tired out, sore and aching from his trip.

He announced it and rolled into the welcoming hammock. There was a folded blanket on it and he simply took off his shoes and, after he was in, removed his coat and made a pillow of it on top the gripsack, wrapping the blanket lightly about him, his gun handy. Dimly he heard them talking, laughing, presently singing bawdy maudlin songs.

CHAPTER FOUR

Thieves' Honor

THE moon was sinking when he woke up suddenly, striving to get rid of the sleep that still drugged him, through which some sense was ringing an alarm inside him.

He rose a little on his elbow but the hammock was yielding, awkward. For a second or two he did not remember he was in one. The wind was blowing hard, breaking up the laguna into waves that caught the sheen of the moon that was the color of a blood-orange. Boughs and palm fronds rustled and whipped. There was a moan like the sound of distant surf and, out of the moan, there came the screech of the skull, mocking and ominous.

Instinctively he listened for snoring, looked down the line of hammocks. He could make out nothing, sight or sound, but he felt there were men squatting in the shadows, stooping, watching, waiting.

There was one back of him, where his hammock swung to the side wall of the porch. He clutched his gun and tried to swing to the floor but the blanket and the meshes of the netted, moving couch betrayed him, fouled and delayed him.

A blow descended. He felt the brief wind of it, knew he was being treated to his own medicine and he ducked as he got his legs free, over the side of the swaying, uncertain bed. The blackjack missed his temple but it almost stunned him. He fell to the porch on all fours, still holding to his gun; whirled on his back, his left hand supporting him while he fired at the tall figure that stooped over him. A stab of flame responded. Lead tore through his neck and he shot again.

Pell crumpled, his second shot smacking into the flooring of the porch. Fenwick had hit him in the belly.

The porch was lively now. They were shooting to finish him. He used Pell for a screen and fired back. He was in a bad place. They were after what they thought was in his sack. Even if he got away they would be after him when they found it empty of valuables; they would guess he had tricked them somehow.

Twice Fenwick fired at the vague figures weaving between him and the moonlight. Twice his aim was perfect. One man caught at the other and they both toppled, crashing into the wire screening. The shadows were thick on the porch and the wind was bringing up clouds that veiled the moon. In the blackness Fenwick rolled off the porch to the ground, through a gap in the screen, kept rolling while the rest, crazed with the liquor, the fury of fighting, spilled blood and the desire for loot, rushed in a jumbled mob, tangled amid the hammocks, to where they thought he still lay. They trampled on Pell's corpse, on the bodies of the two Fenwick had brought down, cursing and confused, striking at each other.

Another got wounded in the fracas and was out of it, leaning against the side of the house, slowly collapsing as the moon came out again and they saw that Fenwick had gone.

Stumpy Sam came out of his kitchen and saw them, his machete naked in his hand, himself naked, his woman back of him. Sam watched the carnage and surveyed the rush. He drew his woman back into the room.

"That skull suah done screech fo' death ternight," he muttered as he heard its eldritch howl above the clamor.

Someone got the prize, the gripsack. The rest rushed after him into the main room.

It was an Australian, wanted for murder in the goldfields, for the same crime in San Francisco and in Chicago—"Sydney Dick" Walton, a burly, uncouth ruffian who might have been the leader before if he had Pell's brains—who had the grip.

"Strike a light, someone," he said. "We'll rip the bloody bag open."

THEY slashed the canvas, tossed out Fenwick's duds, searched them and the bag.

There were no jewels!

"Done!" cried Walton. "Done, by Gawd! Let's look at the blarsted 'ammock."

They rushed outside again to the porch, trampling again on the dead men, pawing, finding nothing, each man suspicious of the other. The wind slammed the door to Sam's quarters.

" 'E's in there. 'E's myde a dicker with Sam."

They pounded on the door, demanding admittance, madmen all.

Sam faced them. His huge, nude body, shining with night sweat, bulked large; his machete glinted in the moonlight.

"What you want of me, gemman?"

"He made a deal with you. Where is he? Where have you hid the jewels?"

Stumpy Sam was calm. He was at bottom, a better man than any of them and he knew it. They were cocked with liquor, and some with drugs. He was a fighter, primitive and sure of his prowess.

"I dunno what you talk about. I dunno of any jewels. I cook fo' you, an' Mister S. pay me fo' it. Pay me good. You shoot me, you lose a mighty good cook but, by Gawd, some of you gwine to git cooked firs'. Cooked—or carved. You clean out." The resolute negro flourished his machete with a swish. One of the men leveled his gun, pulled a trigger that clicked. The clip was empty.

The machete swung in a circle of dull sheen. The man's hand dropped to the floor, severed at the spouting wrist.

"Git out!" said Sam. "Or I done shear you through."

They backed out with the wounded man gripping his forearm in amazement, reeling. Sam closed the door, then opened it again and spurned the lopped hand with his naked foot, kicking it along the porch after them.

Trouble was raging outside. They were accusing each other, shouting incoherently. There was a blow and a shot, the begging yelp of the handless man for something, someone, some way, to stop his bleeding to death. They paid no heed to him. Walton dominated them with his loud, deep voice.

"We got to find Fenwick," he said.

" 'E can't get away unless 'e tries it by water. 'E won't get far, at that. 'E's 'oled up somewhere. 'E must 'ave 'id the swag when 'e was washin' up. 'E 'ad 'is bag with 'im then. 'E'll go after it. When S. comes 'e'll raise 'oly 'ell. Get lanterns."

Both the dugout and the canoe were on the little beach. Fenwick had not dared to try that means of escape. He had lost blood, was losing more. The craft were in plain view if the moon came clear. He was too weak to paddle, swallowing blood, spitting it as he crawled toward the undergrowth like a mortally wounded beast making for covert.

THEY found him cowering in palmetto scrub, his gun empty, his extra clips left in his gripsack.

But he would not tell them what he had done with the gems. Not even when Walton informed him that they had heard from S. He gritted his teeth against their torture.

The wind lashed through the trees and brush. Above them the bleached skull screeched in its place amid the rocking, sapless boughs, shrieking like a witch at a Black Mass revel.

"You might just as well ask that skull," said Fenwick. "You'll get nothing out of me."

A man started to strike him on the head with a gun but Walton stopped him. In the fitful moonshine a twisted smile showed on the face of Sydney Dick.

"Maybe the skull 'll tell *you*," he said. "Or you'll tell the skull. Lash 'im in the tree, mates, lookin' at it. Come sunup, 'e may 'ave the information we want."

Two of them climbed the dead tree and Fenwick, more dead than alive, was hoisted up to them, tied with his face staring into the bony features of the ancient skull. It was a grim jest that fitted their mood. The mosquitos would torture him. He would be willing to tell everything at dawn, not far off now. The dead tree rocked and the skull screeched like a gleeful demon.

"What are we going to do with the stiffs?" asked a man. "Keep 'em to show S. when he gets here tomorrow?"

"Listen," said Walton. " 'Ere's our yarn. Pell starts it all, d'ye see? 'E got finished, too. It was 'is fault. 'E was trying for a getaway with the jewels. I'll make up a tale. Tyke the lot of 'em out to the spand spit where the croc's 'aul out. They'll give 'em burial. Tyke 'im along too," he added, indicating the man who was not yet dead. " 'E can't last. 'E 'll be dead time the big lizards smell 'em and come out of the water with the sun. Come on, let's clean it up. That blighter in the tree 'll talk later. If 'e don't we'll leave 'im crucified till 'e does. We'll dump these stiffs and open another demijohn."

They laid the bodies on the spit where the alligators came to bask. The wind was falling. They stopped at the skull tree. The skull grinned silently with its gaping jaws. Fenwick hung in his bonds.

"Going to spill it, matey?" asked Walton.

Fenwick gathered his strength, spit out blood at them, found his voice.

"You can go to hell!" he told them.

He knew now that S. had intended to take all, that he had come to a trap when he came to Craneo Cay. He heard them go off jeering and his head fell on his neck. That last effort had broken through the wall of his jugular vein, already grazed by a bullet. There came a gush of dark blood, a gurgle in his throat, a death rattle that was mocked by an echo from the skull, welcoming another pirate to the unknown shores.

CHAPTER FIVE

Trent Takes the Trail

TRENT was the first to think of an aeroplane and to secure one the morning after the robbery. He was up as soon as it was light, searching over the swamps and, though he was disappointed, he was not disheartened to see nothing of the fugitive. He gave the man who could plan and pull off such a coup credit for hiding out by day and traveling by night.

But Fenwick had not thought of one thing when he sank the launch. Lake Okeechobee is a thousand square miles in extent but it is universally shallow. The inlet where he had scuttled the launch was little used, and the depth was about three fathoms, sufficient to conceal it from the ordinary observer, or even searcher, but revealing it plainly to a seeker in a plane.

That was Trent's first clue, the second the broken-into-boathouse and stolen canoe, the third the certainty that his man had gone into the glades and the fourth the conviction that he was bound for the refuge maintained somewhere there, the sanctuary of the Overhead and Undercover Association. Trent had not been too sure it existed before, but now he was certain of it and believed it linked up with S. He might be able to kill more than one bird with his stone but that stone must be well flung, for he realized there would be others there, as desperate and dangerous as Fenwick.

That was not going to be easy. He realized he did not possess the skill to trace Fenwick through that maze of waterways and he respected Fenwick's ability to cover his faint trail. Yet it could be done, if he could persuade a Seminole to act with him.

Trent found a negro fisherman at

Palm Beach who had intermarried into the tribe and who took him to a Seminole and acted as interpreter where the Indian's pigeon-English failed.

The Seminole's eyes glittered as Trent went on to hint that he might know the destination of *the fleeing thief* though he could only actually find it by tracing him. The moment it was suggested that there was a band of white criminals hidden there the Indian became eager. But he wanted to know if Trent was authorized by law to use arms against these criminals; if the guide who might be provided could use arms against them, without getting into trouble.

Trent promised not only immunity but a share in the rewards out for these missing men—aside from Fenwick—rewards which would not fail to be paid if the men were delivered either dead or alive.

The Seminole spoke in his own tongue with flashing eyes and the negro translated.

"He say that he'll take the matter up with his chief," the latter said. "He say that the story come to them that white men take Seminole women and make them live with them some place on the Gulfside of the swamp. They scare off some of the men, and some they kill. So he think it sure the chief give you a guide because they are plenty sore on account of the women. Some of them come from this part of the tribe, and they might have done something about it if they hadn't been afraid of getting in wrong with white men. He'll see his chief tonight and he'll meet you here at the same place tomorrow, or send the guide."

THE guide came early in the morning, a copper-skinned Indian with fine aquiline features, of medium height, and powerfully built.

"You like follow one man he go in?" he said. "Can do. We go in my boat. That at Okeechobee. You bring food."

Trent hired a launch to take them to the lake. The boat was a shallow canoe, hewn out of a single cypress log, the workmanship splendid, its shape excellent, uniquely adapted for its work.

It was little short of marvelous to see the way in which Taki, the guide, picked up the trail from the smaller lake named Hicpochee. It was mid-afternoon when they entered the swamps. Fenwick had a start of over thirty hours.

Still more marvelous was the Seminole's unerring following of the sign that Trent often could not see even when it was pointed out to him. The cypress dugout went smoothly and fast under the urge of Taki's paddle and the Indian found where Fenwick's clumsier-handled blade had disturbed the natural position of the water plants. They found places where he had landed and had left more traces than he imagined—impressions, broken twigs, burned matches, ends of cigarettes, sign upon sign that Taki pounced upon and told them they were on the right track.

When at length, on the sixth day, the trail led to the railroad and Taki explained by signs that there was a depot not far off, Trent smiled for the first time as he saw the telegraph wires stretching along the lonesome track. Given a depot, a wire and an operator, he could soon summon force enough to arrest all the malefactors he might find.

Taki's only difficulty came when he had to cast up and down the edge of the swamp on the far side of the track across which they portaged the light craft. The track was raised on an embankment alongside which was a long reach of water on either side. It was late in the afternoon and Trent wanted to push on as he saw his goal in sight.

They spent the night on a hummock. Taki said they were not far from the sea. He pointed out seabirds and the inflow of the tide and Trent could smell the brine. There could not be much farther to go. He slept lightly and rose instantly when Taki touched him on the shoulder. The dawn smell was in the air. The creatures of the swamp were rousing and the sky began to glow as they swallowed a hasty meal and once more took up the trail.

The dugout glided on so silently that it did not disturb the ducks they crept up on, the herons wading, watching for minnows. Trent was alert for indications that they might be observed, looking for signs of watchers. He was ahead of Taki in the dugout. The Seminole tapped him on the shoulder and pointed ahead. They had just swung into a run. The sight was gruesome.

THERE was a spit of sand about which the flood tide was rising. On this spit lay figures that were unmistakeably those of dead men, save one that feebly moved. And, swimming the current as Taki held the dugout against the tide, motionless and quiet, there came the snouts, the horny eye projections of half a dozen alligators, their bodies submerged, the water showing no evidence of the powerful propulsion that brought them on at such a pace.

The foremost reached the spit, hauled out with amazing speed, rising on its short legs, looking like an antediluvian dragon, followed by the rest. What happened was too swift for interference though there was none Trent could have made that would have been efficient. His automatic would have been useless as a popgun against those armored, tremendous monsters. Each seized its prey and scuttled back to the water disappearing

quickly, bearing their food to underground and underwater dens where they would leave it to ripen to suit their tastes.

The foul odor of animal musk came on the faint breeze. It almost sickened Trent, together with the fact he mentioned to Taki.

"One of them was alive."

Taki grunted. There had not been much life left in that man, he thought. He pointed again. At the shore end of the spit there stood a dead tree. Impaled in its branches was a grinning skull.

But that was not the most ghastly fruit it wore. Opposite to it, was a dead man tied in the branches, sagging from his ropes, his face horrible, his clothes dark with gore. A carrion crow flew cawing from the shoulder of the corpse.

Trent saw the face, blotched, twisted, discolored, but he did not recognize it. He had seen Fenwick only in armor with the visor of his helmet down, hiding the gas mask. Yet he was sure that this thing had once been Fenwick. He guessed what had happened in part— that they had tortured and killed him because, in some way, he had hidden the gems.

Those gems should be still ashore. Those dead men the alligators had taken testified to a desperate fight in which rogues must have fallen out. There was a faint plume of smoke back of the dead tree and that meant a meal, a house, men still living.

Trent could never take Fenwick back now. Fenwick had escaped the chair but he had been executed—hanged in a gallowstree.

The Seminole gave a faint hiss, backed the dugout into a low growth along the shore. There were voices, raucous and ribald.

Seven men came out of a little trail that led past the tree and ended at the sand spit. Proper villains they were, drunk, staggering. One had an arm in a sling, another a bandaged head while a third, reeling along, had the end of his arm wrapped in a bloody clout.

Trent looked keenly at the leader. He had seen that rogue's face before. He recognized others, for he was familar with various police galleries. Here was Sydney Dick Walton, long wanted—others who had disappeared.

Here was a haul, if he could land it. Odds of seven to two, and the Seminole with nothing but a knife. There might be more.

Walton was pointing at the empty spit. "All gone, coves!" he cried. "They're men who tell no tales. Now we'll see what Fenwick 'as to s'y."

Trent heard them plainly. This *was* Fenwick then.

"For Christ's syke, the blighter's dead —'E wasn't 'urt that bad— But 'e's a goner. The jewels are 'id somewhere and S. is due today. Tyke 'im down."

They cut the rope brutally and the body fell like a sack of wet wheat. Walton kicked at it.

"Busted a blood vessel," he announced. "Chuck 'im in the drink."

Two of them picked up the body, swung it between them, hurled it into the water. Instantly there was a swirl, hurrying eddies; then only the tidal water running up from the sea.

Trent crouched, tense, his hand on his gun. The odds were too great but he was discounting them, tingling at the sheer brutality. He had learned three things. That this was Fenwick, that the gems were still hidden, that S. was expected. Another probable one—that they would have to give S. an accounting.

The Indian gripped his arm. "By and by," he said. "Not long now. I leave sign. Help come. Seminole come. They come for women."

It was timely, though Trent wondered just how much aid these avenging Semi-noles might be. Firearms were forbidden them. But it was folly to try and arrest the criminals by himself, though he burned to do so. He could go back to the railroad, telegraph. It would take time for a posse to assemble. S. might come and go.

THE sinful seven reeled back into the brush, drunkenly chattering.

"I think they come now," said the Seminole. "Close behind us all time."

He pointed to where a little flotilla came round the bend. Each dugout, and there were three of them, held four men. They were dressed fantastically in red and yellow, wearing some sort of kilts, with plumed headdresses. The flash of their paddles broke rhythmically. Two stroked, two more held what looked like fishpoles. They saw the skull and came straight for it. Trent's guide chirped like a mating bird and they headed in, holding their craft against the stream with paddles set in the mud of the shallows, talking with Trent's man.

"They say one nigger man this place, have got one Seminole woman. No want hurt him. His woman send word he good to her. She like. This nigger man cook this place."

"All right," Trent agreed. It was a time for compromise. "How are they going to fight? Knives? Those men have got guns."

"You see," his guide answered. "Can do."

They hauled out their dugouts, bringing the poles with them, and filed along the trail. They came out into a tiny clearing where butterflies played, and saw the house. Stumpy Sam came out on the back porch and threw some water from a pail, handling it with his half arm cleverly. The Seminoles grunted, softly. Trent understood this was the negro to be spared. The rear of the house was not easily attacked. The kitchen porch ended abruptly. They circled the house, halted in the undergrowth bordering the laguna.

They saw Sam carry in two trays of food and return to the kitchen with a manner eloquent of his dislike of the men he served. He sent his woman in with coffee. As she came out of the main room one of the Seminoles gave a call, and then a second, to which she responded, first by staring and then coming slowly toward them when it was repeated. She squatted down and the leader of the Indians talked with her. Then she got up and went back to the house.

"He tell her," whispered Trent's guide," speak to all Seminole women, tell them we come. We no hurt them, no hurt her man, suppose he keep away. She say her man no like other men."

Trent did not want to storm the house. He was uncertain of his allies' prowess, not of their willingness. He had not yet fathomed the idea of the poles they had brought until he saw them taking tiny shafts from quivers, rolling plugs of cotton about one end of the little darts, careful of the tips which were dark with a gummy substance in which they had been dipped.

Then he knew. These were the blowpipes that the Muskadogees had acquired from the original tribes, the death tubes of the Mayas, the sumpitans of the Orient. At close range, at any distance a dart could reach and cling, piercing the skin.

He waited patiently. Perhaps S. would come and it was not hard to guess how. Trent looked north for a growing speck in the sky but none appeared.

At last the men started to come out, Walton first. He saw that all of them wore guns. Evidently they had been holding some sort of council which was not quite concluded. They came off the porch to the beach where there were crude benches.

Trent let them get seated and then walked out on them.

"Put up your hands!" he said. "I want all of you."

They stared at him and then Walton laughed.

"You want all of us? You? And how many more? You're crazy, copper."

He flipped a gun from his hip and its bullet sung past Trent's ear. His own weapon barked and Walton spun halfway about before he folded up, still firing wildly as he fell to the sand.

"You're all dead men," said Trent, "unless you surrender."

CHAPTER SIX

"S"

THEY looked at him, they looked at Walton, his open mouth full of grit, a hole in his temple. Then they rushed, shooting, trying to shoot.

Darts, like insects charged with venom, came unseen from the thicket where the Seminoles lay. They lodged in the exposed flesh, cheek and neck or hand.

Their bodies slumped, they pitched on their knees with open mouths striving for breath against the poison. It paralyzed their diaphragms and stopped their hearts, jellying their blood.

They sprawled on the sand, stiffening, after they jerked for a brief moment or two like frogs. The colony on Craneo Cay was at an end.

Stumpy Sam did not appear. He trusted his wife's tribesmen but no white officer of the law. With his woman, he went to where the dugouts had been drawn up, took one of them and left.

Trent covered the dead men with canvas that he found. Later, he could go in to Deep Lake depot and have them sent for. They were a good bag but there was better game coming, if not yet in sight. He told the Seminoles, through his guide, that it would be best for them to go. He would arrange for their immunity, for their share of rewards. There was another man yet to arrive, and Trent wanted to meet him solo.

Wondering a little, yet understanding vaguely that this man wanted to capture the other alone, they departed for a later rendezvous that Trent arranged, giving to his guide a signed statement on a leaf from his notebook, to the effect that the Indians had helped him exterminate the crooks on Craneo Cay.

It was afternoon when Trent saw the plane showing swiftly nearer and bigger. The plane hovered over the laguna, then lowered settling at last on the placid water. It taxied to the shore.

There was a hooded pilot with S., also hooded. Trent saw the mounted machine gun; he had to separate them from that. They did not seem startled to get no response from the cay. Perhaps they thought them all drunk. They waded through the shallows to the sand and the pilot hailed the house. It was the same man who had brought the first —and the second—message about Fenwick. He flung out a grapnel anchor to hold the plane against the ebb.

S.—there was no question as to which was he, arrogant, tall, striding like Satan on his native strand—followed. He turned up an edge of the canvas, flipped the stuff back. Saw the corpses!

"Look out, Frank!" he shouted. "Get back to the plane."

But Frank was halfway to the house. As he halted and turned, Trent came out of his concealment.

"The game's up, senator," he said, quietly but clearly.

The identity of S. came to him in a flaming hunch. Partly from his unmistakable carriage, the peculiar lift of the right shoulder, the tilt of the head. Ex-Senator Stroude who had rocketed through national councils and waned like a falling star. The man who might have been President but for his perversions.

S. STOPPED. He took in the evidence of the dead men beneath the canvas, he looked at the solitary figure opposing him. He did not read the riddle but he staked all on a single stroke.

He was armed but he was no marksman. But Frank Fenton, nerveless, consciousless, gunman, pilot and ex-ace, was a dead shot.

"Frank!" he cried again.

There was no need for his appeal. Fenton whirled. He crouched at the hips, firing, his two guns spurting flame.

Probably there were not two men in the United States, criminals or loyal citizens, who could have matched Fenton at his own game. But there was one man who outmatched him. Trent flipped a slug at the gunman, almost carelessly. He was one of the fortunate born with rare coordination, who shoot as they breathe. And Fenton paid the penalty. Twice he spun, his trigger finger twitching, powerless, his eyes dimming until they closed—forever.

Trent held his gun on Stroude, knowing he had got his man.

"I'll fly you back, senator," he said. "I have a pilot's license. Just as soon as I've attended to one or two things—the first of which is to make sure you won't shoot me as we fly. That would be foolish, unless you wanted to crash—and you might. I'll want to stop at Deep Lake first. Suppose you give me your gun."

Stroude was amenable. He let Trent frisk him.

Trent held out handcuffs, snapped

them on. He went further and tied the ankles of Stroude, alias Mr. S.

And then he went to look for the gems.

It seemed like one of those treasure hunts on a sandy cay that are absolutely futile. Fenwick had evidently died rather than tell, yet he could have had little time to find a very remote hiding place.

Stroude disposed of, Trent wound up at the tree where he had seen the skull, and Fenwick's corpse. The skull seemed to have some significance, ancient or modern.

There was a crow on top of it. A wind was blowing from the sea. There came a screech, right from the jaws of the bleached cranium.

Trent investigated. He climbed the dead tree and examined the grisly relic.

He saw the secret of the sound. Some-one ingeniously set a contrivance like a whistle in the maw of the skull. It was like the devices of the Aztecs, akin to the wind-bells of the Orient. When the wind was in a certain quarter and blew with a certain strength, a combination naturally recurring frequently, the skull seemed to screech.

Why? As a warning? Against what?

TRENT climbed higher. The dead boughs could not hold his weight. Long since dried out, they gave way. The tree split at the main crotch of its trunk as he sagged down; it broke loose from the scanty soil in which it had balanced. The trunk was only a hollow shell with shriveled roots that tore loose from the hump of dirt that held them.

There, in the loosened earth, shining through the rotted remnants of the tree, shone gold and gems. Not only those of the Marina Club but ancient jewelry, hoarded in the hollow trunk, not at its base, where Pell had digged.

Fenwick had thrown his loot into the hollow, Pell had dug under the tree, but Trent had unearthed unclaimed treasure.

He looked up. The skull had fallen, rolled until it lay looking up at him. It would screech no more.

Trent examined the gems, ancient and modern.

"I'd better be starting up that gyro," he said. "The senator is due for a heart attack when he sees what I found. He always was ambitious when he sighted money. God knows there are plenty of places for it. It looks as if we might lighten the depression—temporarily."

DOING OUR SUMS

MATHEMATICS have never been our long suit. In fact, if we remember correctly, it took us three frantic terms instead of the usual one to master an elementary geometry course, and the mere thought of anything more advanced than that leaves us trembling.

However, when the problem is no more than adding two and two together, we're right there with the answer—100%. That's right, isn't it? Flynn+Daly+Ware+Dunn=100%. No fractions to carry over—no decimal points or any of those other nuisances that used to worry us so. It's as simple as A B C and why shouldn't it be? Four complete book-length yarns all in the same issue of DIME DETECTIVE MAGAZINE and every one by an ace-high writer of mystery fiction.

And now let us introduce one of the integral components of the problem. We'll let T. T. Flynn—he writes from New Mexico, incidentally—tell us in his own words how he happened to get mixed up in our calculations.

T. T. Flynn

"Born in Indiana—Indianapolis to be exact—with the aura of Riley, Tarkington, Ade and all the other Hoosier writers smoking up the landscape year by year. It seemed a shame not to get some of that easy money, so in the misguided years of youth I started out to be a writer. And at fifteen started hunting material. Did a little of everything, from roaming the seas in engine rooms, fire-rooms and on deck, steel mills, hoboing now and then, taxi driver, railroad work as locomotive inspector, traveling salesman, house to house selling, running a wholesale candy business of my own, and a little spattering of everything else, broken by intense periods of study back at school. Sold a yarn finally, plugged a year before the next one, six months to the third, and then began to bat the ball harder each year. My experience seems no different than most other writers. Years of plugging and disappointment, and then the turn of the tide.

"I work haphazardly, which means any time during the day and night. I use three offices, including an office and home on wheels that I can get out in when I feel like it. My hobbies are travel, hunting, and new scenes and things. Stunt flying ranks high. And swimming off shore during a storm. There's real sport!

"My pet aversions are people who surge up and coo: 'I read one of your stories and I thought it was lovely,' and then look brightly for a sparkling remark from the author. Some day a frank soul will say the yarn was rotten, and be swept off his or her feet by a storm of gratitude. Second aversion is the person who yawns and says: 'I dash off something now and then but don't bother to sell it. I never read any of the cheaper magazines anyway.' Life will doubtless take care of them adequately. I never have found a writer who could.

"*Selah*—may your days be short and your nights long, for the reading of DIME DETECTIVE."

Now turn the page and scan the biggest thrill news that's broken all year.

He Invented a Rupture Appliance and was hailed "Benefactor of Mankind"

C. E. BROOKS, Inventor

Desperate, worried, discouraged over his condition (just as you may now be) over thirty-one years ago C. E. Brooks of Marshall, Michigan, invented his "air-cushion" appliance which brought security, comfort, and freedom of movement to him—results he had sought for years. Good news travels fast. Others similarly afflicted, asked him to make appliances for them.

Today the name of C. E. Brooks is known and revered the world over. And to date more than three million men, women and children of all ages—anxious for similar results—have purchased a Brooks Automatic Air-Cushion Appliance after first trying it for 10 days.

20 IMPORTANT FEATURES
Have Made Brooks the Largest Selling Made-to-Measure Appliance in the World!

Of the twenty outstanding features of the Brooks Appliance, perhaps the most remarkable of all is the "Air-Cushion" principle which in many cases acts as an agent to assist in relieving and curing reducible rupture. This exclusive feature is protected by patents in the U. S. and 13 foreign countries. The Brooks appliance can be secured only direct from our factory at Marshall, Michigan, or from any of our 33 foreign branches.

BROOKS RUPTURE APPLIANCE CO.

---

10 DAYS FREE TRIAL . . .

Over 3,000,000 men, women and children in the U. S. and foreign countries kept a Brooks *after* a 10-day free trial. You have the same privilege—try a Brooks 10 days in your own home with the understanding that you may return it if not entirely satisfied. Send coupon for full details. You'll also be interested in reading our Free Brochure on rupture. Both Brochure and Trial Offer details sent in plain, sealed envelope. Send coupon now!

Send the Coupon Today

> BROOKS APPLIANCE CO.,
> Brooks Bldg., 167-A State Street,
> Marshall, Michigan
>
> Please send me in plain, sealed envelope, Free Brochure and details of your 10-Day Free Trial offer.
>
> Name ....
>
> Address ....
> ....

I'M GLAD I'M AN ARTIST

"When I see fellows in other lines being let out I'm glad I trained my liking for drawing and became an artist. A few years ago I was just like the rest. I had a job and nothing more.

"Now I'm a trained artist—and I've quit worrying. Every Tom, Dick and Harry can't fill my shoes. There aren't so many trained artists—and each of us has his individual style. Art training has certainly helped me to get up above the crowd. If you like to draw, take my advice and enroll now with the Federal Schools and train your talent."

Through the Federal Course you can learn Illustrating, Cartooning, Designing, Lettering, Show Card writing at home. More than fifty famous artists, masters of modern methods, contribute their experience to this course. For 15 years Federal Students have made good. Many Federal Students are now earning $2500 to $6000 a year—some even more.

Why be smothered in the crowd when Federal Training may help you to make a better place for yourself. If you like to draw, you may have art talent. Without obligating yourself in any way find out how the Federal Schools can help people with art ability. This may be your answer to the job problem.

Free Vocational Test

Fill in coupon below and mail for Free Vocational Art Test today. The way to make money is to train your talent. Find out about your ability.

· · · · · · · **Mail Coupon Now** · · · · · · · ·

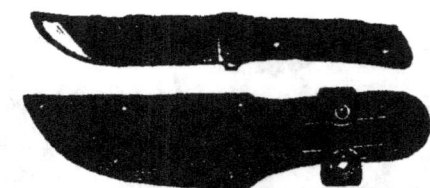

www.ingramcontent.com/pod-product-compliance
Lightning Source LLC
Chambersburg PA
CBHW080912020726
47502CB00008B/2430